TALES

OF THE

LOST

Volume 2 – Tales to Get Lost In!

A CHARITY ANTHOLOGY

For the Save the Children Coronavirus Response

Edited by Eugene Johnson and Steve Dillon

Copyright Notices

For all the Essential Workers who were on the front line during the COVID-19 pandemic; for those lost during this during this horrible time: You are not forgotten.

Contents

Introduction

To Tales of the Lost: Volume II

Mort Castle

LOSS: TEN OBSERVATIONS

1. Minor Loss: The key to my 1980 Chevette. It was on a decorative plastic key tag that had the profile of a wire haired fox terrier. Our dog, Lewis, could have posed for the image.

So you say, "Time to quit looking. It'll turn up."

But you never quit looking, not completely.

And it never turns up.

It's been lost.

It is lost.

And that is that.

And if you vibe any intimations of mortality from that, that's on you.

2. Jack Benny: Jack Benny was born in Waukegan, Illinois. Benny was an American entertainer, who went from modest success on the vaudeville circuit to stardom on radio, television, and film.

Jack Benny died on December 26, 1974.

The entire world has been wrong ever since.

Can you imagine Donald Trump having a place in a world in which Jack Benny lives, squawking for Rochester, playing mediocre violin, implying Dennis Day is a dimwit, pinching pennies, coping with the 1,000 voices of Mel Blanc, and teaching all the secrets of comic timing to Johnny Carson?

I mean, Donald Fucking Trump and Jack Benny occupying the same plane of existence?

I don't think so!

3. Coping with Loss – Part One: There was a time, just before World War II and during it, when Bud Abbot and Lou Costello were the funniest men in the world.

On November 4, 1943, Lou Jr., Costello's son, drowned in the family pool.

That night, Lou Costello performed on the radio with his partner, Bud Abbot.

No one in the live or listening audience knew about the baby's death until after the show, when Bud Abbot explained what had happened and lauded his partner.

The show must go on.

On March 3, 1959, Lou Costello died of cardiac arrest. It was three days before his 53rd birthday.

4. Life's Stages: What do you call that time when you are either dealing with loss or preparing to—or both?

Hmm, are those the <u>Fucked Years?</u>

5. A Musical Interlude: "A-Tisket, A-Tasket" was the breakthrough hit of vocalist Ella Fitzgerald with the Chick Webb Orchestra.

From the lyrics…

A-tisket

A-tasket

I lost my yellow basket

Won't someone help me find my basket

And make me happy again?

In 1942, she performed "A-Tisket, A-Tasket" in her first ever screen role in Abbott and Costello's *Ride Em Cowboy*.

6. Cartoons: Land of the Lost. I refer not to the Saturday morning kids' show but the cartoon released in 1948 (based on a juvenile radio show), though I did not see it until considerably later, probably 1954, probably on *Lunch Time Little Theater* broadcast on weekdays on WGN.

The story: Billy and Isabel are fishing and catch Red Lantern, the talking fish, who takes them to the "Land of the Lost" at the bottom of the sea. The wise old fish shows them the Knives of the Square Table and Tableland, where all the lost dishes and spoons sing and play. Billy finds his lost jackknife.

The cartoon really got me. I think I might have cried. Damned right there ought to be a heaven for lost things. Makes as much sense as anything else.

And if I saw it now, I think I might cry.

7. Snapshot: Home-made poster on the pole. About as high as a kid can reach. Lost dog. "Max."

At the curb. A heap. Fur. Flies.

8. "To an Athlete Dying Young": A Poem by AE Housman.

I've taught all ages of students, from grade through grad school. I've seen the young and talented, sometimes cut down by the workings of The Big Boss who never did give Job much of an answer, if you think about it.

So I'll say AE Housman got some of it right.

A very, very small part of it.

9. Coping with Loss – Part Two: The show must go on… The show must go on… The show must go on. I'm a writer. My show is made of words.

During a remarkable 16 month stretch in my life, my mother died, my father died, a man who taught me to write died, and the man who taught me to teach died.

I did not write anything during that period or for a considerable time thereafter. The show must go on…

Eventually, it did.

And I am a lot older than Lou Costello ever got to be.

10. Tales of the Lost: This is a book of singular insight and compassion and imagination and thought.

It's edited by Eugene Johnson and Steve Dillon.

They understand.

— Mort Castle July 2020

Forever

Tim Waggoner

I'm sitting in my car, looking at a grassy field with a wooden sign rising from the ground that says *Townsend Park*. This is the place where my best friend Alison disappeared when we were both nine years old, and it's the first time I've been back in thirty years. I'm not sure how I expected to feel–nervous, maybe even a little scared–but all I feel is a distant sadness, more like a memory of emotion, a fading echo, than any real feeling.

I get out of my car, lock the doors, then start walking toward the sign. It's mid-December, but the temperature is in the high forties. It tends not to get too cold in Virginia this time of year, not like in Ohio where I live now. There's no snow on the ground and the grass is a dull, washed-out green, not the vibrant color I remember from my last time here. It was spring then, April 23rd, to be precise. The date's seared into my memory.

The park doesn't have an actual entrance, just this sign at the end of a cul-de-sac in a suburban neighborhood. The houses here are upper middle-class dwellings–two stories, with nicely landscaped yards and pools in the back. This town is a bedroom community for people who work in D.C., and while they aren't starving, they don't exactly qualify as wealthy. My parents lived a couple blocks from here, and Alison's lived across the street from us. I don't know if her parents are still there, don't know if they're still alive. I drove past their house before coming here, but I didn't stop. If they are still there, what could I possibly say to them? *Remember me? I'm the girl who was with your daughter when she disappeared. I'm all grown up and have lived the life Alison never got to. How are you doing these days?* But even if her parents still live in the house, I wouldn't stop. The last thing I want to do is talk to Alison's bitch of a mother.

The wind is coming from the east, and although this town is an hour's drive from the ocean, I detect a hint of saltwater in the air, and it makes me smile.

My parents used to take me to the beach in summer, and I would splash in the water and play in the sand for hours. It's been years since I've seen the ocean, and I really should get back there someday.

I walk past the wooden sign and into the empty field. Alison and I used to run back and forth across the grass, racing each other. Although she was smaller than me, she was always faster and I never could keep up. Sometimes we'd lie on our backs and look up at the clouds, tell each other what shapes we saw in them. I saw things like cats and dogs, ordinary, even banal shapes. But Alison saw things like a T-Rex riding a unicycle or a five-headed space alien. She was all imagination and boundless energy that girl, and I wonder what she would be like today if...

If.

If you keep walking straight across the field, you end up in another neighborhood. On the other side of that is a convenience store, and Alison and I used to take a short cut across the field and through that neighborhood so we could go to the store and get slushies. Grape for me, cherry for her. If you head left, though, you'll reach a stretch of woods that fill the park's west side, and I head in that direction now. The woods are a mix of trees—elm, cedar, oak, maple, pine. Most have shed their leaves, but some remain, stubborn holdouts that refuse to acknowledge the reality of the season. I know what it's like to fight the inevitable, and I admire their defiance. The sky's overcast, gray without being too gloomy. It's a balanced sky, one with an equal chance of bringing sun or rain, depending on which way the scales tip. I'm not sure which would suit my mood better, but I'll have to take what I can get. Life's like that, isn't it?

I didn't return to town specifically to visit the park. One of my cousins died in a car accident a week ago, and I attended the funeral this morning. My mom and dad stayed in Ohio. Both are in ill health—Mom's diabetic, Dad has heart trouble—but the truth is they fell out of touch with the rest of the family when we moved from Virginia, not long after Alison's disappearance. Since I'm an only child, and all my grandparents are dead, I was my immediate family's sole representative at the service. It was nice, as nice as a funeral can be, that is, but I spent most of the time thinking about Alison, which felt disrespectful to my cousin, but I couldn't help it. People are gathering at my cousin's house now, to tell her husband and parents how sorry they are as they nibble on finger food and drink stale coffee, weak tea, and warm soda. I know I should be there, but I can't make myself go. I've had enough of death for one morning, and the lure of the park, of *Alison*, is too strong.

When I reach the edge of the woods, I expect to hesitate, to have to muster my courage and force myself to keep going, but I don't slow down. If anything, I pick up speed as I walk past the first tree, dry leaves crunching beneath my shoes, and I continue on.

***

"I win, I win!"

"Not fair!"

We stop at the edge of the woods, breathing hard, faces flushed, sweat gleaming on our skin. We're both wearing T-shirts, shorts, and sneakers, the day gloriously warm, more like summer than spring. I'm eleven and Alison is nine. She's the annoying little sister I never had, and while she drives me crazy at times, I'm drawn to her boundless energy and enthusiasm for life, as if she's a miniature sun, blazing bright, her power feeding me—older, quieter, introverted—making me, at least for the time we're together, more like her. Bold and unafraid. We have a kind of symbiosis: she acts as the devil on my shoulder, tempting me into delicious mischief, while I'm the angel on her shoulder, trying to keep her from taking too many risks. I tether her to reality, she gives me wings to soar.

"We're not supposed to go in there," I say.

She bares her teeth in a wide smile.

"That's why it's *fun*."

She turns away from me and continues on into the woods. This is the moment when I still have a choice. I can stay here and wait for Alison to return or I can leave the park and go home, secure in the knowledge that I won't get in trouble for disobeying my parents. But there's always a moment like this for me when it comes to Alison, when I'm standing at the precipice of a new adventure and trying to work up the courage to jump, never knowing what will happen when I land. Who am I kidding? I always follow her, and I do so now.

She's not very far ahead of me, and I know she went slow to give me time to catch up. I do, and then we're walking together, Alison in the lead as usual, forging a path through the undergrowth. There are established trails in these woods, but Alison prefers to make her own way. Our bare legs are scratched by the thin branches of small trees as we go. The scratches sting, but I try to ignore the sensation. I doubt Alison even feels it. Her mind is too preoccupied with imagining all the wondrous things that might lie ahead of us. An enchanted castle, a fairy village, a dragon's lair… I look at the back of Alison's legs and see bruises. Most are minor, not too dark, but there's a larger one on the back of her left thigh, a purple splotch on her smooth, pink skin. I tell myself she got those bruises from her usual reckless play. She'd tried to perform some ill-advised maneuver—jumping over a lawn chair, riding a skateboard with her eyes closed—and she'd fallen and hurt herself. She was always trying stunts like that, and it was a wonder to me that she wasn't perpetually wearing a cast on one part of her body or another. And while it was quite possible these bruises were the result of another of her misadventures, I know how she really got them. Or rather, who gave them to her. Her mother had a temper, and she lost patience with Alison, her wild child, easily. I wonder what other marks Alison's clothes are hiding, and I feel a deep sense of sadness coupled with helplessness. I wish there was something I could do to help my friend, to fix things for her, but I know there isn't. It's no surprise to me that she doesn't feel the pain of the scratches on her legs. She's felt worse in her short life. Far worse.

There's a light breeze blowing, and the leaves on the trees above us rustle softly, making a sound like a rushing river. I imagine I hear voices as well, whispering words that I can't quite make out. These voices aren't sinister, though. Their tone is soothing, comforting, a balm for the spirit. I wish that time could stand still and I could live in this moment, with Alison, forever.

***

I try to retrace the steps Alison and I took that day, but it was so long ago, and I can't remember exactly where we entered the woods or what route we took. I decide to do what Alison would, and I move forward confidently, no hesitation, as if I know precisely where I'm going. The trees are larger–they've had thirty years to grow, after all–and the undergrowth is sparser than I remember. Most likely the tree canopy blocks the sunlight during the other seasons, stunting the growth of the vegetation below. It strikes me that this is a perfect metaphor for growing older–age hindering new growth–and I think of how different I am from the child that followed Alison into these woods on that long-ago day. I was all potential then, my whole life lying before me. Now I'm a barely adequate literature professor at an unremarkable college, divorced and childless. I used to tell myself that there's still time to start over, that as long as there's life, there's hope, all the platitudes that we fall back on at three in the morning when we can't sleep and the existential angst becomes too much. I don't tell myself there's time anymore because it's not true. Not for me. I feel like an empty shell of the girl I once was, a ghost haunting my own life, and attending my cousin's funeral didn't exactly cheer me up.

A couple months ago, I was watching a true crime program on television called *Suburban Nightmare*. I was shocked to realize the episode focused on Alison's disappearance. There were interviews with her family, police officers who investigated, neighbors who joined in the search for her... I was glad the show's producers hadn't tracked me down. I couldn't imagine talking about that day on camera. I wanted to turn off the program, but despite myself, I was captivated and couldn't stop watching. There was no new information presented, but it was difficult to hear people talk about Alison as if they knew her when *I* was her best friend, practically a big sister to her. Worst of all was having to watch Alison's mother get teary-eyed as she spoke of the last time she saw her darling daughter. Perhaps on some level her grief was genuine, but I remembered the bruises on the backs of Alison's legs that day, and all I could feel for her mother was hatred.

It was so bizarre, seeing one of the pivotal events of my life turned into a thirty-minute (with commercials) show, complete with cheesy reenactments. I suppose that's one of the reasons why I've come here–to purge the emotional residue left behind from watching that program. *A walk through the woods is cheaper than therapy,* I think, and I manage a small smile.

As I move through the woods, I navigate by instinct, following an inner pull that guides me towards my destination. I haven't been here for thirty years, yet there is no floundering, no going about in circles, no turning back and retracing my steps because I've gone in the wrong direction. My soul knows the way, and it leads me there, straight and true.

The trees are older here, taller, set closer together, forming a barrier that's difficult to see through. I slip between a pair of elms and am immediately confronted by a fenced-in area. The fence is chain link, and it's a head taller than me, making it six feet in height, maybe more. There's a door built into the fence, but it's closed and sealed by a rusty padlock. The enclosure is square, the ground within covered with dead leaves, and in the middle is a tall stone monument, perhaps ten feet in height. The white stone is tinged with the gray of age, but its edges are still sharp, its details clear. The top of the monument was carved to look as if a vase rests atop it, with a cloth draped over it and a garland of flowers looped across. The design is meant to look classical, like Greek or Roman architecture, and there's a beauty and elegance to it that takes my breath away for a moment. When I was a child, I wondered what the stone vase was supposed to contain. Water? Wine? A magic potion?

Despite the fence, someone has gotten inside and spray-painted graffiti on the stone's surface in black. A peace sign, and below it four words in capital letters: THEY WILL LIVE FOREVER. This last word is hyphenated, *for* above *ever*, because of the monument's narrow width. The words send a chill rippling down my back, and I look away from them. There's a metal sign bolted to the fence near the door. I've seen it before, read its words, but I walk over to refresh my memory.

Townsend Family Cemetery

Burgess, Virginia

Below this, a pair of names and dates.

Thomas Townsend (1821-1892)

Marie Townsend (1826-1887)

The sign goes on to tell the Townsends' story, a childless couple who lived here during the Civil War and who left their land to the town after they died, with the stipulation that it be turned into a park. *For the children,* the sign says. Relatives commissioned this monument and erected it here, presumably where the couple was buried, to commemorate their generous gift. The entire park was once their property, and the park itself is as much a monument to their legacy as this stone pillar, maybe more so. Alison and I came here many times, and although we were tempted to climb the fence and go inside so we could inspect the monument up close, lay our hands upon the cold stone and think about the people buried there, we never tried. It seemed disrespectful. Even Alison, as curious and impulsive as she was, didn't attempt to scale the fence.

I look at the monument and once more read the words – THEY WILL LIVE FOREVER – and I think back to the true crime show about Alison's disappearance. At the end, the narrator discussed various theories about what might've happened to her. The most prominent was that she'd been abducted by a stranger, taken somewhere and killed, her body disposed of and never found. Another popular theory was that her mother had something to do with her disappearance. The rumor was that Alison hadn't vanished in the park at all, that she'd gone home and her mother, upset for some reason—Alison had been gone too long, she'd returned with mud on her shoes—punished her, perhaps beating her so severely she died. Panicked and facing arrest, Alison's mother, with her father's help, hid her body somewhere and made up the story about Alison's disappearance. Local police had their suspicions, as did the community, but nothing had ever been proven. My parents didn't know what to believe. They were simply relieved that whatever happened to Alison didn't happen to me. Best case scenario, everyone figured, she ran away from her abusive home. Although a young girl on her own would be easy prey, people whispered darkly. Regardless of whatever happened to Alison, no one ever expected to see her again.

And they never did.

***

"Do you think they're *really* buried here?" Alison asks.

She holds onto the fence, fingers grasping metal links, forehead pressing to the chain link, as if she wants to get as close to the monument as she possibly can, maybe even hoping to push her body through the fence if she just tries hard enough.

The monument's stone is a bit whiter than it will be thirty years hence, and its surface is unmarred by graffiti.

I didn't know the answer to Alison's question, but I knew what she wanted me to say.

"Of course they are. They wouldn't put a monument here if they weren't."

She grins and shivers with delicious fear.

"It must be nice." Her tone is wistful.

"What? Being dead?"

She shoots me a look.

"No." She pauses, considers. "Well, that might be okay. You'd get to sleep a lot and no one would bother you."

She puts a slight emphasis on the word *bother*, and I think of the bruises on her body.

"I mean being here all the time," she says. "Living in the woods, trees all around, protected by a fence, peaceful and quiet…"

She falls silent and continues to stare at the monument. Tears begin to roll slowly down her cheeks, and I step closer to her and put my arm around her shoulders. I start crying too, and I stand next to my friend, looking at the monument with her, and for the first time in my young life, it occurs to me that being dead might be—just sometimes—better than being alive.

The padlock on the fence's door—which has only started to rust at this point—snicks open. Our attention is immediately drawn to the sound, and we watch as the door, with a gentle creaking, swings outward of its own accord.

Alison and I look at each other, mouths open, eyes wide with fear. I want to run, run as fast as I can away from here, leave the park, and never come back. And if I was alone, that's precisely what I'd do. But I'm not alone. I'm with Alison, and while it's clear she's afraid, she shows no sign of wanting to leave. Quite the opposite.

She pulls away from me, does her best to wipe the tears from her face with her hands. Her smile is faint and unsteady, but it's there, accompanied by a glint in her eyes that I know only too well.

I shake my head.

"Come on," she says. "It's like we've been invited."

She reaches out to take my hand, but I step back and shake my head harder.

"Don't do it. It's not…" I don't know what to say. Not *right?* Not *safe?* Not *sane?*

Her smile becomes sad.

"I need to do this. I *have* to."

She's asking for my understanding, but I can't give it. After I remain silent for several moments, she leans forward, gives me a quick kiss on the cheek, then whirls about and sprints away from me. I try to grab hold of her to stop her, but she's already moved beyond my grasp. I run after her, chasing her around the fence.

"Stop!" I shout. "Please!"

She reaches the opening in the fence before I do, and she plunges through. I'm almost there when the gate slams shut and the padlock engages once more. I reach the door, grab hold of it, shake it hard, but of course it doesn't open.

Alison has stopped running. She stands inside the enclosure, looking upon the monument once more. Is she regretting her choice? Is she wary? Or is she excited by what's about to happen? Knowing Alison, I figure all of the above.

She turns to look at me one last time, then she starts walking slowly toward the monument. Shadows pool around its base, and from this darkness two figures begin to emerge, human silhouettes, and while they possess no distinguishing feature other than one being taller than the other, I know they are man and woman. A married couple. A *childless* couple. They raise their arms as they glide toward Alison, and I'm too terrified to watch anymore. I turn and run, run, run, and I don't stop running until I reach my house. I collapse into a sitting position on the porch, put my face into my hands and sob.

***

I never told anyone about what I saw that day. I made up a story, said that Alison and I had become separated in the woods. I called and called for her, I said, but she never answered. My parents called the police, and a pair of officers came and questioned me. The police began searching the park and people in the neighborhood volunteered to help, my parents included. I stayed home, fearing that I wouldn't be able to pretend to look for Alison, couldn't deliver a convincing performance, so I stayed home. Alison wasn't found, of course, and she became officially missing, and she'd remain so for the next thirty years. I sometimes wondered what Alison's mother thought about her daughter's sudden disappearance. Was she upset? Scared? Relieved that the child she hated would no longer be a bother to her? I never found out, and I decided it didn't matter. All that was important was that Alison was beyond her mother's reach.

Here I am, an adult, something that Alison never had the chance to become. An adult who returned to town for a funeral. An adult with a secret she didn't share with any of her relatives who attended the service.

"Hey, Alison," I say softly. "It's me, all grown up. I hope you found the peace you were looking for. You deserve it. I could use a little peace myself these days. I'm sick, Alison. I have a tumor inside my head, and it's inoperable. The doctors say I might have a year left, but maybe only six months. It depends on how fast the tumor grows from this point on. I haven't really started experiencing any symptoms yet, at least not serious ones. Sometimes I forget things, and sometimes I get dizzy, but that's it so far. It's going to get worse, though. A *lot* worse. And soon."

The leaves within the enclosure stir slightly. I might put the motion down to the wind, but at this moment, the air is still.

"You found a way to escape all those years ago. Could you help me do the same?" I pause, smile. "For an old friend?"

Nothing happens for several moments, and I begin to think the tumor has affected my brain more than I realized, that it's made me believe impossible things, and if I'm not exactly crazy, I'm not altogether sane, either. But then— just as I'm about to turn away—a pile of leaves near the monument leaps into the air and swirls around several times before compacting into the shape of a child. A *girl* child, I know, although there are no obvious features to indicate gender. The figure comes walking toward me, the dried leaves that comprise its body making soft rasping-crunching sounds as it approaches. I should be afraid of this strange apparition coming toward me, but I'm not. How could I ever be scared of the best friend I've ever had?

When Alison reaches me, she stops and stretches out a leaf-covered hand, her "fingers" formed from wooden twigs. *Nice touch*, I think. I take her hand, crying now, and the twig fingers feel surprisingly warm, as if I'm holding onto flesh-and-blood. She tugs me forward, pulling hard, and I feel my body trying to resist her. She pulls harder, and I experience a sensation of letting go, as if

I've just shrugged off clothes that I'd been wearing too long, and ill-fitting ones at that. I feel light, feel free.

I look down at our clasped hands. Alison's is that of a young girl, and mine is smaller now, fingers slender, skin smoother. I look at Alison's face—we're the same height now—and see a little girl smiling at me. We're both dressed in T-shirts and shorts, as we were on that long-ago day. There are no bruises on Alison's skin that I can see, no marks of any kind, and this fills my heart with joy.

I glance back over my shoulder, expecting to see my adult body lying on the ground, dead, but nothing is there. I'm not exactly sure what's happened to me, but I know *why* it's happened. Alison has invited me to play with her, and I intend to do just that. I squeeze her hand in gratitude.

"Thank you," I say.

She squeezes back then releases my hand and gives me a huge grin.

"Race you to the park sign!" she says and before I can respond, she sprints past me toward the fence's open doorway. Laughing, I give chase. I don't think about my discontent with my job or my failed marriage, and most of all I don't think about my tumor. All these things are unimportant now, so much so it's like they never existed at all.

As I leave the enclosure, I catch a glimpse of two shadowy figures standing near the monument. The taller shadow has its arm around the smaller one, and the Townsends watch me as I face forward once more and pour on the speed. I know I won't catch up to Alison—she's too fast—but that's okay. I'm just happy to run, happy to feel alive...

...happy to be home.

The End

Someone Lost
and Someone Saved

Heather Graham

Kaylyn Connor sat by the bed, holding her father-in-law's hand. She shouldn't have been allowed there, she knew, and she was grateful that she'd accidentally slipped through.

Many patients were there, dying alone. It wasn't through any cruelty—it was to stop the spread of the virus and spare the doctors and nurses from trying desperately to save more people.

But it was obvious she had already been exposed; she'd come in with Papa Drew to emergency because her mother-in-law had been too fragile and hysterical; the paramedics had refused to take her. And Kaylyn had managed to get into the ambulance because he'd been picked up for a suspected heart attack and not the virus. And once she'd been there . . .

Now, of course, she'd have to self-quarantine. For weeks. She wouldn't be at his funeral; she had to be grateful instead that she'd spend his last minutes with him. And she was grateful. And while Evan had been trying to console his mother, she'd managed to get into the ambulance. Their eyes had met for a minute; Evan adored his father. But he knew as well that his dad and Kaylyn had always had something special and there would have been no way for him to stop the ambulance—not as things were—and change places with her. He gave her a sad smile and a little nod; he was glad she'd be with his father. He was grateful his father wasn't going to be alone.

At first, of course, when Papa Drew had experienced moments of being cognizant, she had assured him they'd be going home soon.

He'd known they weren't. But he smiled.

"Yes," he had told her. "I will be going home."

Dr. Hanson walked into the room. He noted her holding Papa Drew's hand, but he didn't say anything. He was geared up, and in his mask and cap and protective wear, his eyes were all that she could see of him. He was such a good man. Kind and empathetic. She knew it had hurt him when he'd told her that Papa Drew's organs were failing.

It was a matter of time.

"He's not in any pain," Dr. Hanson said softly.

Kaylyn nodded. "Thank you," she said softly.

"Normally, I'd have you call your husband and . . ." His voice trailed.

They weren't living in normality.

"It's okay. I understand," she said. She tried to smile. Dr. Hanson was dealing with so much. "I'm okay, and he's okay," she assured the doctor. "He's the greatest guy—born very Irish and very Catholic, but he loved to watch any preacher on TV, studied other religions . . . I've never seen anyone with so much faith."

She wished she had that faith! This hurt; hurt so badly. She'd lost her own parents a few years back; lost a best friend to cystic fibrosis. And now, here, she was losing someone again.

"Faith is beautiful," Hanson said. "I'll be back to check on you, but . . . I'm so sorry. He won't awaken again. He's in a coma. Now, he'll just slip away. You could—"

"I'm grateful to have slipped in here. I'll be here—and I'll do whatever I should do to keep others safe after."

He nodded. She thought that he was offering her a weak smile; it was hard to tell beneath his mask.

Hanson left the room. She was alone. She smiled to herself; Papa Drew had awakened that morning. He'd smiled at her and asked about his glasses; she'd given them to him. He'd asked about a Danish then—not at all impressed with the globular eggs on the plate that had been brought to him. He'd talked, asking about his wife and his son and she'd explained that people just weren't being let in and that hopefully, they'd all soon be together.

He'd smiled then and told her one of his stories. This one had been about chasing a leprechaun through the cemetery—and how he had stopped before he'd caught the little rascal because he'd seen the Mother Mary, staring right at him, and chastising him.

"You don't need to be catching a leprechaun, boy. You've a beautiful family, all the love in the world, and that's far richer than a pot of gold!"

Papa Drew had grinned then. "She was right; my wife, my son—you! And fear not, lass, wherever I may be, I'll be watching the beauty of your babes when you choose to have them!"

"They will love you! Best grandpa in the world!" she'd told him.

And she'd squeezed his hand.

Now . . . she sat. And she waited. Just holding his hand.

She could still feel his warmth; she could see the rise and fall of his chest. He was breathing; he was alive. She could hear his breath.

Then, she couldn't. But she still sat there. His hand was warm.

She loved him.

She hadn't slept in nearly forty hours, and despite all else, she felt her eyes closing. It didn't matter. She was here. She was with him. Maybe he could feel that she tried with all her heart to give him all the love that she could through that handhold.

She did, indeed, wish that she had his faith.

She'd been so close with her mom and so devastated when cancer had taken her. And she'd adored her father, a cop, a good one—really fighting for all good things, like a Superman—truth, justice, and the American Way. But he'd also been all about kindness. They'd never had that much money, but he'd talked to people who did, and he got them to help the homeless he found on the streets, to help at animal shelters and more. He and her father-in-law had been good friends, though they'd teased each often enough. And she wanted to have faith, but . . .

She had bitterness. Her parents had been good people. They had died young. And now, Papa Drew, as they called him, was dying too young, too.

And the world was a mess.

She tried hard to focus on the positive. She was somehow—miraculously—with him. Holding his hand.

She must have drifted to sleep, and into a dream. They were in Ireland—she'd been herself with Evan for their honeymoon, but never with Drew and Katie, her mother-in-law.

But they were all there. Drew had been born in Dublin, but he'd loved the countryside. His family—far, far, back—had owned a place called The Wilds and he'd loved to come there. They were standing there, on the beauty of the high cliffs in a field of rich green grass. The sky overhead was just dotted with white clouds and the breeze was gentle.

Drew was to her left and he looked at her with one of his mischievous grins. "Race you!" he cried, and he was off, running, and she laughed and ran with him and she felt the beauty of the sun and the day and feeling the air and the wonder of the day.

Max caught up and ran into her and they both tumbled down, rolling to the base of the hill that led up to the old castle ruins, and they laughed. Then Drew was there, helping them both to their feet and he smiled at her and said, "Ah, there's the girl! And there's the life! I see the old castle, and the memory is in the heart!"

She woke with a start. Nothing had changed. She was still holding Drew's hand. Nothing had changed. But the dream made her smile.

There was a sound in the hall, and she looked up, thinking that Dr. Hanson had come back.

It wasn't Dr. Hanson. It was an older woman in a hospital gown.

Kaylyn frowned, certain that patients weren't supposed to be moving about the halls.

But the woman made no attempt to come in. She stood in the hallway and looked in and smiled. "Ah, girl! Lucky you are, and lucky he is. These days . . . I adore my grandchildren so! And my children, of course. And I don't worry about myself, I don't. I worry about them."

"I'm—sure they'll be fine," Kaylyn said. She had to say something that was reassuring.

"Well, you see, in my heart, the pain is for the living. They can't hold their loved ones as they leave this world. They want to be with us, as if they can take us to a door of safety. They long to let their love be known. And, yes, indeed, it would be lovely to see sweet faces! But love isn't time or a touch, it's something eternal. I wish they knew I was fine, and I feel their love, with them here, without them here. I'm happy for you . . . my poor daughter! She fears I won't be remembered in a proper way, that there can't be a funeral where I am loved and honored. But I will be okay; it is for them that I hurt, and I wish they knew . . . well, love is sweet, and my life was love, and I carry that with me— with or without whatever might be done in life. Dust to dust, ashes to ashes, but love is eternal. Even when there's loss, that love stays in the heart. I will be just fine. You take care, sweet child! Whatever may be, I had years of love and life, and they were good. You're a young thing. You . . . well, you must now take care of yourself. You must remember that love lives on in the heart."

"Yes, of course."

The older woman looked in at Drew on the bed. "A lovely man?"

"Yes. My father-in-law."

"Ah, an in-law!"

Kaylyn smiled. "They joke you marry a man and not his parents. I love my husband, but I would have married him for his folks and his family. They're amazing."

"And love knows no boundaries of blood!" the woman said. "You take care, child. You take care of yourself. And your husband and those he loves, and you love." She grinned. "And, I believe, you will care for those you meet in life, those you pass—those strangers who need a seat on the bus, or a sandwich since they live on the street. You will do fine, I believe."

Kaylyn smiled. She couldn't help herself. "Well, thank you. I hope so. But, you know, you have just met me—I could be a horrible human being!"

"But you're not."

"You know that?"

"Oh, yes, I do. I know that well!"

Kaylyn grinned. "Well, thank you, then. Now, I'm worried about you. Shouldn't you be lying down? Are you feeling better? Will you get to leave soon?"

"I will be leaving soon," she said.

"Wonderful!" Kaylyn said.

She didn't reply, but said instead, "Well, do your best, child. Try to make those left behind see that in the end, fanfare is nothing. It's what existed in life that mattered, the love. And the love was there, with all of us, to the end—and then, it's there beyond!"

The woman lifted a hand and gave Kaylyn a sweet and mischievous smile. "I guess I had best get back before . . . well, I guess I had best get back. Don't want to get caught, you know?"

Kaylyn laughed. "No, don't get caught."

The woman was gone. And Kaylyn, still holding Drew's hand, missed her. The exchange had been nice. She wished she would have asked the woman her name. She was a sweet little spitfire!

Nothing. Nothing different.

She leaned back in her chair again. She was so tired. But so glad to be there.

Coffee would have been nice.

But, in truth, she knew she wasn't allowed to roam the halls, and the nurses and orderlies were overworked; she didn't want to ask anyone for anything.

She thought about some of the things the woman had said, and she thought about Drew's wonderful sense of life and humor. He'd become an engineer in "real life." But he'd worked in dinner theater for years and was a patron of one of their local theaters. He had taught kids drama for years at the theater and had studied with some of the most wonderful teachers when he'd been young. She knew he'd done a stint at a Marcel Marceau school in France and worked several years behind the scenes on Broadway. He'd talked about teaching sometimes.

"I had a teacher who was of the 'tree' method. You know. You are the tree—be the tree! But, most of the time, a cast is an ensemble. Yes, you are the character, be the character. But every time a character enters a scene, the real question is this—what does that character want? Motivation drives us all. Be the tree, but remember, you need to know what it is that the tree wants! Now, this doesn't have to be bad. Sometimes the tree just wants to make sure that everything is all right with all the other trees in the forest. Then, of course, you have that tree wants the sunshine all to himself. But most trees are decent, and still—what the tree is looking for, what it wants, separates it from other trees!"

"This tree would really like coffee!" she said softly.

His hand moved; she felt it. He squeezed her hand.

She smiled. "I think you told me that trees sometimes accepted the fact they weren't going to get what they wanted, and they could rip up the scene because of it—or accept the matter and move on, changing direction—growing. The best characters, you told me once, are those that grow throughout a book, a play, or a movie. Right?"

She thought he would squeeze her hand again.

He didn't. Or, did he? She didn't know what she really felt, what she saw, and what was real, and what was a dream when she dozed off. No, she felt his hand. And he did squeeze hers!

"You know," she said, determined to be bright, "I had this great dream about all of us taking a vacation together. Of course, you've been in Ireland—

you were born there, and you've been back a dozen times. But I dreamed about all four of us being there, and we were running in the grass and it was so beautiful! When you're better and this is all over, we're going back. All of us!"

She was sure that, once again, she felt his hand squeeze hers.

Maybe he could get better!

But as that thought struck her, she saw orderlies moving through the hall, two young men, all in their anti-contamination apparel, masks and paper gowns.

The hospital was full.

They could be going anywhere.

Dread filled her as, a moment later, they appeared in the hall again. They had one of the small stretcher beds that moved through the hall, bringing the sick to and from tests . . .

And to the morgue.

This time, they were moving a bed. A sheet covered the body on the bed. All of it; the head and face were covered.

She knew this time, the body was heading to the morgue.

Dr. Hanson was there, saying something to one of the orderlies.

He saw her watching.

He stuck his head in the and asked her, "Are you doing all right, Kaylyn?"

"I'm—fine," she said, and she smiled. "Some people are . . . well, maybe getting better."

"Yes, hopefully, many will get better."

"Don't be angry, but one of your patients was out. Moving. I'm hoping she's going to be all right. She was very sweet. An older woman."

He stared back at her.

"Really! I shouldn't have spoken. Don't be angry! She was so sweet. So kind."

He was still just staring.

"Dr. Hanson, seriously, she didn't come in; she didn't do anything wrong—"

"Kaylyn, no one was moving about the hall. There's only one older woman here, and, well, she wasn't moving around."

"Oh, but she was! Don't be angry—"

"Kaylyn, maybe we should get you out of here."

"No, no! I'm here now. It's a miracle I'm here, but I'm staying!"

He nodded. Then, even behind his mask, she saw that he sighed.

"I'm so sorry; you didn't see a woman. I hope you were sleeping—and dreaming."

"But Dr. Hanson—"

"That was Mrs. Abigail Harrison. And she wasn't moving, Kaylyn. Um . . . that was Mrs. Harrison that the orderlies just . . . brought from her room."

She'd been the body beneath the sheet in the bed heading to the morgue.

Kaylyn fought hard to conceal her thoughts, fears, and emotions.

"Ah, I see. Well, I guess I have been dreaming. Nice dreams, so, no problem!" Kaylyn said cheerfully.

Dr. Hanson came on into the room, stopping to check on Papa Drew.

He looked over the bed at Kaylyn.

"You know," he said softly, "you could leave. He's in a coma, and I think . . . well, you understand his organs are failing him. He'll be gone very soon; he won't regain consciousness before then. This must be very difficult for you. Miserable."

Kaylyn shook her head. "No, I understand I'm lucky to be here—"

"And, well, of course, whether you were or weren't here, you know, you, your husband, and your mother-in-law must be in quarantine for the next several weeks and test negative after that."

"Yes, of course."

He looked at her, shaking his head. "You know, you expose yourself every minute that you're here."

"I know."

"Maybe—"

"Dr. Hanson, I don't know how I managed to get in here. My husband . . . well, I know he wished it had been him, but he's glad that it's at least me, and . . . I'm not going."

Hanson lowered his eyes and nodded.

"You're here, so, well, you're here. I'll keep checking in," he promised.

He left her.

She continued to hold Papa Drew's hand. Her eyes began to close again.

Christmas, two years ago. The silly Santa game . . . a twenty-dollar gift given, and a twenty-dollar gift received. There had been a good group with Papa Drew and Granny, her and Max, Max's brother and his brother's wife and their kids, and her sister and her husband and their kids and her brother-in-law's parents. She'd done the buying for several of them, some really cool on-sale toolboxes and music sets—and, at the end, when she was short one gift—a ridiculous pair of elf slippers. Papa Drew had wound up with the ridiculous elf slippers, and he'd loved them! He'd put them on, found someone's Santa hat, and danced around for the kids, delighting them all.

The memory made her smile, even in a state of being half awake and half asleep.

Memories were great. He had a way of talking to little ones, of entertaining them. She and Max wanted children and intended to have them, but they had both been trying to establish themselves with their work first—kids in just a year or two. They were still in their mid-twenties, so they had time.

No, they didn't.

Not for their children to know the wonder of the man who had been their grandfather.

Happiness nearly turned to tears.

They had video; they had memories. She knew she would be able to tell her children just how wonderful this grandfather had been—and, of course, their other grandfather, her dad, a man she had all but hero-worshipped, and she had loved her mom so much!

They were lost.

No, never lost.

"And Mom, Dad, you were the best! I had friends with parents who were abusive, if not physically, mentally. And friends with parents who really didn't care. And friends with okay parents, but no one as wonderful as you, so, I'm so grateful! Grateful that I had you for the time that I had you—better than all the time in the world with someone else!"

She was startled to see that Dr. Hanson was standing by the door again.

She lifted a hand to him. "It's okay. Yes, I'm talking to myself. I'll keep it down. I promise!"

He gave her a thumbs-up sign.

Despite that, she wondered if she hadn't worried him a little. He was probably overwhelmed with the cases he was handling—not to mention the normal amount of heart attacks, liver failure, and broken body parts that might also need healing.

But he headed on out.

She closed her eyes again.

Easter. Another big family event, this one held by Papa Drew and Granny every year in their backyard, after church, and any stray friend of anyone who had no other plans was welcome to attend.

And there was Papa Drew—in a ridiculous giant bunny suit, all to entertain the kids, and the adults as well.

He wasn't perfect, and she knew that. People didn't belong on pedestals. They all had their faults and without them, they wouldn't be human. Papa Drew loved to play poker—and sometimes, he lost a few hands too many and Granny would chastise him. But that was okay; she loved him anyway. And he tried his hardest to make it up to her while arguing they were both retired—they had worked hard all their lives and the world allowed them to play.

And, of course, he was such a spiritual man. A Christian at heart, and so Granny liked to warn him that if the Second Coming happened, he'd be in trouble because Christ wouldn't be able to find him at the poker table.

And Granny would tell him that yes, that was fine—except that, while the house was paid off, they were still expected to pay their taxes every year!

He promised her he would never lose the taxes, and he would never lose the money they needed for the family, either. And she would just wave a spoon in the air and head back to the kitchen.

They'd had such a good life, and she hoped she had appreciated it, and she knew she had never thought just to be thankful for such days.

And now . . .

She blinked furiously. She had reached a state where she wasn't sure if she was awake or asleep, drowsing or dreaming.

She smiled to herself. She had, at least, stopped speaking aloud. Hanson wouldn't have to worry about her.

She closed her eyes. Really, there was nothing she could do except try to rest, even sleep, because there was nothing else she could do; she was here, and she was holding Papa Drew's hand.

She squeezed his hand again and said, "I love you so much. And Max loves you, and Granny loves you . . . everyone loves you so much. You . . . we'll always love you. Always!"

He couldn't hear her, of course. He was in a coma.

But maybe he could hear her.

She talked to him. She remembered Christmas and Easter to him, and all the times that had been so good. And she laughed and thanked him for Max, because Max was the best husband ever—oh, they were human, too. They had their fights, but they ended quickly. Max was . . .

"You raised an amazing son!"

He didn't respond. But she wanted to believe he heard her. She'd read that people in a coma could hear what went on around them.

Smiling, she leaned back. She closed her eyes. She started to drowse, awake enough to make sure she never released his hand.

She didn't know how much time had passed; she must have drifted off again and this time, without dreaming.

Because she suddenly felt movement; Papa Drew's hand, still clutched in her own.

She opened her eyes and sat straight with a start.

Papa Drew was not lying back in his bed. He was sitting up, and he was just as straight as she was.

He was looking across the room, at the corner. There was a window to Kaylyn's right, and the TV was up high in the corner, but . . .

He wasn't looking at the TV.

He was staring into the corner, smiling.

His eyes were open. He was smiling. He looked . . . so happy.

Kaylyn looked where he was looking. She could see nothing, and yet . . .

There was something there . . . something, someone. She could not see anything, and yet she had the strangest sense that there was . . . something.

She stared at Papa Drew. He was still smiling.

He started to release her hand, but then he didn't. He reached up with his free hand, his left hand, and he stretched it across the room, still smiling.

Still with his eyes opened.

Kaylyn felt chills race up and down her spine, and yet . . .

Chills, but she wasn't frightened. Chills that said yes, something is there.

Papa Drew's smile grew bigger still.

Then his left arm fell back to his side. He turned to her, still smiling, and he whispered, "I love you, and my boy, of course, and my wife. Love you!"

He squeezed her hand.

Then he fell back, eyes closed.

His hand was still in hers, but there was something different about it.

Kaylyn jumped up, searching the bed for the control, hitting the call button.

Seconds later, Dr. Hanson was in the room.

"He sat up, doctor; he sat up and talked! But then he laid down again, and I . . . but he did wake up! He sat up in bed . . . he talked to me. He squeezed my hand. Is there a chance—"

Hanson had been working over Papa Drew.

He stood, and she saw the truth in his face before he spoke.

"I'm so sorry, I believe he passed right after I left the room."

"No, he sat up and talked. I swear, I saw him."

The doctor looked at her sorrowfully.

"Kaylyn, you poor dear. You've been here with him, with us. And so tired! You must have slipped off to sleep again, and, of course, that's lovely, you'll have a memory, even if the memory was a dream."

He didn't believe her.

But then, he didn't believe she'd seen the woman in the hall, either.

But she had! She hadn't been dreaming, had she?

No!

She glanced at her arm; she still had goosebumps.

Not bad, goosebumps, and she had felt a bad chill.

She smiled. "No, you don't understand. Drew was one of the most spiritual men I ever knew. I say spiritual because he was Catholic, but he'd go to any church, listen to a priest, a rabbi, an imam, a preacher—you name it—if they were giving a sermon on kindness and caring. I think that . . . I think that someone came for him. And I think he greeted them, that he knew he was going, he knew someone would come . . . I . . ."

"Kaylyn, of course. Someone came for him. He has passed. I think you need to say goodbye, and someone will get you to the exit where they'll . . . well, we have a medicinal disinfectant which isn't a true guard against a virus, but . . . and don't forget. You must remain quarantined now for two weeks and then test negative. Have home delivery, please, and, after your husband gets you, please have him stay home, too." He hesitated. "You all must—for other people."

"Of course."

"I sound so . . . harsh, and I'm so sorry and . . . I'll call your husband and tell him his dad has passed and it's time he comes for you. And I'll give you . . . another five minutes here, a real goodbye. An orderly will come to escort you."

"Thank you," she told him.

He hesitated and then nodded.

"I mean, thank you, seriously, and all the doctors and nurses and hospital workers and janitors—thank you. With everything in me. Thank you."

She knew that he smiled. "Thank you," he told her.

And he left.

When he was gone, she stood. She held her father-in-law's hand, and it was true—he was gone. There was a difference.

The spirit of the man no longer rested in the body.

And still she folded his arms and laced his fingers in prayer. He'd like that, she knew.

"I love you," she murmured.

Of course, there was no answer.

"I will never forget you. And my children will know all about you."

She looked around the room again, and, in the end, focused on the corner.

There was nothing there now. Absolutely nothing there.

In a minute, the orderly arrived. He had empathy; he was polite. He was also getting her out of the hospital. He had brought her a clean mask to wear just to get out of the hospital, and with his gloved hands he gave her a new pair of gloves and a tiny container of hand sanitizer.

"I'm so sorry," he told her. "And again, you don't know how lucky you were! We aren't letting people in. I think someone thought you were part of rescue. You were masked and I guess your sweats are the same color as some uniforms and . . . anyway, he had you, and you had him, and that may not help when you've lost someone, but—"

"It helped," she said. And she thanked him, too.

Max, of course, was crying. He was alone, and he was anxious to get back to his mom. She did her best to console him.

But he had to cry awhile, and she knew it. She somehow realized that feeling loss made people human, and those who felt it so keenly had the ability to be human—and humane.

It was later when he came to her, his mom in bed, needing time then to be alone, and took her into his arms. "I'm so glad you were with him," he said, "and so sorry, too. You've faced so much loss, and my dad . . . I know you loved him. Another loss."

She thought about his words. And she thought about the woman in the hallway, the words she had said.

And she thought about Papa Drew.

She hadn't been dreaming.

She had seen him sit up. And if angels would come for anyone in the world, surely they would come for him.

She wrapped her arms around her grieving husband.

"Another loss, and yet something gained," she said.

Max looked at her frowning.

"I lost your dad, yes. But he gave me something so beautiful before he left."

"That was—"

"Life and love. The memories of life and love, the memories that shape us, and give to us. But he gave me even more!"

"More?"

And she found she could give him a real smile. "Hope, my love. Your dad gave me an incredible gift; he gave me hope."

The End

The Lady of Styx

Stephanie M. Wytovich

Split-faced, wearing a neckline of blood
the bones of my forest whisper
into pockets of moonlight, the flutter
of batwings a harmony to torn throats,
to ripped-out screams.

With a stomach full of stones,
I walk barefoot on the corpses of my sisters,
drown in irony, the waters of my rage
a cyclone, a force-fed monster born
from last words, from quiet moments
of prayer.

Bent-necked and flaccid, I succumb
to graveyards made of pain and hair,
the ashes of burnings thick in my mouth:
I lick the earth poison, weave crowns
of fresh henbane as I sing songs of
death, bury coins in the dirt.

I watch them rise, their bodies cold,
luminescent in sleepless flight,
I slit my wrists with elder, bleed
my name into the wind. The sky opens,
removes the shrouds from their faces,
with them, I walk into the dark, its arms
a familiar embrace.

20th Century Ghost

Joe Hill

The best time *to see her is when the place is almost full.*

There is the well-known story of the man who wanders in for a late show and finds the vast six-hundred-seat theater almost deserted. Halfway through the movie, he glances around and discovers her sitting next to him, in a chair that only moments before had been empty. Her witness stares at her. She turns her head and stares back. She has a nosebleed. Her eyes are wide, stricken. My head hurts, *she whispers.* I have to step out for a moment. Will you tell me what I miss? *It is in this instant that the person looking at her realizes she is as insubstantial as the shifting blue ray of light cast by the projector. It is possible to see the next seat over through her body. As she rises from her chair, she fades away.*

Then there is the story about the group of friends who go into the Rosebud together on a Thursday night. One of the bunch sits down next to a woman by herself, a woman in blue. When the movie doesn't start right away, the person who sat down beside her decides to make conversation. What's playing tomorrow? *he asks her.* The theater is dark tomorrow, *she whispers.* This is the last show. *Shortly after the movie begins she vanishes. On the drive home, the man who spoke to her is killed in a car accident.*

These, and many of the other best-known legends of the Rosebud, are false... the ghost stories of people who have seen too many horror movies and who think they know exactly how a ghost story should be.

Alec Sheldon, who was one of the first to see Imogene Gilchrist, owns the Rosebud, and at seventy-three still operates the projector most nights. He can always tell, after talking to someone for just a few moments, whether or not they really saw her, but what he knows he keeps to himself, and he never publicly discredits anyone's story... that would be bad for business.

He knows, though, that anyone who says they could see right through her didn't see her at all. Some of the put-on artists talk about blood pouring from her nose, her ears, her eyes; they say she gave them a pleading look, and asked for them to find somebody, to bring help. But she doesn't bleed that way, and when she wants to talk, it isn't to tell someone to bring a doctor. A lot of the pretenders begin their stories by saying, You'll never believe what I just saw. *They're right. He won't, although he will listen to all that they have to say, with a patient, even encouraging, smile.*

The ones who have seen her don't come looking for Alec to tell him about it. More often than not he finds them, comes across them wandering the lobby on unsteady legs; they've had a bad shock, they don't feel well. They need to sit down a while. They don't ever say, You won't believe what I just saw. *The experience is still too immediate. The idea that they might not be believed doesn't occur to them until later. Often they are in a state that might be described as subdued, even submissive. When he thinks about the effect she has on those who encounter her, he thinks of Steven Greenberg coming out of* The Birds *one cool Sunday afternoon in 1963. Steven was just twelve then, and it would be another twelve years before he went and got so famous; he was at that time not a golden boy, but just a boy.*

Alec was in the alley behind the Rosebud, having a smoke, when he heard the fire door into the theater clang open behind him. He turned to see a lanky kid leaning in the doorway—just leaning there, not going in or out. The boy squinted into the harsh white sunshine, with the confused, wondering look of a small child who has just been shaken out of a deep sleep. Alec could see past him into a darkness filled with the shrill sounds of thousands of squeaking sparrows. Beneath that, he could hear a few in the audience stirring restlessly, beginning to complain.

Hey, kid, in or out? *Alec said.* You're lettin' the light in.

The kid—Alec didn't know his name then—turned his head and stared back into the theater for a long, searching moment. Then he stepped out and the door settled shut behind him, closing gently on its pneumatic hinge. And still he didn't go anywhere, didn't say anything. The Rosebud had been showing The Birds *for two weeks, and although Alec had seen others walk out before it was over, none of the early exits had been twelve-year-old boys. It was the sort of film most boys of that age waited all year to see, but who knew? Maybe the kid had a weak stomach.*

I left my Coke in the theater, *the kid said, his voice distant, almost toneless.* I still had a lot of it left.

You want to go back in and look for it?

And the kid lifted his eyes and gave Alec a bright look of alarm, and then Alec knew. No.

Alec finished his cigarette, pitched it.

I sat with the dead lady, *the kid blurted. Alec nodded.*

She talked to me.

What did she say?

He looked at the kid again, and found him staring back with eyes that were now wide and round with disbelief.

I need someone to talk to, she said. When I get excited about a movie I need to talk.

Alec knows when she talks to someone she always wants to talk about the movies. She usually addresses herself to men, although sometimes she will sit and talk with a woman—Lois Weisel most notably. Alec has been working on a theory of what it is that causes her to show herself. He has been keeping notes in a yellow legal pad. He has a list of who she appeared to and in what movie and when (Leland King, Harold and Maude, *'72; Joel Harlowe,* Eraserhead, *'77; Hal Lash,* Blood Simple, *'85; and all the others). He has, over the years, developed clear ideas about what conditions are most likely to produce her, although the specifics of his theory are constantly being revised.*

As a young man, thoughts of her were always on his mind, or simmering just beneath the surface; she was his first and most strongly felt obsession. Then for a while he was better—when the theater was a success, and he was an important businessman in the community, chamber of commerce, town planning board. In those days he could go weeks without thinking about her; and then someone would see her, or pretend to have seen her, and stir the whole thing up again.

But following his divorce—she kept the house, he moved into the one-bedroom under the theater—and not long after the 8-screen cineplex opened just outside of town, he began to obsess again, less about her than about the theater itself (is there any difference, though? Not really, he supposes, thoughts of one always circling around to thoughts of the other). He never imagined he would be so old and owe so much money. He has a hard time sleeping, his head is so full of ideas—wild, desperate ideas— about how to keep the theater from failing. He keeps himself awake thinking about income, staff, salable assets. And when he can't think about money anymore, he tries to picture where he will go if the theater closes. He envisions an old folks' home, mattresses that reek of Ben-Gay, hunched geezers with their dentures out, sitting in a musty common room watching daytime sitcoms; he sees a place where he will passively fade away, like wallpaper that gets too much sunlight and slowly loses its color.

This is bad. What is more terrible is when he tries to imagine what will happen to her if the Rosebud closes. He sees the theater stripped of its seats, an echoing empty space, drifts of dust in the corners, petrified wads of gum stuck fast to the cement. Local teens have broken in to drink and screw; he sees scattered liquor bottles, ignorant graffiti on the walls, a single, grotesque, used condom on the floor in front of the stage. He sees the lonely and violated place where she will fade away.

Or won't fade... the worst thought of all.

Alec saw her—spoke to her—for the first time when he was fifteen, six days after he learned his older brother had been killed in the South Pacific. President Truman had sent a letter expressing his condolences. It was a form letter, but the signature on the bottom—that was really his. Alec hadn't cried yet. He knew, years later, that he spent that week in a state of shock, that he had lost the person he loved most in the world and it had badly traumatized him. But in 1945 no one used the word "trauma" to talk about emotions, and the only kind of shock anyone discussed was "shell—."

He told his mother he was going to school in the mornings. He wasn't going to school. He was shuffling around downtown looking for trouble. He shoplifted candy-bars from the American Luncheonette and ate them out at the empty shoe factory—the place closed down, all the men off in France, or the Pacific. With sugar zipping in his blood, he launched rocks through the windows, trying out his fastball.

He wandered through the alley behind the Rosebud and looked at the door into the theater and saw that it wasn't firmly shut. The side facing the alley was a smooth metal surface, no door handle, but he was able to pry it open with his fingernails. He came in on the 3:30 p.m. show, the place crowded, mostly kids under the age of ten and their mothers. The fire door was halfway up the theater, recessed into the wall, set in shadow. No one saw him come in. He slouched up the aisle and found a seat in the back.

"I heard Jimmy Stewart went to the Pacific," his brother had told him while he was home on leave, before he shipped out. They were throwing the ball around out back. "Mr. Smith is probably carpet-bombing the red fuck out of Tokyo right this instant. How's that for a crazy thought?" Alec's brother, Ray, was a self-described film freak. He and Alec went to every single movie that opened during his monthlong leave: *Bataan, The Fighting Seabees, Going My Way.*

Alec waited through an episode of a serial concerning the latest adventures of a singing cowboy with long eyelashes and a mouth so dark his lips were black. It failed to interest him. He picked his nose and wondered how to get a Coke with no money. The feature started.

At first Alec couldn't figure out what the hell kind of movie it was, although right off he had the sinking feeling it was going to be a musical.

First the members of an orchestra filed onto a stage against a bland blue backdrop. Then a starched shirt came out and started telling the audience all about the brand-new kind of entertainment they were about to see. When he started blithering about Walt Disney and his artists, Alec began to slide downwards in his seat, his head sinking between his shoulders. The orchestra surged into big dramatic blasts of strings and horns. In another moment his worst fears were realized. It wasn't just a musical; it was also a *cartoon*. Of course it was a cartoon, he should have known—the place crammed with little kids and their mothers—a 3:30 show in the middle of the week that led off with an episode of The Lipstick Kid, singing sissy of the high plains.

After a while he lifted his head and peeked at the screen through his fingers, watched some abstract animation for a while: silver raindrops falling against a background of roiling smoke, rays of molten light shimmering across an ashen sky. Eventually he straightened up to watch in a more comfortable position. He was not quite sure what he was feeling. He was bored, but interested too, almost a little mesmerized. It would have been hard not to watch. The visuals came at him in a steady hypnotic assault: ribs of red light, whirling stars, kingdoms of cloud glowing in the crimson light of a setting sun.

The little kids were shifting around in their seats. He heard a little girl whisper loudly, "Mom, when is there going to be *Mickey?*" For the kids it was like being in school. But by the time the movie hit the next segment, the orchestra shifting from Bach to Tchaikovsky, he was sitting all the way up, even leaning forward slightly, his forearms resting on his knees. He watched fairies flitting through a dark forest, touching flowers and spiderwebs with enchanted wands and spreading sheets of glittering, incandescent dew. He felt a kind of baffled wonder watching them fly around, a curious feeling of yearning. He had the sudden idea he could sit there and watch forever.

"I could sit in this theater forever," whispered someone beside him. It was a girl's voice. "Just sit here and watch and never leave."

He didn't know there was someone sitting beside him and jumped to hear a voice so close. He thought—no, he knew—that when he sat down, the seats on either side of him were empty. He turned his head.

She was only a few years older than him, couldn't have been more than twenty, and his first thought was that she was very close to being a fox; his heart beat a little faster to have such a girl speaking to him. He was already thinking, *Don't blow it.* She wasn't looking at him. She was staring up at the movie, and smiling in a way that seemed to express both admiration and a child's dazed wonder. He wanted desperately to say something smooth, but his voice was trapped in his throat.

She leaned towards him without glancing away from the screen, her left hand just touching the side of his arm on the armrest.

"I'm sorry to bother you," she whispered. "When I get excited about a movie I want to talk. I can't help it."

In the next moment he became aware of two things, more or less simultaneously. The first was that her hand against his arm was cold. He could feel the deadly chill of it through his sweater, a cold so palpable it startled him a little. The second thing he noticed was a single teardrop of blood on her upper lip, under her left nostril.

"You have a nosebleed," he said, in a voice that was too loud. He immediately wished he hadn't said it. You only had one opportunity to impress a fox like this. He should have found something for her to wipe her nose with, and handed it to her, murmured something real Sinatra: *You're bleeding, here.* He pushed his hands into his pockets, feeling for something she could wipe her nose with. He didn't have anything.

But she didn't seem to have heard him, didn't seem the slightest bit aware he had spoken. She absent-mindedly brushed the back of one hand under her nose, and left a dark smear of blood over her upper lip... and Alec froze with his hands in his pockets, staring at her. It was the first he knew there was something wrong about the girl sitting next to him, something slightly *off* about the scene playing out between them. He instinctively drew himself up and slightly away from her without even knowing he was doing it.

She laughed at something in the movie, her voice soft, breathless. Then she leaned towards him and whispered, "This is all wrong for kids. Harry Parcells loves this theater, but he plays all the wrong movies— Harry Parcells who runs the place?"

There was a fresh runner of blood leaking from her left nostril and blood on her lips, but by then Alec's attention had turned to something else. They were sitting directly under the projector beam, and there were moths and other insects whirring through the blue column of light above. A white moth had landed on her face. It was crawling up her cheek. She didn't notice, and Alec didn't mention it to her. There wasn't enough air in his chest to speak.

She whispered, "He thinks just because it's a cartoon they'll like it. It's funny he could be so crazy for movies and know so little about them. He won't run the place much longer."

She glanced at him and smiled. She had blood staining her teeth. Alec couldn't get up. A second moth, ivory white, landed just inside the delicate cup of her ear.

"Your brother Ray would have loved this," she said.

"Get away," Alec whispered hoarsely.

"You belong here, Alec," she said. "You belong here with me."

He moved at last, shoved himself up out of his seat. The first moth was crawling into her hair. He thought he heard himself moan, just faintly. He started to move away from her. She was staring at him. He backed a few feet down the aisle and bumped into some kid's legs, and the kid yelped. He glanced away from her for an instant, down at a fattish boy in a striped T-shirt who was glaring back at him: *Watch where you're going, meathead.*

Alec looked at her again and now she was slumped very low in her seat. Her head rested on her left shoulder. Her legs hung lewdly open. There were thick strings of blood, dried and crusted, running from her nostrils, bracketing her thin-lipped mouth. Her eyes were rolled back in her head. In her lap was an overturned carton of popcorn.

Alec thought he was going to scream. He didn't scream. She was perfectly motionless. He looked from her to the kid he had almost tripped over. The fat kid glanced casually in the direction of the dead girl, showed no reaction. He turned his gaze back to Alec, his eyes questioning, one corner of his mouth turned up in a derisive sneer.

"Sir," said a woman, the fat kid's mother. "Can you move, *please?* We're trying to watch the movie."

Alec threw another look towards the dead girl, only now the chair where she had been was empty, the seat folded up. He started to retreat, bumping into knees, almost falling over once, grabbing someone for support. Then suddenly the room erupted into cheers, applause. His heart throbbed. He cried out, looked wildly around. It was Mickey, up there on the screen in droopy red robes—Mickey had arrived at last.

He backed up the aisle, swatted through the padded leather doors into the lobby. He flinched at the late-afternoon brightness, narrowed his eyes to squints. He felt dangerously sick. Then someone was holding his shoulder, turning him, walking him across the room, over to the staircase up to balcony-level. Alec sat down on the bottom step, sat down hard.

"Take a minute," someone said. "Don't get up. Catch your breath. Do you think you're going to throw up?"

Alec shook his head.

Joe Hill

"Because if you think you're going to throw up, hold on till I can get you a bag. It isn't so easy to get stains out of this carpet. Also when people smell vomit they don't want popcorn."

Whoever it was lingered beside him for another moment, then without a word turned and shuffled away. He returned maybe a minute later.

"Here. On the house. Drink it slow. The fizz will help with your stomach."

Alec took a wax cup sweating beads of cold water, found the straw with his mouth, sipped icy cola bubbly with carbonation. He looked up. The man standing over him was tall and slope-shouldered, with a sagging roll around the middle. His hair was cropped to a dark bristle and his eyes, behind his absurdly thick glasses, were small and pale and uneasy.

Alec said, "There's a dead girl in there." He didn't recognize his own voice.

The color drained out of the big man's face and he cast an unhappy glance back at the doors into the theater. "She's never been in a matinee before. I thought only night shows, I thought—for God's sake, it's a kid's movie. What's she trying to do to me?"

Alec opened his mouth, didn't even know what he was going to say, something about the dead girl, but what came out instead was: "It's not really a kid's film."

The big man shot him a look of mild annoyance. "Sure it is. It's Walt Disney."

Alec stared at him for a long moment, then said, "You must be Harry Parcells."

"Yeah. How'd you know?"

"Lucky guesser," Alec said. "Thanks for the Coke."

Alec followed Harry Parcells behind the concessions counter, through a door and out onto a landing at the bottom of some stairs. Harry opened a door to the right and let them into a small, cluttered office. The floor was crowded with steel film cans. Fading film posters covered the walls, overlapping in places: *Boys Town*, *David Copperfield*, *Gone With the Wind*.

"Sorry she scared you," Harry said, collapsing into the office chair behind his desk. "You sure you're all right? You look kind of peaked."

"Who is she?"

"Something blew out in her brain," he said, and pointed a finger at his left temple, as if pretending to hold a gun to his head. "Six years ago.

During *The Wizard of Oz.* The very first show. It was the most terrible thing. She used to come in all the time. She was my steadiest customer. We used to talk, kid around with each other—" His voice wandered off, confused and distraught. He squeezed his plump hands together on the desktop in front of him, said finally, "Now she's trying to bankrupt me."

"You've seen her." It wasn't a question.

Harry nodded. "A few months after she passed away. She told me I don't belong here. I don't know why she wants to scare me off when we used to get along so great. Did she tell you to go away?"

"Why is she here?" Alec said. His voice was still hoarse, and it was a strange kind of question to ask. For a while, Harry just peered at him through his thick glasses with what seemed to be total incomprehension.

Then he shook his head and said, "She's unhappy. She died before the end of *The Wizard* and she's still miserable about it. I understand. That was a good movie. I'd feel robbed too."

"Hello?" someone shouted from the lobby. "Anyone there?"

"Just a minute," Harry called out. He gave Alec a pained look. "My concession-stand girl told me she was quitting yesterday. No notice or anything."

"Was it the ghost?"

"Heck no. One of her paste-on nails fell into someone's food so I told her not to wear them anymore. No one wants to get a fingernail in a mouthful of popcorn. She told me a lot of boys she knows come in here and if she can't wear her nails she wasn't going to work for me no more so now I got to do everything myself." He said this as he was coming around the desk. He had something in one hand, a newspaper clipping. "This will tell you about her." And then he gave Alec a look— it wasn't a glare exactly, but there was at least a measure of dull warning in it—and he added: "Don't run off on me. We still have to talk."

He went out, Alec staring after him, wondering what that last funny look was about. He glanced down at the clipping. It was an obituary— her obituary. The paper was creased, the edges worn, the ink faded; it looked as if it had been handled often. Her name was Imogene Gilchrist, she had died at nineteen, she worked at Water Street Stationery. She was survived by her parents, Colm and Mary. Friends and family spoke of her pretty laugh, her infectious sense of humor. They talked about how she loved the movies. She saw all the movies, saw them on opening day, first show. She could recite the entire cast from almost any picture you cared to name, it was like a party trick—she even knew the names of actors who had had just one line. She was president of the drama club in high school, acted in all the plays, built sets, arranged lighting. "I always thought she'd be a movie star," said her drama professor. "She had those looks and that laugh. All she needed was someone to point a camera at her and she would have been famous."

When Alec finished reading he looked around. The office was still empty. He looked back down at the obituary, rubbing the corner of the clipping between thumb and forefinger. He felt sick at the unfairness of it, and for a moment there was a pressure at the back of his eyeballs, a tingling, and he had the ridiculous idea he might start crying. He felt ill to live in a world where a nineteen-year-old girl full of laughter and life could be struck down like that, for no reason. The intensity of what he was feeling didn't really make sense, considering he had never known her when she was alive; didn't make sense until he thought about Ray, thought about Harry Truman's letter to his mom, the words *died with bravery, defending freedom, America is proud of him*. He thought about how Ray had taken him to *The Fighting Seabees*, right here in this theater, and they sat together with their feet up on the seats in front of them, their shoulders touching. "Look at John Wayne," Ray said. "They oughta have one bomber to carry him, and another one to carry his balls." The stinging in his eyes was so intense he couldn't stand it, and it hurt to breathe. He rubbed at his wet nose, and focused intently on crying as soundlessly as possible.

He wiped his face with the tail of his shirt, put the obituary on Harry Parcells' desk, looked around. He glanced at the posters, and the stacks of steel cans. There was a curl of film in the corner of the room, just eight or so frames—he wondered where it had come from—and he picked it up for a closer look. He saw a girl closing her eyes and lifting her face, in a series of little increments, to kiss the man holding her in a tight embrace; giving herself to him. Alec wanted to be kissed that way sometime. It gave him a curious thrill to be holding an actual piece of a movie. On impulse he stuck it into his pocket.

He wandered out of the office and back onto the landing at the bottom of the stairwell. He peered into the lobby. He expected to see Harry behind the concession stand, serving a customer, but there was no one there. Alec hesitated, wondering where he might have gone. While he was thinking it over, he became aware of a gentle whirring sound coming from the top of the stairs. He looked up them, and it clicked—the projector. Harry was changing reels.

Alec climbed the steps and entered the projection room, a dark compartment with a low ceiling. A pair of square windows looked into the theater below. The projector itself was pointed through one of them, a big machine made of brushed stainless steel, with the word VITAPHONE stamped on the case. Harry stood on the far side of it, leaning forward, peering out the same window through which the projector was casting its beam. He heard Alec at the door, shot him a brief look. Alec expected to be ordered away, but Harry said nothing, only nodded and returned to his silent watch over the theater.

Alec made his way to the VITAPHONE, picking a path carefully through the dark. There was a window to the left of the projector that looked down into the theater. Alec stared at it for a long moment, not sure if he dared, and then put his face close to the glass and peered into the darkened room beneath.

The theater was lit a deep midnight blue by the image on the screen: the conductor again, the orchestra in silhouette. The announcer was introducing the next piece. Alec lowered his gaze and scanned the rows of seats. It wasn't much trouble to find where he had been sitting, an empty cluster of seats close to the back, on the right. He half-expected to see her there, slid down in her chair, face tilted up towards the ceiling and blood all down it—her eyes turned perhaps to stare up at *him*. The thought of seeing her filled him with both dread and a strange nervous exhilaration, and when he realized she wasn't there, he was a little surprised by his own disappointment.

Music began: at first the wavering skirl of violins, rising and falling in swoops, and then a series of menacing bursts from the brass section, sounds of an almost military nature. Alec's gaze rose once more to the screen—rose and held there. He felt a chill race through him. His forearms prickled with gooseflesh. On the screen the dead were rising from their graves, an army of white and watery specters pouring out of the ground and into the night above. A square-shouldered demon, squatting on a mountain-top, beckoned them. They came to him, their ripped white shrouds fluttering around their gaunt bodies, their faces anguished, sorrowing. Alec caught his breath and held it, watched with a feeling rising in him of mingled shock and wonder.

The demon split a crack in the mountain, opened Hell. Fires leaped, the Damned jumped and danced, and Alec knew what he was seeing was about the war. It was about his brother dead for no reason in the South Pacific, *America is proud of him*, it was about bodies damaged beyond repair, bodies sloshing this way and that while they rolled in the surf at the edge of a beach somewhere in the Far East, getting soggy, bloating. It was about Imogene Gilchrist, who loved the movies and died with her legs spread open and her brain swelled full of blood and she was nineteen, her parents were Colm and Mary. It was about young people, young healthy bodies, punched full of holes and the life pouring out in arterial gouts, not a single dream realized, not a single ambition achieved. It was about young people who loved and were loved in return, going away, and not coming back, and the pathetic little remembrances that marked their departure, *my prayers are with you today, Harry Truman*, and *I always thought she'd be a movie star.*

A church bell rang somewhere, a long way off. Alec looked up. It was part of the film. The dead were fading away. The churlish and square-shouldered demon covered himself with his vast black wings, hiding his face from the coming of dawn. A line of robed men moved across the land below, carrying softly glowing torches. The music moved in gentle pulses. The sky was a cold, shimmering blue, light rising in it, the glow of sunrise spreading through the branches of birch trees and northern pine. Alec watched with a feeling in him like religious awe until was over.

"I liked *Dumbo* better," Harry said.

He flipped a switch on the wall, and a bare lightbulb came on, filling the projection room with harsh white light. The last of the film squiggled through the VITAPHONE and came out at the other end, where it was being collected on one of the reels. The trailing end whirled around and around and went *slap, slap, slap.* Harry turned the projector off, looked at Alec over the top of the machine.

"You look better. You got your color back."

"What did you want to talk about?" Alec remembered the vague look of warning Harry gave him when he told him not to go anywhere, and the thought occurred to him now that maybe Harry knew he had slipped in without buying a ticket, that maybe they were about to have a problem.

But Harry said, "I'm prepared to offer you a refund or two free passes to the show of your choice. Best I can do."

Alec stared. It was a long time before he could reply. "For what?"

"For what? To shut up about it. You know what it would do to this place if it got out about her? I got reasons to think people don't want to pay money to sit in the dark with a chatty dead girl."

Alec shook his head. It surprised him that Harry thought it would keep people away if it got out that the Rosebud was haunted. Alec had an idea it would have the opposite effect. People were happy to pay for the opportunity to experience a little terror in the dark—if they weren't, there wouldn't be any business in horror pictures. And then he remembered what Imogene Gilchrist had said to him about Harry Parcells: *He won't run the place much longer.*

"So what do you want?" Harry asked. "You want passes?"

Alec shook his head.

"Refund then."

"No."

Harry froze with his hand on his wallet, flashed Alec a surprised, hostile look. "What do you want then?"

"How about a job? You need someone to sell popcorn. I promise not to wear my paste-on nails to work."

Harry stared at him for a long moment without any reply, then slowly removed his hand from his back pocket.

"Can you work weekends?" he asked.

In October, Alec hears that Steven Greenberg is back in New Hampshire, shooting exteriors for his new movie on the grounds of Phillips Exeter Academy—something with Tom Hanks and Haley Joel Osment, a misunderstood teacher inspiring troubled kid-geniuses. Alec doesn't need to know any more than that to know it smells like Steven might be on his way to winning another Oscar. Alec, though, preferred the earlier work, Steven's fantasies and suspense thrillers.

He considers driving down to have a look, wonders if he could talk his way onto the set—Oh yes, I knew Steven when he was a boy—wonders if he might even be allowed to speak with Steven himself. But he soon dismisses the idea. There must be hundreds of people in this part of New England who could claim to have known Steven back in the day, and it isn't as if they were ever close. They only really had that one conversation, the day Steven saw her. Nothing before; nothing much after.

So it is a surprise when one Friday afternoon close to the end of the month Alec takes a call from Steven's personal assistant, a cheerful, efficient-sounding woman named Marcia. She wants Alec to know that Steven was hoping to see him, and if he can drop in—is Sunday morning all right?—there will be a set pass waiting for him at Main Building, on the grounds of the Academy. They'll expect to see him around 10:00 A.M., she says in her bright chirp of a voice, before ringing off. It is not until well after the conversation has ended that Alec realizes he has received not an invitation, but a summons.

A goateed P.A. meets Alec at Main and walks him out to where they're filming. Alec stands with thirty or so others, and watches from a distance, while Hanks and Osment stroll together across a green quad littered with fallen leaves, Hanks nodding pensively while Osment talks and gestures. In front of them is a dolly, with two men and their camera equipment sitting on it, and two men pulling it. Steven and a small group of others stand off to the side, Steven observing the shot on a video monitor. Alec has never been on a movie set before, and he watches the work of professional make-believe with great pleasure.

After he has what he wants, and has talked with Hanks for a few minutes about the shot, Steven starts over towards the crowd where Alec is standing. There is a shy, searching look on his face. Then he sees Alec and opens his mouth in a gap-toothed grin, lifts one hand in a wave, looks for a moment very much the lanky boy again. He asks Alec if he wants to walk to craft services with him, for a chili dog and a soda.

On the walk Steven seems anxious, jingling the change in his pockets and shooting sideways looks at Alec. Alec knows he wants to talk about Imogene, but can't figure how to broach the subject. When at last he begins to talk, it's about his memories of the Rosebud. He talks about how he loved the place, talks about all the great pictures he saw for the first time there. Alec smiles and nods, but is secretly a little astounded at the depths of Steven's self-deception. Steven never went back after The Birds. *He didn't see any of the movies he says he saw there.*

At last, Steven stammers, What's going to happen to the place after you retire? Not that you should retire! I just mean— do you think you'll run the place much longer?

Not much longer, *Alec replies—it's the truth—but says no more. He is concerned not to degrade himself asking for a handout—although the thought is in him that this is in fact why he came. That ever since receiving Steven's invitation to visit the set he had been fantasizing that they would talk about the Rosebud, and that Steven, who is so wealthy, and who loves movies so much, might be persuaded to throw Alec a life preserver.*

The old movie houses are national treasures, *Steven says.* I own a couple, believe it or not. I run them as revival joints. I'd love to do something like that with the Rosebud someday. That's a dream of mine, you know.

Here is his chance, the opportunity Alec was not willing to admit he was hoping for. But instead of telling him that the Rosebud is in desperate straits, sure to close, Alec changes the subject . . . ultimately lacks the stomach to do what must be done.

What's your next project? *Alec asks.*

After this? I was considering a remake, *Steven says, and gives him another of those shifty sideways looks from the corners of his eyes.* You'd never guess what. *Then, suddenly, he reaches out, touches Alec's arm.* Being back in New Hampshire has really stirred some things up for me. I had a dream about our old friend, would you believe it?

Our old—*Alec starts, then realizes who he means.*

I had a dream the place was closed. There was a chain on the front doors, and boards in the windows. I dreamed I heard a girl crying inside, *Steven says, and grins nervously.* Isn't that the funniest thing?

Alec drives home with a cool sweat on his face, ill at ease. He doesn't know why he didn't say anything, why he couldn't *say anything; Greenberg was practically begging to give him some money. Alec thinks bitterly that he has become a very foolish and useless old man.*

At the theater there are nine messages on Alec's machine. The first is from Lois Weisel, whom Alec has not heard from in years. Her voice is brittle. She says, Hi, Alec, Lois Weisel at B.U. *As if he could have forgotten her. Lois saw Imogene in* Midnight Cowboy. *Now she teaches documentary filmmaking to graduate students. Alec knows these two things are not unconnected, just as it is no accident Steven Greenberg became what he became.* Will you give me a call? I wanted to talk to you about—I just—will you call me? *Then she laughs, a strange, frightened kind of laugh, and says,* This is crazy. *She exhales heavily.* I just wanted to find out if something was happening to the Rosebud. Something bad. So—call me.

The next message is from Dana Llewellyn, who saw her in The Wild Bunch. *The message after that is from Shane Leonard, who saw Imogene in* American Graffiti. *Darren Campbell, who saw her in* Reservoir Dogs. *Some of them talk about the dream, a dream identical to the one Steven Greenberg described, boarded-over windows, chain on the doors, girl crying. Some only say they want to talk. By the time the answering machine tape has played its way to the end, Alec is sitting on the floor of his office, his hands balled into fists—an old man weeping helplessly.*

Perhaps twenty people have seen Imogene in the last twenty-five years, and nearly half of them have left messages for Alec to call. The other half will get in touch with him over the next few days, to ask about the Rosebud, to talk about their dream. Alec will speak with almost everyone living who has ever seen her, all of those Imogene felt compelled to speak to: a drama professor, the manager of a video rental store, a retired financier who in his youth wrote angry, comical film reviews for The Lansdowne Record, *and others. A whole congregation of people who flocked to the Rosebud instead of church on Sundays, those whose prayers were written by Paddy Chayefsky and whose hymnals were composed by John Williams and whose intensity of faith is a call Imogene is helpless to resist. Alec himself.*

After the sale, *the Rosebud is closed for two months to refurbish. New seats, state-of-the-art sound. A dozen artisans put up scaffolding and work with little paintbrushes to restore the crumbling plaster molding on the ceiling. Steven adds personnel to run the day-to-day operations. Although it's his place now, Alec has agreed to stay on to manage things for a little while.*

Lois Weisel drives up three times a week to film a documentary about the renovation, using her grad students in various capacities, as electricians, sound people, grunts. Steven wants a gala reopening to celebrate the Rosebud's past. When Alec hears what he wants to show first—a double feature of The Wizard of Oz *and* The Birds—*his forearms prickle with gooseflesh; but he makes no argument.*

On reopening night, the place is crowded like it hasn't been since Titanic. *The local news is there to film people walking inside in their best suits. Of course, Steven is there, which is why all the excitement . . . although Alec thinks he would have a sell-out even without Steven, that people would have come just to see the results of the renovation. Alec and Steven pose for photographs, the two of them standing under the marquee in their tuxedoes, shaking hands. Steven's tuxedo is Armani, bought for the occasion. Alec got married in his.*

Steven leans into him, pressing a shoulder against his chest. What are you going to do with yourself?

Before Steven's money, Alec would have sat behind the counter handing out tickets, and then gone up himself to start the projector. But Steven hired someone to sell tickets and run the projector. Alec says, Guess I'm going to sit and watch the movie.

Save me a seat, *Steven says.* I might not get in until *The Birds, though. I* have some more press to do out here.

Lois Weisel has a camera set up at the front of the theater turned to point at the audience, and loaded with high-speed film for shooting in the dark. She films the crowd at different times, recording their reactions to The Wizard of Oz. *This was to be the conclusion of her documentary—a packed house enjoying a twentieth-century classic in this lovingly restored old movie palace—but her movie wasn't going to end like she thought it would.*

In the first shots on Lois's reel it is possible to see Alec sitting in the back left of the theater, his face turned up towards the screen, his glasses flashing blue in the darkness. The seat to the left of him, on the aisle, is empty, the only empty seat in the house. Sometimes he can be seen eating popcorn. Other times he is just sitting there watching, his mouth open slightly, an almost worshipful look on his face.

Then in one shot he has turned sideways to face the seat to his left. He has been joined by a woman in blue. He is leaning over her. They are unmistakably kissing. No one around them pays them any mind. The Wizard of Oz is ending. We know this because we can hear Judy Garland, reciting the same five words over and over in a soft, yearning voice, saying—well, you know what she is saying. They are only the loveliest five words ever said in all of film.

In the shot immediately following this one, the house lights are up, and there is a crowd of people gathered around Alec's body, slumped heavily in his seat. Steven Greenberg is in the aisle, yelping hysterically for someone to bring a doctor. A child is crying. The rest of the crowd generates a low rustling buzz of excited conversation. But never mind this shot. The footage that came just before it is much more interesting.

It is only a few seconds long, this shot of Alec and his unidentified companion—a few hundred frames of film—but it is the shot that will make Lois Weisel's reputation, not to mention a large sum of money. It will appear on television shows about unexplained phenomena, it will be watched and rewatched at gatherings of those fascinated with the supernatural. It will be studied, written about, debunked, confirmed, and celebrated. Let's see it again.

He leans over her. She turns her face up to his, and closes her eyes and she is very young and she is giving herself to him completely. Alec has removed his glasses. He is touching her lightly at the waist. This is the way people dream of being kissed, a movie star kiss. Watching them, one almost wishes the moment would never end. And over all this, Dorothy's small, brave voice fills the darkened theater. She is saying something about home. She is saying something everyone knows.

The End

Scritch-Scratch

Ben Monroe

Nicole Jackman was putting a dangly earring in her left ear as she entered the room. "Babe, can you zip me?" she called out, then she noticed she couldn't see her husband Ray. Then a bang and an "Ow!" and she realized he was under the bed.

She walked around the foot of the bed and saw he had his head and arm stuck under it from the side he slept on. He was still only wearing his undershorts and undershirt. "Drop something?" she asked.

Ray slid out from under the bed and rolled over onto his back. Dust bunnies clung to the white cotton of his shirt. "Hey, wow, you look great," he said as he rubbed his head.

"Thanks," she said. "Zip me up. We need to get going, and you're not even dressed yet."

He got to his feet as she turned around, gathered her long black hair in both hands and lifted it up off her neck. Ray gripped the zipper of her floral print dress and tugged it up until it came to a close just below her shoulders. He gave her a kiss on her shoulder as she dropped her hair. "Do we have to go to this thing?" he asked.

"Yes," she said, turning back to him. "It'd be rude to cancel at the last minute, and you know that."

"Yeah, but on the other hand, if we stayed home, we wouldn't have to go at all."

"Nice try, smartypants," she said. "I need to show my face, and I want you to meet some of my new colleagues. Besides, it'll be good to get out of the house. You can't stay cooped up in here forever."

"Says you. I'm happy being a mysterious loner."

"We'll just go and show our faces, say some hellos, and then leave early," she said. "Who knows, maybe you'll make a new friend."

"I already have friends," Ray replied. He crossed the room to his dresser, opened a drawer on the top level and got out a pair of black dress socks.

She nodded, and then walked around to the side of the bed. "Yeah, but they're all back in California. You need Texas friends." She tilted her head and looked down at the floor. "What were you looking for, anyway?"

"You seen my dad's cufflinks?" he asked.

She shook her head. "Nope. Are they what you were looking for under the bed?"

"Thought maybe they had rolled under there. Or somewhere else, maybe," Ray said, and then started rooting through her walnut jewelry box which rested on top of the dresser. "Just can't find them since we moved." Ray didn't have much in the way of jewelry of his own and the only ones he really cared about were his wedding band, and the ivory cufflinks his dad had given him on his wedding day. They were his grandfather's before that.

"You kept them in there, right?" Nicole asked, pointing to the box.

"Yeah, I never take them out. Hope they didn't get lost in the move," he said. He poked a few other cufflinks aside, as well as a quarter that was tucked in with them. "This yours?" he asked, holding the coin up.

Nicole looked over with little interest. "Nope," she said. "It's not mine. When was the last time you wore them?" she asked, peering into the tiny compartments of the box.

"Hell, I don't remember," he said. "Maybe at Jim's wedding?" Then he took the two knobs of the lower tray between his fingers and slid it out. He raised the lip and slid the tray free of the box, then peered inside. Nothing.

"Anything?" Nicole asked, looking around his head into the dark slit.

"No," he said, standing straight. "Thought maybe they'd jiggled into the insides of the box or something." He stared at the box for a moment, as if looking at it hard would cause the ivory studs to suddenly materialize out of thin air.

As he watched the thoroughly inert wooden box, he heard a scratching above him. Like tiny nails raking on wood. Ray looked up just as Nicole did. It would be just his luck, he thought, to have moved into a house infested with rats.

The move had been hard on him, but he'd known it was for the best. When Nicole had been offered her dream job teaching upper division English at UTA, moving out to Texas was a no-brainer. Ray's work had been a series of dead end jobs, and he figured he could find those just as easily in Texas as California. And housing costs were so much lower that they could afford to buy a place. A little out in the boonies, but it was theirs. And it made Nicole happy, and that's all he really cared about. But now rats. Or whatever slinks into a house and makes a nest in a Texas attic.

"You hear that?" she asked.

Ray nodded. "Thought we had a clean report from the inspector," he said. The scratching stopped. "What do you think? Rats?"

Nicole stared at the ceiling. "I suppose," she said. "Let's not worry about it now, though. We need to get going. Fashionably late is one thing, but showing up as everyone else is leaving is something else entirely."

"Okay, Professor," Ray replied. "I hear you loud and clear. I'll pick up some traps in town tomorrow."

Nicole rubbed his shoulder, then kissed him on the cheek. "Sounds great. Figure it all out tomorrow. One little rat can't cause much trouble. In the meantime, just wear one of your shirts with buttons. No need to get too fancy."

"Yeah, that's fine," Ray replied, then walked to the closet and picked out a burgundy long-sleeved shirt. It was still in the dry cleaner bag from the last time he'd taken his shirts in to be pressed. When they'd packed, he just folded most of his clothes in whatever state they were and shoved them into moving boxes. Unpacking had been simply that in reverse. "Just figured I never get a chance to wear them, might be fun."

"I applaud your commitment to fanciness," Nicole said as she slipped down the hall to the bathroom. A moment later he heard the slight thud and click of the door closing behind her.

Ray pulled the shirt from the plastic bag and started to undo the buttons. As he did he noticed the dust bunnies clinging to his undershirt. He picked at a few balls of fuzz, and then heard the scratching overhead again. Ray looked up, tilting his head slightly to try and get a better read on the source of the sound. He walked around the room slowly, trying to step lightly so as not to cover the sound of scratching overhead.

The sound stopped. He traced the crease where the walls met the ceiling with his eyes until they came to rest on the vent cover on the far wall, just over the oak headboard of the king-sized bed which filled the center of the room. Beyond the grate, he saw the slats which controlled the air flow, darkness beyond them. Then a glitter, a deep, purple sparkle as something beyond them caught a twinkle of light and vanished.

Ray was staring at the grate, wondering if he'd seen anything at all, or if it was just a trick of the light when Nicole entered the room again.

"Babe, come on," she said. "We're going to be late if you don't get dressed."

He pulled his eyes away from the grate and looked at her. She was radiant, her black hair spilling over her shoulders, over the trace of her neck, and he instantly forgot about twinkling lights in the air vent. "Yow, you look amazing," he said, stepping toward her.

Nicole laughed as she took a step back. "Yeah, I know. Now get dressed or we'll miss the party."

He dressed in silence, keeping his ears open for more scritching or scratching from the attic, but nothing came. After he was done, Ray cast one last look over his shoulder toward the vent cover then turned off the light as he walked out of the room. As he walked down the hall, he imagined a rat or raccoon, something small and sinister in the space overhead. The kind of something that raised the hairs on his neck, and caused his skin to crawl. But he heard nothing more.

***

Ray held Nicole's hand as he drove down the gravel driveway of the Mason's house. A few pickups and other sports cars were parked in front of the house, and a half dozen people still lounged on the front porch.

The party hadn't been nearly as bad as Ray anticipated. It was still the same sort of high brow academia chatter he'd gotten used to over his years with Nicole. He always thought it was weird being in a room full of professors. Mostly they wanted an audience, not a conversation. So, Ray had defaulted to his usual behavior of sipping at his beer and nodding without bothering to try and contribute to the conversation.

"See, I told you it wouldn't be so bad," she said as she squeezed his hand. "You owe me one."

"Sorry I was such a grump," he said. "I had a good time. Just this whole move has me feeling sort of off-kilter."

"Well, we're almost done moving in. I start work next week and setting up the house is going well. Things'll get back to normal soon enough."

The drive from the Mason's to their house was across Austin, and then through the suburbs, finally down a two-lane road with scattered low houses occasionally on either side. The closer they got to their new home, the further apart the houses were. Ray once again thought about how different things were now. From the cramped bustle of the Bay Area to out in the sticks.

The night was warm and humid with the threat of thunderstorms looming. "I love the wildflowers," Nicole said as they drove along. The full moon overhead cast a blue glow over fields awash with flowers on either side of the road, and sparse copses of pecan and ash trees past them. "Wonder how long they'll last?"

Ray took a deep breath, breathing in the faint scent of honeysuckle, and a dim, distant tang of lighter fluid and barbecue smoke. "Probably not much longer," he said. "Summer's supposed to be a real bitch around here."

Ray felt a sting on his neck and slapped it. His hand came away with a thumbnail-sized smear of blood and a fat mosquito crushed in his palm. "Cripes. Remind me to pick up bug spray tomorrow. I'm getting eaten alive."

A few minutes later they saw their new home through the trees. They'd left the porch light on, and as they approached the house saw it was occluded with a thick caul of bugs. Huge ones, too. Ray'd read about the size of the bugs in Texas, but didn't believe it until he'd seen them firsthand just a week back. He'd been driving along Highway 40 coming into Texas, hauling their life's belongings in a U-Haul trailer behind them. He had the window down and was singing along to some Mellencamp when he heard a crack and something smacked him in the side of the head. He felt something plop into his lap, looked down and saw the head of a grasshopper the size of his thumb. Almost drove off the side of the road. After that, he kept the windows up, and his mouth closed while he was driving.

He pulled the car into the driveway and parked in front of the house. It was a wide, two-level ranch style home, the kind they'd never have been able to afford back home. Ray caught himself thinking about that. How long until Texas starts to feel like home?

"You okay?" Nicole asked, looking at him.

"Hmm? Oh, yeah," he said, snapping out of his thoughts. "Just still adjusting, thinking about the move, the future. All that stuff."

"Come on," Nicole said as she opened the door and got out. "I just want to take a shower and get to bed. If you're good, maybe you can join me."

Ray popped the car door open. "Don't have to ask me twice," he said.

As Ray walked toward the porch something caught his eye. Next to the side of the house something poked out from under the orange berries of the sumac bushes planted around the perimeter. Something slim and gray. He let go of Nicole's hand, and then walked toward it.

"What is it?" she said, looking after him.

"Not sure," Ray replied as he walked toward the corner of the house. Flies buzzed around the bush as he approached it. Once he got closer, he squatted down, balancing himself with one hand. With his other he moved the tiny branches aside and found a coyote. It was lifeless, just a limp gray shape, its head twisted at an unnatural angle and its muzzle smeared with dark, drying blood.

"Dead coyote," Ray said. "Should we call animal control?"

"I think you call sanitation," Nicole replied. "Let's go inside and we can figure it out." She slapped at something on her arm. "Come on, I'm getting eaten alive." She walked onto the porch and unlocked the front door.

Ray stood up, keeping his eyes on the dead canine. Something was wrong with its muzzle. It was strangely misshapen. It looked flatter than he thought it should be. "Yeah, go on in," he said. "I'll be right behind you."

When he heard the screen door slam shut, Ray snapped a slim branch off the sumac bush. With the broken end, he prodded the coyote's mouth open. When he levered the jaws apart, he saw what was odd about it. The coyote had no teeth. Looking closer, he saw black sockets, still oozing blood where teeth should be.

He stood up, turned to walk back to the house and heard a quick scratching overhead. Ray looked up just in time to see a shape, something small and dark, skitter around the roof and under the eaves. Ray dashed around the house, keeping his eyes on the roof where the thing had disappeared. Just as he came around the corner, he saw the shape squeeze into a crack where the roof and the wall met.

He watched the crack for a minute to see if the thing would emerge, but nothing came out. Ray walked back around to the front of the house and up the steps to the porch. As he approached the screen door, a cloud of bugs flew from the porch light. He swatted them away as he opened the door and entered the house, making sure to keep his mouth closed.

"Nicky?" he called out as he walked down a short hallway looking for her. "Looks like maybe a rat or possum or something in the attic."

He came into the kitchen where he saw Nicole standing by the sink, phone pressed to her ear. She mimed "shushing" him with one finger.

"You can't come out tonight?" she was saying. Then she nodded and said, "Sure, okay. Tomorrow then." She took the phone from her ear and tapped the off button with her thumb.

"Who's that?" Ray asked.

"Sanitation," she said. "Tried animal control, but apparently they're only for live animals. Sanitation said to leave it alone, and they'll send out someone in the morning to pick it up."

Ray shrugged. "I guess that's fine," he said. "Should I put a tarp on it or something? Kind of worried it might attract scavengers."

Nicole let out a quick laugh. "What'll they do, kill it more?"

He smiled, "No, I just mean we don't want other critters around here thinking we've got an all you can eat buffet set out for them, and they start hanging around looking for snacks."

"Gotcha," she said. Then, "What was that you said about rats?"

"Oh, when I was out there, I saw something crawling up the side of the house and into the attic. There's a little gap up where the roof and wall meets."

"Ugh," she said. "Maybe that's what we heard earlier?"

"That's my guess," Ray said. "I'll look around tomorrow when I put up the traps. And if they don't take care of it, we can call animal control."

"Okay, well I'm going to bed," she said. "We'll sort it out in the morning."

She kicked off her shoes and picked them up by the straps over the heels. As she climbed the stairs she turned to see Ray staring out the screen door. "Hey, don't ruminate too long, okay?"

He turned and smiled up at her, a tired smile, the one she knew meant he'd had enough of people for one day. "No, I'll be right up," he said. "Just going to make sure everything's locked up. This is chainsaw cannibal country, you know."

"Pretty sure that movie was all made up," she said, and then disappeared up the stairs. A moment later he heard the bedroom door click closed.

Ray wandered through the downstairs of the house, locking every door, checking the latches on every window. Just as he was about to go upstairs himself, he remembered the fireplace in the living room, and made sure the damper was fully shut. Rats, possums, hell could even be a chupacabra for all Ray knew. All he really knew was whatever it was, he wanted it out of their home.

For a few minutes he stood in the middle of the living room, listening intently. Listening for any scritch or scratch. But the house was silent and still.

By the time Ray rose the next morning he could already tell it was going to be a scorcher. Sunlight streamed through the east-facing windows of the kitchen while he scrambled eggs over the stove. He took a sip of coffee and was just putting it back on the countertop when the doorbell rang. "Shit," he muttered, taking the frying pan off the stove and setting it to the side.

He walked down the hall and opened the front door. A round man with graying hair stood before him. He was carrying a beat to hell clipboard, wearing workman's coveralls, and Ray noticed the sanitation department's logo on his chest. "Oh, hi," Ray said. "You here about the coyote?" In the distance, he heard the buzzing croak of insects in the grass.

"Yessir," the man said in return. He looked down at his clipboard and then at the street numbers next to the door. He ticked something off on the form on the clipboard. "Care to show me where the animal is?" he said. Past the man, in the driveway next to Ray's car was a pale green pickup truck with the same sanitation department logo painted on the side. Ray noticed a collection of black plastic garbage bags in the bed of the truck.

Charlie, Ray thought, seeing the guy's name stitched just below the department logo.

"Of course," Ray said, and stepped out of the house. Morning heat hit him hard, causing beads of sweat to pop up on his forehead. "Gonna be a hot one, huh?" he said to Charlie.

"If you say so," Charlie said, stepping aside as Ray walked down the porch steps.

"Just over here," Ray said as he walked along the side of the house. "Saw it last night as we were coming home." But when he approached the bush, he saw nothing under it. "It was right here," he said. He turned to Charlie. "Weird, huh?"

Charlie looked at the ground and pointed. "Drag marks," he said, and walked to the corner of the house.

Ray followed as Charlie disappeared around the corner. He saw the drag marks in the dirt, and smear of blood every few feet. A moment later he rounded the corner and saw Charlie standing a few feet in front of him. Ray was about to make a joke about the chupacabras. But then Charlie turned as he heard Ray approach and said, "Buzzard."

The backyard of the house was a well-tended lawn surrounded by a low fence. Bushes and flowers had been planted around the fence, lending a bit of elegance to the dirt patch surrounding it. And in front of the flowers, a mop of glossy brown feathers crouched over the prostrate form of the dead coyote and a thin trail of dry blood drops every few feet.

Charlie bent down, picked up a handful of grit from the dusty ground and tossed it at the shape. Pebbles hit it, and instantly wide wings sprouted. The grotesque bald head of a turkey vulture popped up, a strip of red, oozing meat in its beak. It turned to them, opened its beak and let out a dire, gurgling hiss. Its wings beat at the air and the buzzard hopped a few feet away before taking flight away from them.

"Well now," Charlie said, stepping forward nonplussed by the birds. "The fucker was going to drag your coyote off into the trees, eh?" Then he paused, looked over at Ray and said, "Pardon my French."

"Don't sweat it," Ray said.

Charlie walked to the coyote and poked it with the toe of his boot. A moment later, "Yeah, that's a coyote for sure. Let me get a bag," he said, and walked back to his truck.

Ray turned back to the body of the small doglike animal. They'd lived in Texas only a week, and he'd seen a few of these from a distance, but never up close until this one. His eyes went back to the creature's mouth, and the missing teeth.

He heard a whooshing *snap!* behind him, and turned to see Charlie shaking open a large black plastic bag. He was wearing leather work gloves now, covered in dark red smears and splotches. He handed the open bag to Ray. "Here hold this," he said.

Ray took the bag, holding it wide open as Charlie picked up the coyote's body, already stiff with rigor, and dumped it unceremoniously into the bag.

Ray turned his head as a wave of foul air erupted from the bag.

Charlie twisted the neck of the bag around, then tied it into a knot. "Okay, that's it," he said, turning back to his truck.

"Do I need to sign anything?" Ray asked.

"No sir," Charlie said. "All done and done."

"Well, thanks," Ray called after. He watched as Charlie tossed the bag into the back of his truck. It hit with a solid, yet somehow sickeningly meaty, wet *thud.*

The truck grunted off in a cloud of dust. Ray headed back around front. He wanted to wash his hands and get something cold to drink. As he walked past where the coyote had been under a bush the night before a sparkle below the bush near where the animal's head had been caught his eye. A brief silver glimmer. He squatted down and pushed the bushes aside, careful not to get any of the gore-soaked dirt on his jeans.

As he leaned forward, he saw what had caught his attention: a silver dollar, half-buried in the dirt. He picked it up, rubbing the dirt off with his thumb.

"Weird," he said, turning the coin over between his fingers. It had a stamped profile of Eisenhower on it, and the date was marked 1973. He stood, slipped it into his pocket and walked back into the house.

When he got back inside, he found Nicole sitting in the breakfast nook in a dark red terry cloth bathrobe, her hair up haphazardly. It was what he sometimes referred to as her "Don't talk to me until I've had my coffee" look. She was sipping at a mug as he entered the kitchen.

"Trash guy come?" she said as he entered.

"Yup, all done," Ray replied. "Interrupted a buzzard having breakfast."

Nicole looked at him over the rim of her mug. "Too early," she said. "I don't want to hear about it."

"Well, the guy dumped the thing in a bag and took it away before the buzzard could finish it up." He turned on the sink's faucet then took the coin out of his pocket and washed it and his hands under the running water. "Did you lose a silver dollar?" he asked her.

She looked up and said "Nope, why?"

He tossed the coin to her. "Found it near the coyote. Thought it might've been yours."

"No," she said, turning it over in her hand. "Never seen it before. Must've been the previous owners. Or who knows?"

Ray dried his hands on a cloth towel hanging from a metal ring near the sink. "Guess that's an extra buck closer to owning this place," he said.

Nicole smiled at that, and went back to her coffee.

"I'm going to run into town," Ray said. "Pick up a few rat traps and then take them up into the attic. Need anything while I'm at the hardware store?"

She shook her head. "No, thanks."

"Okay," he said. "Back in a bit."

***

Ray was comparing rat traps in the local Ace Hardware store when an older man wearing a thick red canvas Ace apron approached him. "Got rats?" he said. "Or something bigger? .22'll take care of that."

Ray turned to the man. "Rats, I think. Been hearing them in the attic, and only saw one from a distance. And in the house, so don't think I'll be shooting at them."

"Never stopped me," the man said. "How big?"

"Looked pretty big," Ray replied. "But I saw it from a distance. I can hear it crawling around in the attic, and last night I saw it climbing up the wall outside. Looks like it's getting in through a crack or something."

"Gotcha," the man said. "Well, those're good," and pointed at the plastic bag Ray was holding with two wooden and plastic Victor rat traps. "Use peanut butter on them though. No cheese. Rats 'n mice'll snatch the cheese without setting off the trap. Peanut butter, they gotta work at that. More chance they'll set it off."

Ray nodded, then took a second pair of traps from the peg on the display. "Okay, peanut butter it is. Thanks."

"Yeah, no problem. See if you can figure out where they're getting in from. Staple some chicken wire over the crack and that'll slow 'em down for a while. Remember the .22 though. Pick 'em off before they get to the house."

Ray turned to leave and then had a thought. "Oh, hey, what do you know about coyotes or other animals around here?"

"Know that coyotes are all the hell over the place once you get out of town. Buzzards and grackles, too. Why, what do you want to know?"

"There was a coyote outside my house last night. Dead. But it looked like it didn't have any teeth. The muzzle was all bloody like something had pulled them out or something. Any thoughts?"

The man thought about that for a moment. Ray could see him rolling his tongue around in his mouth like he was counting his teeth while he was thinking. Then, "Beats me. Maybe the varmint pissed off the tooth fairy."

A thin laugh escaped Ray's lips. "Yeah, must be it," he said. "Okay, well, thanks for the tip on the peanut butter."

The man flipped Ray a two-fingered salute motion off his forehead and went back to work.

"Alright, you little fucker," Ray muttered while looking at the bags of traps. "Let's get rid of you, once and for all."

After he paid for the traps and was leaving the store, he called Nicole. "Babe? We got any peanut butter?"

***

An hour later, Ray had collected peanut butter from a Safeway on the way back to the house as well as a six pack of beer for later and was opening the trap door access panel to the attic. He stood on a ladder with a plastic shopping bag in his free hand. In it were the rat traps, a flashlight, a jar of peanut butter and a plastic spoon. Before his head popped into the attic, the smell hit him. The sour, yeasty animal smell that told him something had turned the attic into its nest. "Oh, ugh," he gagged.

"What is it?" Nicole asked. She was holding the ladder and felt it shimmy as Ray turned away from the smell.

"Just stinks," he said. "Something's definitely been using the attic as its toilet."

"Gross," Nicole said. "You sure you want to go up there? I could just call an exterminator."

He shook his head. "No, not yet. Let me just take a look around. I'll set the traps and we'll see if that takes care of it. The guy at the hardware store said I should look around to see if we can find where the rat's coming in from and cover it with chicken wire."

Ray heaved himself up into the attic putting the plastic sack of equipment next to him. The smell was worse when he was fully inside, something foul, lurking in the eaves and baking in the attic's stifling heat. Once he was sitting on the edge of the opening, he reached out and flicked on the light switch. A pale yellow light filled the small chamber, and he saw tiny brown pellets scattered around like buckshot. *Buckshit*, he thought to himself and grimaced. "Can you grab my work gloves?" he called down. "Don't want to touch the wrong thing and end up with the hanta virus or something."

"Sure, hang on," Nicole called up.

Ray looked around at the sparse attic. Most of the floor was layered in clouds of puffy pink insulation crammed between the wooden frame of the floor. Sheets of plywood were nailed into the framing along the center of the space, forming a walkway to get from one side to the other. There was an AC unit in the center, with aluminum ducting tubes going from it into the house's vents. He stood up, and realized the roof was only an inch or so over him. Ray stepped around to the other side of the AC unit as he inspected the ducting. Once there, he saw a fist-sized hole in the aluminum tube. He got the flashlight out of the plastic shopping bag and shined it into the hole. The edges were ragged, like they'd been chewed out. A bluish crust adhered to one sharp fang-like protrusion, like something viscous had splashed onto it and dried while dripping down.

"Babe? Got your gloves," Nicole called. Ray looked away from the hole. A moment later they flew up through the access opening and flopped onto the plywood floor around it.

"Thanks," he replied, and stepped over to retrieve them. She was down below, visible through the opening as he pulled the brown leather gloves on. "Hey, could you look around and find the inspection from when we moved in. There's definitely something living up here, and looks like it's been here before the inspector came. I want to make sure I didn't miss something."

"Okay, I'll find it. Call me if you need anything."

He interlaced his fingers and pressed the gloves down snugly onto his hands as he walked along the plywood walkway, scanning from one side of the attic to the other. At the far end he felt a slight breeze, and realized he was on the side of the house he'd seen the rat or possum clambering up the wall the night before.

When he got to the wall, he looked up. Where the wall met the ceiling he saw a gap in the wood. It was a foot above his head, right at the tallest point of the ceiling, and skinny. Only a few inches deep, but big enough that a big rat or possum could easily crawl through. He got on his tiptoes to look at it, and saw it was tattered and gnawed just like the hole in the air ducting. He took off a glove and slid the fingers of his left hand inside the opening. Empty space beyond his reach, and a brief warm breeze trickled around his fingers.

"Okay, you little fucker," Ray said, his words sounding strangely dead in the small chamber. "Let's get this over with."

Ray placed the bag at his feet, and got out the packages of traps. One by one he smeared dollops of peanut butter on the catch of each trap, armed them, and placed them at the corners of the plywood platform.

When he had placed the last trap back near where he'd come in, Ray noticed that the fiberglass insulation had been torn up a bit in the corner.

He inched out along the joist to investigate. Using one hand he braced himself on the ceiling as he worked his way to the corner, squatting down as he got out to the edge where the sloping roof met the wall. Reaching out with his free hand he pulled up the insulation and recoiled.

Below the cloud of pink, grimy fiberglass lay a menagerie of tiny skulls. Leathery skin still attached to some of them, but most picked clean, or worn smooth. The skulls looked to be from numerous species, some rat-like, others maybe small dogs or cats, possums. Ray wasn't sure of what animals they were, but one thing was certain: all of them were missing their teeth.

"What the hell?" he muttered. He pulled the insulation back a little more and saw a tiny silver hasp among some other bits of metal. After a moment he realized they were the metal from various pieces of jewelry: the studs, backings and loops of earrings, the cut thread and clasp of necklaces. Then he saw the peg of one of his missing cufflinks. The ivory button was missing, but he was sure that was one of the ones he thought had rolled under the bed.

And then he noticed a pouch wedged between the pile of skulls and the corner where the joists came together. It was black leather, a little bit bigger than his fist. He lifted it and heard a clinking within as something inside shifted. Ray opened the bag, peered inside and saw it was filled with coins. Upending it into one hand, out spilled quarters, silver dollars, something that looked ancient and black with age. When he lifted it to get a better look, it seemed to have the faint profile of a Roman emperor stamped on it.

Then he heard a furtive, claws-on-wood scratching behind him. The skin on his back became gooseflesh as he spun around just in time to see a long, thin, dark tail disappear into the crack he'd been investigating just a few minutes before.

"Babe!" he called out. "We're going to need to call an exterminator!"

No answer came.

He dumped the coins into the plastic bag, scooped up the scraps of metal jewelry and shoveled them into the plastic bag. He stood up, approached the opening to the attic and called down, "Nicole! Hey, I'm coming down, can you hold the ladder?"

Ray waited a minute but she didn't answer. He thought she must be in the bathroom, or maybe out in the garage. He dropped the bag and it hit the landing below him with a dull metallic *thunk!*, spilling its contents. He sat on the edge of the hatchway and lowered himself down until his feet were resting on the top of the ladder, then stepped down while balancing himself against the lip of the opening with his hands.

"Nicole?" he called out again as he descended the ladder. When he got to the bottom, he picked up the items spilled from the bag and jewelry and shoveled them in as well.

As he came around the corner and into the opening to the kitchen he stopped. The room was dim, the sun was going down. And in the center of the room Nicole lay on the kitchen floor, her back to him. A dark puddle seeped around her head, her long hair in disarray and matted into it.

"Nicky!" he shouted and leapt into the room. Ray jumped over and then down on one knee in front of her. Her eyes were wide open, glazed over. Blood oozed from her mouth. He slid his hand under her neck to raise her head from the floor. Her mouth fell slackly open, and a runnel of bright crimson poured from it. He saw that her teeth were missing.

"Oh my God, oh my God," he repeated, looking around the kitchen, trying to make some sense of what was happening. He cradled her head in his hand as he reached into his pocket for his phone. As he raised it to his ear he heard a scuttling behind him.

He turned to look and then something was on his back, something small with digging claws scaled his spine, his shoulders, grabbed his hair, and then a piercing, stinging pain at the back of his neck. A burning that flooded his neck and skull and spread lower. His body went slack and he slumped to the ground, facing his wife, head bouncing off the floor. But he felt nothing.

His eyes were fixed on Nicole and hers on him. He couldn't move, but as he watched her, saw a single tear drip from her eye, roll along the side of her face, glittering dully in the waning light, and plop onto the floor. She was still alive.

As Ray watched her helplessly, something dropped to the floor between them. It was the size of a large cat, but humanoid in form. It had dragonfly-like wings folded against its back, and a large leather sack slung over one shoulder. As it turned toward him, he saw the dim light catch in glittering purple eyes in a wide face that was an awful parody of humanity. A broad, thin-lipped, but horribly toothless mouth grinned at him from under a needle-like nose, and those awful solid violet eyes. A long, whiplike tail tipped with a piercing barb slid around the floor behind the thing, dripping a trail of bluish venom that stank faintly of vinegar as it twitched back and forth.

The creature stood on two tiny bare feet and padded slowly toward Ray. He heard the familiar scratching as the nails of the thing's tiny toes scraped along the floor.

It inched closer, reaching into its bag and pulled out something long and thin. Ray's eyes were focused past the terrible imp, and it was becoming a blur as it moved toward him. But as the creature stood in front of Ray, he realized what it was the thing held in its rat-like paws.

They were shining steel pliers.

The End

Cracks

Chris Mason

A year after his brother went missing, a flyer appeared in Jake's letterbox. The glossy page of A4, destined for the bin with the rest of the junk mail, caught his eye at the last minute. In large black print across the top it promised – *YOU LOSE IT, WE'LL FIND IT!* A new business had opened up on the high street. They were offering a 15% discount for the first ten customers, and a guarantee of 'your money back' if they failed to deliver. It was a long shot, but Jake thought it worth investigating.

The following day after school, he rode his bike into town. In his pocket he had twenty-eight dollars and thirty-five cents, all he'd managed to save over the past twelve months. Stacked behind glass at the local Op shop, a collection of mint condition *Dark Tower* comics with a thirty dollar price-tag waited for him. They'd have to wait a while longer for him now. He might have had them already if he'd been brave enough to ask his parents for the extra two dollars. But two dollars in the Smith house was the difference between having milk on his cereal or going without. Times were lean, had been since his dad got sick and his mum got laid off at the factory. Processing chicken carcasses had not been her career of choice, but the long shifts had meant they'd been able to afford an occasional treat. Now it was down to the basics. Every fortnight, Jake's mother took the three-hour-round bus trip to the Centrelink office so she could argue her case with a pinched-faced woman who had as much empathy as a hammer. Simply put, there were no jobs to be had for anyone, let alone a forty-year old woman living in the back of beyond where the unemployment rate was far too high for the government to admit. Her pleas made no difference. Payment of benefits remained as precarious as her husband's health. Jake was pretty sure his father had thought more than once about going out to the shed and throwing a rope over a beam. If he could have got out of bed, he probably would have. When it rained shit, the Smith family always seemed to get caught without an umbrella. First, Rhys had disappeared.

Now, Jake's father was heading for the exit, courtesy of the big C. So, when Jake entered the strange little shop on the corner of Fury lane and High street, it was no surprise he had a lump in his throat and a knot in his stomach.

A tinkle of bells announcing his arrival, he stepped into the small cluttered space at the front of the shop. From behind the counter, a man peered over his spectacles at him. Jake stared back. The shopkeeper looked like the sheriff from an old black-and-white B grade western. He was weasel thin with a pencil moustache and wore a satin waistcoat, a silver fob chain looping between buttonhole and pocket.

"Well, hello there, young sir."

"Hi," said Jake, his voice squeaking on the nervous upward inflection. He browsed the rows of shelves. There were boxes of assorted scarves, caps and gloves; a rack of coats; plastic tubs containing keys, eyeglasses, and watches; a mountain of soft toys and drink bottles; containers dedicated to dummies, dog leads and dentures. In one corner was a stand of umbrellas, in another, a wire basket containing balls of every size and colour. Towards the rear of the shop, Jake spied a dozen cages containing birds—budgerigars, cockatiels, peach faced parrots.

"Anything I can help you with?" asked the shopkeeper.

"Umm... I'm not sure." Jake was beginning to feel like this was a stupid idea after all.

"If you're looking for something in particular, I have more out back. Books, bags, shoes... an abundance of remote controls and phones. Contact lenses... Dogs." The man smiled.

"A flyer was put in our letterbox. It said—"

"You lose it, we'll find it," said the man, his smile widening into a toothy grin with a splash of gold in it.

"With a money back guarantee?"

"I assure you, my success rate is extremely high, but yes, your money back if I can't deliver on what I promise."

Jake moved towards the counter where he spied a collection of rings, chains and bracelets. "What type of things do people usually ask you to find?"

"Things of sentimental value... jewellery mostly, although I'm also kept quite busy these days with keycards and passwords."

Jake nibbled on his bottom lip, shifted from one foot to another. It was now or never. "What about time?"

The man stopped smiling. "Well, that depends."

"On what?"

"If it's lost or misplaced."

"What's the difference?"

"Missing is one thing, but *lost* is quite another."

"Oh," said Jake.

The man held out his hand. "Lawrence Tredreau, at your service."

Jake shook it. "I'm Jake. Jake Smith."

"Something tells me you have a story to tell, Jake."

Jake's eyes glassed over, and he nodded.

"Well, come around here and pull up a stool." Tredreau indicated for the boy to come behind the counter. When Jake hesitated, the shopkeeper added, "I don't bite, and the door is that way if you want to use it."

Did Jake want to leave? No, he didn't think so, not yet, not before he found out if Tredreau could help. Jake climbed onto a stool near the cash register, a large boxy thing that looked quite ancient. Beside it was its modern equivalent, a sleek black EFTPOS terminal.

"How much time are we looking at?"

"About thirteen hours," said Jake.

"Can you be more specific?"

"From Saturday, March 28 of last year to Sunday 29; between five in the afternoon and six the next morning. Approximately."

Tredreau scribbled the details on a notepad.

"Anything else pertinent to this particular period?"

"My brother."

"How old?"

"Eight... No, Rhys would be nine now. He's missing—"

Tredreau pursed his lips, thinking. "The police are involved?"

"Yes." Jake went back to chewing on his lip. "They haven't been much help."

"And?"

"They don't believe me when I tell them what I saw. The bits I remember, anyway. It's why I need you to find those thirteen hours."

"And if I can find your time...?"

"Then I might be able to find Rhys. Or at least find out what happened to him...and me." A tear spilled down Jake's cheek. He swiped it away, but it was useless. The dam had opened. Tredreau took a clean folded handkerchief from his pocket and offered it to Jake. "How about you start at the beginning."

Jake hitched in a breath and wiped his face. When he'd composed himself, he told the shop owner his story.

A year ago, Jake's mother still had her job and his father couldn't tell you where his pancreas was. Same as every Easter, they'd gone to the showgrounds to enjoy the local harvest festivities. Perhaps it had been small town naiveté, but Jake's parents had deemed it entirely appropriate for him to supervise his younger brother while navigating the show rides and food stalls. Eleven was practically an adult out in the country where kids grew up with air rifles strapped to their backs, and knew how to separate the steers from the cows come market day.

Jake and his brother had taken their last Ferris wheel ride for the day and were heading towards the popcorn stand on the other side of the oval when it happened.

"He's here," said Rhys.

"Who is?"

61

"The man from the boat."

Jake frowned. "What are you talking about?"

"He's come to take me home."

"What?"

"See, there he is." Rhys pointed.

Jake's eyes followed the finger. The person Rhys was referring to was not hard to miss. An extraordinarily tall man in a broad-brimmed hat cut through the crowd, making his way towards them. In front of him, people parted like the red sea, totally oblivious to the corridor of late afternoon sun forming between the stranger and the two boys. Jake put his hand on his brother's shoulder.

Rhys slapped it away "Don't."

"Rhys, what's going on?"

With the sun at his back, the man's long shadow reached the boys before he did; thin arms and fingers trailing dark lines across the sawdust laid down to prevent the ground being trampled into mud.

"Stay out of his shadow," Jake warned, instinct telling him the shadow was as great a threat as the man. Rhys took no heed and stepped forward, planting his feet firmly in the centre of the dark shape bleeding into the ground.

The sharp caw of a crow split the air. The man kept coming; walking with a sway in his step, the hem of his coat collecting sawdust. The boots he wore had shiny silver tips on the toes. Jake squinted up into the sun. He couldn't see the man's face, a halo of golden light making the hat appear even larger. Rigid with fear, the taste of sweet yet bitter toffee apple rising in the back of his throat, Jake made a thin whining sound. There was no doubt in his mind that he was in the presence of something truly evil. The thought of this man coming to collect Rhys scared Jake to death. Yet Rhys gave no indication he felt the same way. The crowd in the showground seemed not to be bothered either.

The encounter was not something Jake would ever forget. Which made it all the more surprising that he had little to no memory of what came later.

"Interesting. What else do you remember about the man?" Tredreau asked.

"His head was too big," said Jake.

Tredreau nodded. "Go on."

"It got bigger. I don't know, maybe because he was bending down towards us it seemed that way. I still couldn't see his face. I don't think he had one." Jake wiped sweat from his palms. "The other thing I can't stop thinking about was the way Rhys smiled at him, as if he'd met this man before. Knew him really well. How could that be? And the thing he said about the man being there to take him home. I didn't like that at all."

Jake recalled how the sky had blackened and the noise of the crowd had turned into a deep swooshing sound, like giant waves hitting sand. He'd again tried to pull Rhys out of the man's way, but his brother wouldn't cooperate.

"This is the bit that gets really crazy. Rhys opened his mouth and the man blew smoke into it. It was disgusting. Why would he do that? Rhys didn't seem to mind a bit. He started giggling like it was a party trick." Jake paused. "And then... how do I explain it... they both sort of faded."

"Faded?"

"Yeah." Jake's eyes widened. "Like the air just sucked them up."

Tredreau waited.

"After that it's one big blank. They found me the next morning wandering along a creek over near Palmerston. I don't know how I got there. And I don't know how I ended up with these bite marks on me. See?" Jake rolled up his sleeve and let Tredreau see the semicircles of pink scarring.

"Hmm. I'm going to ask you a question. It's very important you have a good think before you answer."

Jake had a feeling what was coming. The police had asked him over and over if he'd in fact led his brother away from the showground, done something awful to him out in the scrub. Isn't that what big brothers did when their younger sibling annoyed the crap out of them? Of the two hundred people there that day, not a soul could confirm Jake's story. All eyewitness accounts told how Jake and his brother had last been seen leaving the Ferris wheel together, heading in the direction of the Horticulture tent. No one could verify the presence of a tall man in a hat, and no one saw the boys with anyone besides their parents or each other.

"Did you smell anything?" Tredreau asked.

"What?"

"At the moment your brother disappeared, was there a smell?"

Jake frowned. Now that he thought about it, there had been. *How did he know?* Jake had told no one. His eyes met Tredreau's. "Yes," Jake whispered, "the air smelled kind of salty, like the sea." It had been strong too. *How was that even possible?* They were four hundred miles inland.

Tredreau folded his arms across his chest and nodded, as if it all made perfect sense. Jake didn't know why he was sharing all of this with Tredreau. Perhaps it was the earnest twinkle in Tredreau's eye. Perhaps it was simply because he was willing to listen.

"There are plenty of rumours flying around," said Jake after a while. "Mrs. Hupperts—our neighbour—she says the Lord knows the truth and my dad is going to get what's coming to him. Mum got cross at her, swearing and everything. Told her anyone can get cancer, and she should go crawl back under her rock."

"Ah, Alice Hupperts. She came in yesterday looking for her personality. Didn't find it, but I did have the parcel her sister sent to her back in July."

Jake gave him a tiny smile. It faded quickly. "I know my parents blame themselves. Sometimes, I think they blame me."

"I'm sure that isn't true."

It didn't seem that way to Jake. His parents rarely spoke to him these days outside of the day-to-day minutia. They didn't talk much to each other, either.

"What do *you* think happened?" Jake asked.

Tredreau looked at the floor and then up again. "You slipped through the cracks."

"Cracks?"

"Oh, yes. And cracks can be quite tricky. They're a lot deeper than they look."

"I don't understand."

"Here, let me show you." Tredreau rolled a coin along the counter. It disappeared into the thin slot between a tray of cufflinks and a box of fountain pens. When he moved them both aside, the coin was gone.

Jake frowned. "That's a trick."

"Is it?"

He waited for Tredreau to produce the coin in a traditional magician's sleight-of-hand exercise. When it didn't happen, Jake said, "Okay, you got me. Where did it go?"

Tredreau held his hands out, palms up in a 'you-tell-me' gesture.

"Cracks?"

"Correct."

"Then, how do you find stuff?"

"Well, sometimes things turn up in the last place you look."

Jake followed Tredreau's eyes and saw that the coin was back on the counter.

"But more often than not, I need to go hunting in the Bottoms."

"Of the cracks?" Jake sighed. Cracks? Bottoms? As he'd thought, it was a ridiculous idea. Tredreau was nuts. "I'm sorry. I think I've wasted your time."

Tredreau drummed his fingers on the counter. "Thirteen hours? An unusual request, but I do believe I can be of some assistance."

"Ah, I don't think so."

"What about Rhys?"

The reminder was a punch in the gut. Jake wrestled with the idea that Tredreau was peddling pure nonsense. But then, was it any stranger than what had happened a year ago?

"You really think you can help me?"

Tredreau nodded. "Of course."

Jake took the money out of his pocket and slid the pile of coins and notes across the counter. "It's all I have."

Tredreau put the cash in the till without counting it. "Come back tomorrow at a quarter to five."

Jake was almost to the door when he turned back. "What about the man in the hat?"

"Oh, him," Tredreau replied. "Nasty piece of work."

"So, he *did* have something to do with all of this?"

"I dare say he's the one responsible for why you ended up... where you ended up."

Jake swallowed.

"And while I think of it, thank you for reminding me. You better bring a box of matches."

***

Jake arrived on time. Tredreau locked the front door and turned the sign in the window from 'Open' to 'Closed'.

"Follow me," he said. Tredreau led Jake past the counter and through a door into a large storage area where there were more shelves loaded with boxes and baskets, all overflowing with second-hand goods. They didn't stop, exiting instead through the rear of the shop into a laneway.

"Stay right there," Tredreau instructed. He walked out into the middle of the lane and turned, the sun at his back. Jake froze. The long shadow stretching out in front of the man looked all too familiar.

No. No. No.

"Jake, I know this doesn't look good, but I'm not going to hurt you. If you want to find out what happened to you and your brother, you must step into my shadow. It's the only way."

Jake groaned. "I've made a mistake. A big fat mistake."

"No, you haven't. Do you honestly think I'd stay in business if I harmed my clients? Of course not. I'd be run out of town."

Jake shook his head. He'd only met the man the day before. He didn't really know him at all. "Who are you?"

"Someone who wants to help."

"How do I know if you're lying?"

"Ah, well that is always the great dilemma—who to trust." Tredreau put his hand over his heart. "I promise—cross my heart and hope to die—I'm not the monster who took your brother. Let me be perfectly clear. I *find* things. I don't collect them."

Jake wasn't sure what to do. He couldn't remember what had happened between the showground and the creek. He only knew it wasn't good. The marks on his body proved that. *Did Rhys do this to me?* Not knowing what had occurred in the hours Jake had gone missing consumed every hour of his day. He couldn't concentrate, he barely ate, and he couldn't sleep without waking up throughout the night in a cold sweat. Try as he might, he also couldn't get rid of the voice in his head that kept asking: *What did you do, Jake?*

"I understand you have reservations, but courage is the order of the day. Otherwise, we go back inside and I'll give you a refund. What will it be?"

"Wait, I'm thinking."

A thousand other things churned in Jake's mind, not least of all what might happen to his parents if, a year after his brother, he too disappeared. The police had interrogated them with the same scepticism they'd afforded Jake. But, what if Tredreau *could* help him. And what if…and this was a huge *if*…Rhys was still alive somewhere and Jake could bring him home? What Jake would give to see his father smile again; to lift the blanket of grief for one tiny moment before the cancer took it all. And maybe…just maybe…his father might love him, like before.

With great trepidation, Jake stepped forward.

***

The world wobbled and a great whooshing noise brought the smell of the sea. Jake tumbled through space. His eyes stung, and the taste of salt brushed his tongue. He landed on sand. A beach stretched out before him, a dull flat sea to his left, low dunes to the right. The sky above was clear. It contained no sun…no moon…no stars. Everything appeared washed in perpetual twilight. Beside him stood Tredreau, looking much taller than he had in his shop. He took the fob watch on its silver chain out of his pocket and checked the time. "Thirteen hours. Right, we'll need to move fast, no dilly-dallying. Anything look familiar?"

Jake scanned the shore and shook his head. Aside from the overwhelming feeling this was a bad place, he had no clue as to where he was. *Had he been here before?*

"Stay close," said Tredreau, setting off. Not wanting to be left behind, Jake fell in quickly behind him.

As they walked, Jake noticed the ground was littered with all manner of things: odd socks, Tupperware lids, beach towels, jigsaw pieces, hair accessories. They'd only gone a short distance when Jake, unable to help himself, stooped to pick up a cricket ball. The red leather was autographed.

"Leave it," said Tredreau. "Take something that isn't yours down here and you're bound to attract something that'll want it back."

Jake dropped the ball. He watched it roll towards the water's edge where it met a lone sneaker. He couldn't tell if the tide was in or out. The water looked grey and miserable.

"Does everything end up here?" Jake asked.

"Depends. Some things don't want to be found. Ever. But in general, much of what I'm looking for I pick up along this stretch."

"I don't see my brother," said Jake.

"That's because humans can't stand still. Always gets them into trouble. Your Rhys should have stayed put."

"He's been gone a year!"

"Not down here, he hasn't."

In the distance, Jake spied a dark shape approaching.

Tredreau sighed. "Seems we're not the only ones out and about today. I probably should warn you. Whatever you do, do *not* run."

The contents of Jake's stomach did a somersault. An image of him fleeing a broiling cloud of black popped into his head. The scars left by tiny teeth began to throb. *Is that what had happened? He'd tried to outrun the monster who'd taken his brother, and in the process, he'd left Rhys behind?* He shuddered.

"Are you alright?"

"I think I just remembered something."

"Good. Proves you *were* here."

No it wasn't good. It wasn't good at all.

The thing drew nearer. Jake squinted into the gloom, trying to work out what it was that was coming. Some type of cage on wheels being hauled across the sand by a ragged creature, bent over and shuffling. As it came closer, Jake realised the cage was full of cats, all of them black except for the scrawny tabby on top, mewing loudly.

"Evening, Joyce," said Tredreau.

The creature lifted its head and Jake could see now it was an old woman, wearing a cloak made from pelts that looked suspiciously feline. She looked up at him and his heart skipped a beat. Her face dripped with wasps, a hideous beard of pulsing fat bodies and wings.

"Evening, Lawrence." Her voice was scratchy and thin. "You interested in taking a gander at this lot? I've got a few new ones in."

"Not today. I'm looking for a boy."

"Like that one?" She pointed at Jake.

"Yes. A little younger though."

Her eyes lit up. "I seen 'im."

"Excellent."

"I seen 'em both. The pair was fightin'. Going hard at it, too."

"We were?" said Jake, although he knew it to be true. He and Rhys had fought often. While Jake was the older of the two, it made little difference, with Jake usually coming off second best. Rhys knew exactly where his brother's weak spots were, and not all of them were physical.

"Where is the boy now?" Tredreau asked Joyce.

"He went with O."

"Hmm. That is a pity."

Joyce sniffed and a wasp disappeared up her nose. "How come you got this one with you?"

"Long story."

She leaned forward and poked Jake with a finger. "You want to trade 'im?"

"I'm not for sale," said Jake, horrified.

The wasps lifted from her swollen chin and swarmed around him. It took everything he had to hold still.

She gave him a toothless grin and said, "I see you been taught some manners since the last time."

Jake had no idea what that meant.

Tredreau kissed her ancient cheek. "Nice to see you again, Joyce, but we ought to get on. Thanks for your help."

The wasps resettled, this time forming a crown on the woman's head. "O, he don't like visitors."

"I'm aware," said Tredreau. He nodded politely and they were on their way.

***

They kept walking, the shifting sand making progress slower.

As the minutes slipped by, more memories came to light; Rhys yelling, his small pale fists punching at Jake; the faceless man in the broad brimmed hat dragging a net; a fishhook, sharp and gleaming.

Jake could hardly breathe. More came. Rhys screaming; Rhys thrashing; Rhys biting... biting... *biting*; Rhys's face floating away on a tide of hate; then Jake wading out of the creek, a cigarette in his mouth and a crow riding on his shoulder.

"Stop," said Jake.

Tredreau turned.

"I want to go back."

"Why?"

"I can't do this."

"You already have."

It was true.

"But... what if what happened is all my fault."

Tredreau studied him carefully. "I think it wise not to get ahead of yourself on that score, but if it's any consolation, I doubt it."

Silence.

Finally, Jake asked, "Who is O?"

"He's the one who took your brother from the showgrounds."

"And me. He took me too."

"Uh-huh."

"You said he's a collector. What does he collect?"

"What do you think?"

"Children?"

Tredreau laughed, but there was no humour in it. "O doesn't stop there. If it's got a pulse, he'll grab it."

Jake frowned. "How did I get away from him?"

"I guess that's why we're here. To find out."

There was something Tredreau was not saying. Jake could feel it in his marrow. "You think O let me go, don't you? Why?"

There was a long pause. "I'm not sure he wanted you in the first place. I suspect he was only after Rhys. And generally, he doesn't double dip in the same gene pool. Not at the same time, anyway."

This stung more than it should have. Why Rhys and not him? Why was Rhys so damn special?

A crack of lightning split the sky. The beach turned white, then the colour of ash again. Thunder rolled across the sea towards them.

"Incoming. We need to find shelter," said Tredreau. "Quick, this way."

Jake followed Tredreau into the dunes, picking up the pace as they fled the coming storm. They found a concrete bunker, long deserted and covered in graffiti. As soon as they were inside, the heavens opened. The sound of rain, heavy on the roof, was interspersed with thuds as other things fell from the sky. Jake watched from the gun hole, a long slit in the wall facing the beach. Three sheep hit the ground, bleating. Then came wallets, combs, walking sticks; a rainbow of plastic, and—bizarrely—streams of digital data: a downpour of unsaved zeroes and ones, plummeting into the sea. When the rain stopped, the beach looked like a tsunami had hit it. A dozen shapes emerged from the dunes pulling shopping carts across the sand.

"C'mon let's keep moving," said Tredreau.

Jake turned in the direction of the beach, eager to see the spoils of the storm.

"Not that way. O won't be out there. He'll be on his trawler."

Jake reeled, sharp pain erupting behind his eyes. The flashback was terrifying—a ship's deck, greasy with oil and blood, the hold brimming with human cargo. Then more vivid: a gaping pit filled with bodies, limp as fish; Rhys down there with a hook, scrambling over the stew of pale flesh, his tiny teeth chattering.

Tredreau glanced at him. "Another memory?"

Jake burst into tears.

"That bad, huh?"

Jake was quiet for some time. Finally he spoke. "I hated him."

"Rhys?"

He nodded. "When Rhys came into a room, he brought chaos with him. Everything was always about what he wanted." He hitched in a breath. "The police said if it was Rhys that bit me he must have had a reason. But Rhys never needed a reason. He was always hurting me. Poking, pinching, punching... he did it all the time." Jake was suddenly angry, something he hadn't felt in a long time. "But did anyone ever say anything?"

"You mean your parents?"

"They thought because he looked like an angel that he was one. But my little brother had the devil in him. No one saw it but me."

"O saw it."

Jake stared at Tredreau.

"It's why he likes boys like Rhys."

Jake's anger turned to confusion. "If you knew that, then why did you bother bringing me back here?"

"You employed my services, remember. And this has never been about Rhys. Not really."

Jake wasn't listening. "I'm his older brother. I should have been able to protect him."

Tredreau gave him an exasperated look. "I think you probably tried."

"It wasn't enough."

"Jake, you need to understand the reason Rhys is with O has little to nothing to do with you. You are not to blame for your brother's choices."

"I don't think he knew how to make the right ones."

"Probably so. But it wasn't your job to teach him."

Jake breathed deep. "Everything changed after that day. I can't help it. I feel empty inside. Rhys took everything."

Tredreau's eyes softened.

Jake looked away. He had nothing left to say.

***

They pushed on through the dunes for another few hours, the sand eventually giving way to foggy marshland. Jake's feet sunk into the thick grey mud. With each step his heart sunk, too. In this place, Jake recalled clearly, the man who'd taken Rhys. Here, he'd had no shadow. The wide brim of his hat, the swirling smoky veil beneath, all hid the man's face well, but Jake had caught glimpses of it. The eyes were soulless, the mouth a cruel chasm. Worse, when he returned Jake's stares, it was as if he were looking right through him, as if Jake wasn't there at all. He'd never felt so small and insignificant.

Rhys, on the other hand, had been entirely comfortable in O's presence and followed him up the beach, willingly. To Jake, this was unbelievable. The man wasn't their father. He wasn't their friend. Why would Rhys behave this way? Jake was used to making excuses for him. Rhys was young. Easily distracted. He'd even gone as far as saying Rhys was not quite right in the head. But did it explain this? No, something else was at work here, something far more disturbing.

Is that why you killed him? The thought was as insidious as the suggestion it might be true.

Think, Jake. Think! What happened?

He'd gone after them.

But what did you do?

He'd pleaded with Rhys to stop the madness. Nothing he'd said had made the slightest difference.

WHAT DID YOU DO?

The sight of the trawler, a line of crows on the bow had filled him with dread. And then as he'd got closer, he'd seen the contents of the nets on deck. Horrified, he'd screamed till his throat was raw. The catch of the day, a hideous tangle of human flesh, presented no such problem for Rhys. He'd bounded towards the gangplank like a child in a playground, eager to get to the slide. In one last desperate attempt to stop him, Jake had body slammed Rhys to the ground. It was then, in the fight to keep him down, that Rhys had sunk his teeth into him. He'd kept biting until Jake, howling in pain and frustration, let go.

Oh God, why did I let him go?

Rhys had boarded the trawler without looking back. It was the ultimate betrayal.

***

Tredreau took a rest on the dock. It gave Jake a chance to take in their surroundings without the panic of his previous visit. The body of water was not the sea, but an inlet, dark and stagnant. The trawler sat there, a brooding sinister presence, looking no less terrifying than the first time Jake had seen it. He doubted it had sailed in a while: the hull rusted to a dull red, the wheelhouse empty. O was nowhere to be seen, nor Rhys. Crows, perched starboard, were the only audience to Jake's return.

"I don't need to go any further," said Jake.

"Are you sure?"

"What's the point? I get it now. Rhys was gone before he even got here. He's not coming back."

"I'm sorry."

"Don't be."

A bell clanged and O appeared on the deck, gliding across it like a snake on oil.

Jake watched him, trembling.

"I've come to discuss the situation with the boy," Tredreau called.

It occurred to Jake, Tredreau wasn't talking about Rhys. He felt the contents of his bowels liquefy. Had he come all this way only to have Tredreau blindside him now?

"May I come aboard?" Tredreau asked.

O gestured for him to proceed. Tredreau was almost to the gangplank when Rhys climbed out of the hold. He looked older, tired. The boy set his cold eyes on Jake and scowled. "What are you doing here?"

"I've come back for you."

"Why?"

Jake blinked. "It's Dad. He's sick."

"So?" There wasn't an ounce of emotion on the young boy's face. In that moment, Jake didn't know if he could hate his brother more.

"*So?* Rhys... he's dying."

"You deal with it. Now fuck off and leave me alone."

"You don't mean that." The words felt hollow. Of course he meant it. "Come home, Rhys... please." And there, again, the thread of hope wrapped tight around his throat. He couldn't give up even though he knew it would destroy him.

The answer was short and sharp. "NO."

Jake turned to Tredreau, who'd remained quiet during the exchange.

"Can you do anything?"

Tredreau shook his head.

Jake bit his lip. Every muscle in his body tensed. It was now or never. "Fine," he snapped and pushed past the man who'd brought him back here. Tredreau didn't try to stop him, instead stepping aside. Jake stormed up the gangplank with his belly on fire.

"Get out of my way," he yelled at Rhys, his voice so loud even he wondered where it had come from. The look of shock on Rhys's face was priceless. If Jake could have photographed it, he would have. But he had other business to attend to.

When Jake came before O, he was shaking. The rage that had propelled him dissolved rapidly into terror. What was he, crazy? O had the power to suck the life out of him; grind his bones to dust and trade his soul to the highest bidder. It was not a thought Jake wanted to linger on. He held true.

"You took something from my family. You took something from *me*. I don't expect you to give it back. But I *do* expect you to pay for it," said Jake.

O looked down at him, the smoky haze masking his face, barely disguising a spark of interest in Jake.

From behind, Jake heard Tredreau chuckle. "The boy makes a good point, O."

Eons passed before there was a rustle of fabric, and a dead hand emerged from the folds of the long coat. O pressed a silver coin into Jake's palm.

Jake turned, and doing his best not to drop to his knees and vomit, made his way back down the gangplank. He didn't look at his brother, couldn't bear to. Rhys had lost his way and now Jake had to find his. He marched into the dunes, a new boy.

***

Tredreau found Jake on the beach, gazing at the sea. A pink cardigan floated on the tide.

"I think I'm ready to go home."

"I think so, too."

Jake, his face shiny with tears, faced Tredreau. "All this time I thought I'd done something bad. Really bad."

"Uh-huh."

"But I hadn't."

"For what it's worth, I never once believed you could have done such a thing."

"Killing my brother... or standing up to O?"

"Violence is not in your nature. Fighting for what is right *is*."

"I thought I was going to shit myself."

"Well, it's not every day you get to bargain with Death. You have quite a flair for business."

"The bit I don't understand is this is the second time he's let me go."

"O doesn't need to keep you here."

"Why?"

"Guilt creates its own kind of hell." He gave him a wink. "But only if we let it."

"You're not like him. Like O, I mean."

"You seem surprised."

"Well I—"

"Good exists, Jake. Same as bad."

While Jake thought on this, a different kind of memory surfaced.

"Last time, after I got back to the beach, I smoked a cigarette. Joyce gave me one to calm me down."

"Did she now? She must have been in a good mood. Normally she'd sling you in the cage with the cats."

"What I want to know is how did I get home?"

"Check your pocket."

Jake pulled out a box of matches. "Oh."

"I'm guessing Joyce gave you a light too."

Jake remembered. As soon as Joyce struck the match, two things had happened. Wasps had swarmed out of her mouth...and he'd run, the lit cigarette stuck to his bottom lip. The beach had swallowed Jake before the wasps could reach him.

"Ah, I didn't make it back to the show ground because I didn't stay put. That's why I ended up miles away in the creek."

Tredreau nodded.

"One of his damned crows from the boat came along for the ride, though. If it's still around when I get back, I'm going to take a slingshot to it."

"I hope you've given up smoking since then."

Jake gave him half a smile. "I never said I was perfect."

Tredreau checked his watch. "Right, time to go. I'll try and direct you a little closer to where you live this time."

Jake struck a match. The light flared around him, and in the blink of an eye he was flat on his back, surrounded by wheat. The paddock was two blocks from home.

He'd been gone for just under nine hours.

***

When he walked through the door, it was obvious his mother was worried sick. His father was in the hospital. They drove all the way in silence. She didn't want to know where he'd been, and he was happy not to have to tell her.

Bedsides, Jake could see the light in his father's eyes fading fast. He kissed him on the forehead, and for one fleeting moment there was recognition.

"Rhys? Is that you?"

Jake choked back a tear. He hesitated before softly answering, "Yes, it's me."

He sat with his father until he could no longer bear it. Before Jake left, he whispered in his ear: "It's okay. I love you, Dad. You can go to sleep now." They were all the words he had.

Tredreau was waiting for Jake out in the corridor.

"It isn't fair," said Jake, his eyes red where he'd rubbed them raw.

"I never said I could give you fair," said Tredreau. "Are you going to be alright?"

Jake shrugged.

They sat together, watching the clock on the wall.

"If it's any help, I think you're a boy who'd be handy to have around. I have a storeroom that's long overdue for a clean out. I'd pay above minimum wage. What do you think?"

Jake wiped his nose with the back of his hand. "Sure, I could do that."

"Down the track, and with the right training, you'd be looking good for promotion." Tredreau gave him a nudge. "Acquisitions."

Jake had no intention of crossing O's path again, or Joyce's for that matter, and said so.

"Do you still have the coin he gave you?"

Jake had completely forgotten about it. He produced it from the pocket of his jeans.

"Can I see?"

"Sure."

Tredreau inspected the coin. "He paid well."

"Whatever it's worth, it will never be enough." Jake took it back.

"No, it won't, but it will more than cover the funeral costs, with plenty left over to set you and your mother up for a few years to come.

At that moment, Jake's mother appeared, sobbing. She had a wad of tissues in one hand, his father's shoes in another. The doctor with her, beckoned to Jake.

"She needs me," said Jake.

Tredreau nodded.

And for the first time in a very long while, Jake felt like he had the courage to deal with whatever came next.

The End

Three Rooms, With Heliotrope

Kaaron Warren

When this first started, I wondered how long I could go without washing my hair. I still haven't washed it. My scalp itches a bit, and I have to keep it off my face or I get greasy cheeks. But it doesn't matter. No-one's looking. No-one can see.

My name is Joanie and I am twenty-seven years old.

I may be the last person alive on earth.

AFTER SEVEN WEEKS UNDERGROUND, SUBJECT IS SHOWING SIGNS OF EXTREME DISORIENTATION.

After six months, apparently, your hair begins to cleanse itself and you end up with the sort of soft hair shampoo dreams of giving you. It's good to preserve the water anyway. I'm not sure how much is left. Peter looked after all of that.

He's gone, now. I thought I heard a cat meow, and he slipped through the safety chute to rescue it. He never came back.

I wonder what it's like up there? Is the sun still shining? Is there anybody alive, and how are they suffering, what with the radiation and the food'd be mostly off by now?

The sun must be out because my little heliotrope plant has tilted its flowers. It always faces the sun. If I stand next to the plant and tilt my face the same way, close my eyes, I can almost feel the warmth on my skin.

I've been underground for so long.

Why didn't Peter include any form of communication device? He was a fool.

My name is Joanie and I am twenty-seven years old.

I wonder how long the food will last. That was one thing Peter did right. Down come my meals, three a day, ready to be heated whenever I want them. I feel hungry, which is strange.

AFTER FOURTEEN WEEKS UNDERGROUND, SUBJECT'S CIRCADIAN DAY HAS SHIFTED TO 36 HOURS.

The walls are all white here. Three rooms, a nice little three-room apartment, though if a Real Estate agent was selling it they'd call it four, count in that kitchen type thing. Or even five; call the alcove where the Heliotrope sits a second bedroom.

I can walk the square of the lounge room in sixteen steps, if I climb over the lounge suite, a beige, stained set which carries the dents of many sleeping heads. The stains I guess at. Peter liked to save money, and buying a good lounge suite for a bomb bunker we may never use would have seemed wasteful.

A couple of bookcases, built in, on either side of the TV that doesn't work. Not only doesn't work, but has no works. Just the screen and the box on the outside. I suppose it's meant to make me feel at home. Normal. The bookcases are crammed full, an amazing selection of books about love and marriage and romance etc. Enough books to last—well, I could have done with them during my pregnancy, all I read were baby books.

Oh, my child. My child. How could I have let them take her? She would have been happy here, with just her Mum. But they took her off to be with the other children, somewhere safe. Why didn't Peter do something? I didn't like to ask, afterwards. He hates being questioned.

Off she went, waving out the window of the bus like she was going off on an excursion, her little pink fingers waving so quickly I could barely see them. Oh, the poor little thing without a Dad. Well, she's got me. I'll find her when the doors swing.

Peter's got a bullet in his brain.

I wish I hadn't heard that cat.

He was always clever with science, that's how he built the bunker, and the computer or whatever it is that sends food down when I want it. And the fake TV. He always said I watched too much, but look at him! After a shift he'd sit in front of it for hours without talking.

But his brain got tired in that job of his. All that information, all those planets with new rocks, the chemistry and physics of it all. Too busy to worry about what was happening at home. On earth.

This is how it happened.

We had given up on Nuclear War, oh yes. We had seen the movies and heard the environmentalists and the scientists. All the great nations agreed, we would not destroy the world through Nuclear War.

That took care of the great nations, for as long as they agreed.

But there are small nations, too, ones the great nations didn't even consider.

It took the kidnapping of two little children for the war to start. Two little children, living with their mother. She had escaped their father, given them her idea of a life of freedom and opportunity.

Her husband did not agree. He was King of a small principality, and he had many resources at his disposal. He had his children found, carried across the sea, brought to him.

The mother's government did nothing. World peace too precarious, control too tenuous.

So she hired some people to get her children back.

"At any cost," she told them. Those words were famous now. The people she hired killed her ex-husband, the King, to get the children back and there, it began.

Half the world wept: half rejoiced. The two halves separated, in anger, and the last great war began.

"At Any Cost," said the headlines, their irony too obvious to be clever, as the world began to burn.

Everyone blamed her. That poor woman who only wanted her children back.

I don't know any more. I have had no news, no word, since I walked into this small world and heard the doors shut. They will not open till it is safe.

I'm sure Peter wouldn't have thought of heliotrope. I must have asked for it. I'm so glad it's here. I worship my little sunworshipper.

It's a bit like a bachelor flat. I keep expecting a man with sideburns to come out of the bathroom with his shirt undone and offer me a drink.

Which would be nice, actually. Even a sweet sherry.

I wonder if they'll still make sweet sherry. Whoever they are. There won't be many of us, I don't suppose. Maybe I'm it. I'm the last. Ha! Imagine how that'd piss Pete off. The Dumb Bitch is alive and well, the last human to be so.

Time to eat.

Well, I don't know what time it is, there're no clocks. All I've got on my arm is a fading watch strap mark.

My name is Joanie and I am twenty-seven years old. It makes me miss the sun, that disappearing pale strip. We used to get sock marks, at school, sit there for hours sunbathing our legs, ending up with white feet and brown legs.

I don't know where this meat is coming from. Peter said all animals would be dead or contaminated. Maybe it's the cat I heard, but I've been eating it for ages and a cat doesn't have much meat on it. And there's no tail or claws. And it tastes like veal. I always hated veal. Soft, weak, fleshy. Someone told me once that human meat tastes like veal.

AFTER TWENTY-FOUR WEEKS UNDERGROUND, SUBJECT IS REFUSING TO EAT.

The worst thing about being under here, apart from no windows, no sun, no body, no booze, no drugs—no, because of none of those; I have to think. All those things I never thought because I hated them.

"You dirty little girl," says my mother. I don't know how she got through the doors.

"It wasn't me," I say. I'm eight. She's just been told by my sister that I've been telling all the children in the street about sex. It wasn't me. It was my sister.

"Dirty little girl," my mother says. Then she goes away.

I hate having to think.

AFTER TWENTY-FIVE WEEKS UNDERGROUND, DIET CHANGED TO INCLUDE ONLY VEGETABLES. SUBJECT RESUMED EATING.

Someone is playing music. Though I can't track its source. I thought it was coming out of the bath plug hole, but when I stuck my ear over it, I could only hear calls and screams for help. I hadn't thought about people trying to get in. They know I'm safe and they want to be safe with me. Safe with Mummy.

Where is my daughter?

My name is Joanie. I am twenty-seven years old, but I may have missed a birthday.

I breathe my own old air, smell my own sweat. I haven't showered yet. My hair is a solid hanging curtain; I draw it back and brush it every day. No tangles. And I don't really smell any more. I've discarded clothing. It's warm in here. All that nuclear energy bubbling away, I suppose. And my clothes were mostly synthetic anyway. Hard to find real cotton these days.

I'm not putting on any weight, which is strange, because the only exercise I'm doing is sixteen steps around the lounge room. Peter always said I'd go to fat in a flash. He called me fatso. Fatso fatso till I got a gun and shot him heard a cat he went to investigate, he hasn't come back.

At times I love being alone. I can sing all my favourite songs, bang around the room with a plate and spoon, marching 16-time to the beat.

They had marches, for a while. When we were getting ready for war, waiting for the men to come back from battling space to battle with each other. A hundred thousand citizens, marching in time. Shouting for victory in our time. Didn't they know? It may have started with promises, no nuclear force. But then one country cheated, and they all started, and Pete and I hardly had time to send our child away and hide underground in this ill-equipped bachelor's apartment.

Maybe he thought he'd be here without me, fantasised about leaving me behind, and our daughter. In a race, I'd beat him anyway. Soft, weak and fleshy, for all his intelligence and knowledge.

He was a good scientist, though.

I think I may be pregnant. Well, I can't be. Peter hadn't come near me for months. (Fatso, fatso) and I've been here all alone for ages. I had a period when I first came in, and I'd had a few before that. Not for ages, though. I must be due for another. I may even have missed a couple. If I'm pregnant, it must be a phantom lover, a sweet boy straight off a ship and into my arms.

Must be the radiation. I must have been touched. Peter must have let some air in when he went to get the cat. It's affected my insides.

AFTER TWENTY-EIGHT WEEKS UNDERGROUND, SUBJECT'S BODY HAS CEASED TO MENSTRUATE DUE TO ALTERED BODY CLOCK. MEAT PRODUCTS RETURNED TO SUBJECT'S DIET.

Lord Heliotrope is facing the sun. I face the same way. Imagining the rays, etc. It smells of vanilla, my little plant, makes me dream of milkshakes in huge metal cups.

We've had seven hymns and the vicar is just about to make his sermon up as he goes along. I count the flowers on the altar, and the number of people I can see without moving my head at all. I add up the numbers of the hymns. I divide them.

I open my eyes and my bachelor pad doesn't seem as boring for a minute.

My name is Joanie and I am twenty-seven years old.

I went to the pictures alone, just once. I hated it. Every time something occurred to me, I found a clue or heard a new fact, saw a handsome face or noticed a flaw, I bent to the empty seat beside me, my eyes still on the screen. A noise of appreciation to no-one. I nudged air with my elbow. It wasn't till the end I got used to having no-one to nudge, no-one to make noises to. The people around me carefully stared ahead as they left. I imagined they thought me insane.

There is no-one to laugh when I sing a song I wrote; a funny song. What's the point? I remembered something marvellous from my childhood. Does a memory, not repeated, not told, no longer exist? Never happened? A song, with no audience, is it wasted?

When I was a child and space was out there, the adults talked about war and thought they would never have another. But I remember my father, his racism, his hatred of anybody but us. God, I'd forgotten. I brought home a friend; her dark skin fascinated me in school, the way she shone in the sun and knew the names of the planets. I took her home for tea–I didn't think.

My father spilt his coffee on me. When I screamed in pain, he stroked my hair and said, "You'd better run off now," to my friend, who stood terrified.

I had forgotten where my scarred thigh came from.

AFTER TWENTY-NINE WEEKS UNDERGROUND, SUBJECT'S CIRCADIAN DAY IS FORTY-EIGHT HOURS, THE LONGEST EXTENDED DAY RECORDED.

There was a boyfriend, before Peter, who I have not thought of since. That whole time is blank–I've lost whole chunks of memory trying to forget that boyfriend. He was a pacifist; I remember his death now, he drowned, dived into a river and drowned. I wasn't there. I wasn't told. I didn't know.

He drowned, dived into a river, the sound of cheers behind him, I would guess; everything he did was surrounded by cheers and adulation. I always felt obliged, after lovemaking, to tell him how wonderful it had been, how magnificent he was. The night before he died, I said nothing; I remember now, his wounded eyes, full of failure. That's why I wasn't with him at the river; I couldn't face him after my cruelty.

I have never felt responsible for him drowning. I had nothing to do with it. He would have dived in anyway, got his fingers caught in weeds and drowned. Was he going to prove to his friends he had been all the way to the bottom? It is what he would have done if I had been there, whether I had adored him the night before or not.

His funeral was a dull affair; only his mother and I wept; we loved him truly.

Afterwards, I set about forgetting everything about him and the time we had spent together.

AFTER THIRTY WEEKS UNDERGROUND, SUBJECT IS EXPERIENCING WEIGHT LOSS DUE TO THE LONG PERIODS BETWEEN EACH OF HER THREE MEALS A 'DAY'.

I haven't showered since I've been here, did I say? I feel I should preserve the water, who knows how much there is. The only rain may be acid rain out there. Perhaps the plants are gone, the trees. Perhaps there is no air to breathe, and I am alone in my clever cell. Thanks, Peter. Your final torture to me. Leaving me alone in this home, this tin, or plaster. I don't know. I scratched the walls to see but nothing.

My hands are scarred, and my arms, long scratches which couldn't heal cleanly in this place without sun.

You always kept your fingernails long, raggedy, for such a meticulous man.

AFTER THIRTY-FIVE WEEKS UNDERGROUND, SUBJECT CRIES THROUGHOUT THE THIRTY-SIX HOURS SHE REMAINS AWAKE, AND SLEEPS FITFULLY THROUGH TWELVE HOURS.

It's nice to have a pet. They are so grateful when you feed them, they look at you with lilac eyes and exude a scent of vanilla, like a milk shake when there was milk. Or a white jelly bean, which no-one but me liked, so I would get them all, suck them till the flavour was gone then let the remaining gelatine slide down my throat. My dad told me I was eating horse's hooves. I suppose I was. My loving pet always faces the sun.

I have no clock. Peter said all time would stop, after the bomb. Clockwork cannot operate in a chaotic state, he said, expecting me not to ask. But time tumbles on, taking me along. My body knows: I could always wake without an alarm clock. My heliotrope faces the sun, but the sun is strange. The earth is spinning faster. The sun rises and sets twice a day.

Twice I have killed. I left a child alone, while I went out for cigarettes.

"Joanie, Joanie."

"Shut up."

"I wanted a bath, so I'd be clean and you would hug me."

"You didn't have to be clean."

"Yes. You left the house because I was too dirty. But the bath was bigger than when Mummy put me in it. There were no arms for a ladder."

"I told you I'd only be gone for a minute."

"A minute is enough."

That blonde hair, soft like seaweed in the water. The taps running hot and cold, but too much hot. Always turn on the cold tap first. Always keep both feet together when sitting. Never talk to strangers. A baby-sitter should never leave the child alone and go out for cigarettes.

Yes, Mother.

I mean it , Joanie. You'll be hurt, and then where will I be?

I remember the look she had when I told her about the drowned child.

"Thank God I wasn't responsible. Thank God she died in YOUR care."

I was only fifteen.

I'm twenty-seven now.

I suppose my mother is dead.

Is there little doubt the world is ending when the curses upon us are so great? My daughter, taken from me, my husband taken (gone away) and me left to carry on. Why me? Are my genes so good I've been selected to start again? Will there be others? Men? Will I see men again, make another baby, or are they all gone? Are there only women left, and we'll raid the sperm banks and raise our children in a new, matriarchal world?

AFTER THIRTY-EIGHT WEEKS UNDERGROUND, SUBJECT IS MASTURBATING CONSTANTLY AND WITHOUT APPARENT PLEASURE.

My name is Joanie and I am twenty-seven.

Bloody Peter's left the toilet seat up again. Why can't he just put it down? Why did he shout? I thought he didn't feel pain. I thought he wouldn't bleed— he was always disdainful of my blood, when my flesh was opened by his cruel hands.

Space did that to him. They were machines, in space; if they acted like humans, mistakes could be made and they would die. Perhaps he found it hard to be human again, once he had returned to me.

I have realised what meat I am eating.

AFTER FORTY WEEKS UNDERGROUND, SUBJECT HAS STOPPED EATING. DIET ADAPTED TO DISINCLUDE MEAT PRODUCTS. SUBJECT RESUMED EATING.

Peter is gone.

I forgot; I was setting the table for dinner, and I went to the cutlery drawer and I pulled out two sets of knives and forks. It wasn't until I was halfway to the table that I realised he wasn't there, would never be there, and that there was no point even using utensils because civilisation is gone and I've always wanted to eat with my fingers.

All is habit.

Soon the massive doors will open, as soon as it is safe. I've been here a long time. If I concentrate, stare, they will open sooner.

AFTER FIFTY-TWO WEEKS UNDERGROUND, SUBJECT RELEASED.

Final nine weeks spent in a virtually motionless and completely naked position directly in front of the doors. Subject was carried from Project Room 6 and cleaned. She has not yet spoken and is unaware of the completion of her sentence.

As a test case, the punishment appears somewhat equal to the many years in a traditional prison. However, there is no sign of rehabilitation as she only sporadically remembers the crime. For the most part, she believes her husband died accidentally.

Subject is presently being held in a detention cell at Your Hospital for the Disturbed. Meanwhile, we will continue with the Project, in deference to the pressing needs of the Present Government to find an alternative to long-term imprisonment.

My name is Joanie and I am twenty-seven years old. I have been placed in a room underground as part of an experiment. It's very small. My husband Peter volunteered me for the job, which is well paying. I'll kill him for that when I get out.

The End

The Revival of
Stephen Tell

John Palisano

"You are cordially invited to witness the Revival of Stephen Tell."
—Roxanne Dualilly

Oscar put the invite away and looked out the door of the converted storefront one last time. People walked up and down Burbank boulevard, oblivious. Families strolled by eating pastries from Porto's Bakery boxes. The air smelled of spring. A woman dressed like a fashion model rushed past. A small terrier trotted along, turning its head, and then away.

They had no clue what was about to happen only inches away.

"It's going to be okay," Martha squeezed his hand. "This is going to be unbelievable."

His stomach tightened when the door shut. He felt the same way whenever his wife wanted to go to Six Flags. He hated the roller coasters. It never seemed safe. He didn't like heights. He didn't like the falling feeling. Oscar sensed a similar sensation as he sat on a folding chair close to the room's barely-functioning air conditioner.

He looked around. The others chatted, but he couldn't make out what anyone was saying. Most all were couples, and most seemed to come from different walks of life. He was happy to see a few other Latinos in the room, too. If the whole thing turned out to be bunk, which he was sure it would be, he'd be able to count on them to joke about it with. There was a black couple. An Asian couple. He nudged his wife. "Not too many white people here," he said. "What's up with that?" Oscar spotted a husky, pale man with red hair in the back, studying his invite, an empty chair next to him. The man wiped his brow. *I'm not the only one cooking in here. Good. It's not just my nerves.*

"You know how it is nowadays," Martha said. "Everyone's trying to make things more representative of the real world. It's good, isn't it?"

"Whatever," he said. "Doesn't change anything outside of this room, though."

She smiled and he remembered the way her eyes came down a bit on the edges when she did. It was what made him fall in love with her—thinking and dreaming of her eyes when she smiled—way back when. That's how Martha was able to talk him into coming to her strange magic shows and sideshows. "She looks normal, Papi," his son had said. "But she's into all that weird horror and Goth stuff."

Oscar was much more into soccer. That was his thing. *I do this for her, I get to watch the game later, no hard time about it.*

There was a woman near the front of the room. She was tall and blonde and looked like she would have been well put-together coming out of the birth canal. Behind her, a large red curtain divided the venue.

He had to pee, but managed to change his focus. *Just nerves, man. Keep it together. Come on. This is easy stuff.*

Oscar wanted to look at the invite again. Martha had put it away in her bag as soon as they'd arrived. She liked to keep everything in mint condition. He remembered it, though—knew what it said—knew what she told him was going to happen.

"They're going to revive him," she'd said. "Right in front of our eyes. He's going to die and we're going to bring him back."

He didn't believe her. Not fully. There always seemed to be some sleight of hand involved, even if it wasn't clear. They'd experienced it several times at close-up magic sessions at the Magic Castle. She'd even gotten involved with some of the other magicians, and they'd gone to private parties. Of course, everyone used the parties to try out their latest and greatest gags.

They were invited to the Revival. "Stephen Tell's dark," she'd explained to him. "He's touched with the other side. The regular magicians don't like him. They think he's into evil. Occult. Not good stuff."

"Meh," Oscar had said. "Aren't they all?"

There had been something about the entire thing, though, that had rubbed him nervous. For some reason, it didn't feel safe. It wasn't a card trick in a parlor. It wasn't filmed in front of a television crew and audience. They'd arrived at the one-off storefront with little fanfare. "Maybe they're going to drug us so we can all be sacrifices to the aliens or something," he'd joked.

Martha had poked him in the ribs. "Oh, stop that. Do you know what an honor it is to be asked to be a part of a Revival like this? They're going to need each of us to be on point in order for this to work. If you're not into it, I can always ask David."

That was all she'd needed to say. David was a younger magician who'd gotten friendly with Martha. He'd overheard her telling a friend she thought he was so handsome and hot and smart and funny.

Oscar joked with her about it, but there was no way he wanted her to spend any more time alone with him if he could help it. *Mama didn't raise a fool. I know where spending time together as friends can lead.*

"Excuse me, everyone," said the woman in front. "We are going to shut the doors and begin shortly. Mr. Tell is almost ready."

Her voice and poise were immaculate.

The good thing about it almost starting is that we're that much closer to it ending, he thought.

Martha cupped a hand to his ear. "That's Roxanne Dualilly," she said in a whisper. "She's been his partner for fifteen years."

"Oh," he said, not sure what to think. "Cool."

Oscar wanted to be back home—he pictured his TV and his Netflix, felt his favorite comfy chair in the living room. *Soon. Very soon.*

Roxanne made her way to the side of the room. She pulled a dark cord that went up to the ceiling. There, a series of pulleys turned.

The curtain opened.

A man stood on a small platform. Around him, a frame made of what appeared to be aluminum rods seemed to keep him upright. He was bound to it.

The crowd sighed and gasped. Oscar couldn't tell which. *Did I make a noise, too?* He looked to Martha. She appeared lost, her focus razored in on the man.

Roxanne stepped close to the man, turned to the crowd and nodded. "My fine friends, I'm sure you've all heard of Stephen Falcon Tell," she said. "Today we will be experiencing a revival."

Stephen Tell didn't seem to be moving. His body remained still. Oscar tried to see if the man was breathing, but didn't see any signs.

From that point onward, his heart wouldn't stop racing. He felt as though he'd fallen off the edge of a building, or gone over the first hill on a roller coaster. *He's dead, or almost dead. What the hell has she brought me into? This is not fun at all. This isn't cool. It's awful.*

He tried to get Martha to look over to him, but her focus remained laser-tight on the scene in front of them.

Stephen Tell's eyes opened. He looked around the room, searching for everyone's connection. He looked directly at Oscar. *His eyes are dark and endless. Don't look at me anymore. Please don't. I don't even want to be here. Don't call on me or call me up or any of that stuff.*

Tell's eyes moved on.

"Good afternoon, my friends," Stephen Tell said, his voice clear and strong. "Thank you for coming to my revival."

There was soft applause. Stephen raised a hand. "Thank you all," he said. "What I am going to need from everyone is your undivided focus. I am going to give you a glimpse into the great beyond . . . into what there is beyond this life . . . but I am counting on each of you to bring me back."

He looked to the crowd. His bright eyes looked right at Oscar. "Each one of you is going to hold onto a piece of me . . . all the pieces will need to come together."

His eyes left Oscar's and met someone else's.

"If any single one of you weren't here, I wouldn't be able to come back," Stephen said. "And I am grateful for each of you. And I am grateful for you coming on this journey into the unknown with me."

There's no music. No fanfare. It all seems so quiet and small, Oscar thought. *How are they going to pull this off?* He looked to Roxanne, who remained still, her hands folded at her waist. *What is your role? Are you the one who's pulling the strings behind the scenes?*

Stephen looked at her. "I am ready if you are," he said.

"I am," she said.

With that, Stephen Tell shut his eyes. Roxanne turned to him and watched him. She stepped forward. "Mr. Tell is now slowing his heartbeat," she said.

Of course he is, Oscar thought. *They're really making this dramatic, aren't they?*

Roxanne watched Stephen. Oscar wanted to know what signs she was looking for proving he'd crossed over. Oscar thought the man looked like he was asleep. *How the heck are they going to show us what's in the great beyond? How are we going to see into the beyond? It looks like he will, but what about us? What proof are we going to have, other than his word? He could make it all up.* Oscar looked around the room at the others. The others were rapt. Even the man in back of them . . . the one who'd been distracted earlier . . . stared forward. The man blotted his sweating forehead with a tissue. *He's having a worse time of this than me.*

Roxanne made her way to Stephen's side. "We're ready," she said.

Tell went still. Oscar stared, trying to see any signs of life. Breathing. Blinking. Eyes moving behind the sockets.

He could tell nothing.

He's just in a deep meditative state. Not unique. Millions of people have done this. Totally explainable.

Roxanne looked at the assembled. "Is everyone ready?"

No one said anything, but it seemed everyone nodded. Oscar looked at his wife. She was rapt; she didn't even offer Oscar a glance.

"Okay," Roxanne said. "Here we go."

She placed her hands to the left side of Stephen Tell's head. Her right hand cupped near the crown, as she placed the other under his chin.

She pulled.

A large piece of his head moved.

Oscar's heart felt like it might have stopped. *That looks pretty damn real. Not sure a special effect could do that. But maybe it could? Special makeup effects?*

He felt chills running from his belly to the base of his neck. He didn't want to believe it, but he sensed something intangible. Oscar believed it was real. *I don't know why.*

Then there was something else that went down. Roxanne worked the side of Stephen Tell's head and the section moved even farther away from the rest of his head.

She's opening it like a door. How is that even possible.

The whole side of Stephen Tell's face had almost detached, staying in place by only one edge. Oscar scanned his face. No movement. No signs of life. *But he is still alive. He is still here. This is one hell of a trick. I don't see any mirrors. Or smoke. Projections.* He scanned the room, looking for hidden projectors or cameras . . . something which would explain the impossible act he was witnessing. He spotted nothing.

Roxanne dropped her hands and went around back of Stephen, stepping toward the other side of his head. "We're a third of the way there," she said.

At the other side, she repeated the process of unsnapping the side of his head and then pulling the flap free.

Still no signs of life. Nothing. There's got to be a catch. Maybe it wasn't him when we first came in. It's possible they projected his face onto this dummy and then turned it off when he shut his eyes. That would have worked. This could be a very realistic fake body we are looking at. We weren't thinking about it. That could very well be it.

Stephen opened his eyes. He was present. He was alive. He was not a projection or a fake, Oscar knew.

This is like when people get extreme body modification. That's what they've done here. Somehow, this is like he is pierced. Got to be something like that.

"Two of the three pieces have now fanned out," Roxanne said. "When we do the third, it will put Mr. Tell into a kind of coma. The physiological nature of the event will be clear once we turn him around and you can see."

Roxanne then turned Tell round and undid the back of his head. It reminded Oscar of a Bento box, unfolded.

How is he still alive? This can't be real.

With Stephen Falcon Tell's head folded open, dots escaped, blowing out like dust on a breeze. He opened the other side of his head and they could see the fleshy insides of his skull. They could see pockets and cavities—it did not look the way he'd always seen the inside of a head to appear. It looked groomed, as though manicured and curated to not be off-putting or disgusting. The fact that it was not made Oscar's stomach turn worse.

His brain unfolded, too. The gray matter . . . the forms . . . have been somehow unwrapped and are moving with the sides of his head. What about the blood vessels? The neurons? The connective tissues? How is the skull open like that? Any kind of germ can get in there. Skulls aren't moveable. He'd die of gangrene or something within a few weeks of having been cut open.

Tell's eyes and face went still.

Was he in pain? Did he know? Oscar wanted to throw up. Had this man just committed suicide?

The strange dots moved across the room. He watched as they went toward others . . . the sweating man toward the back had a hand over his head. He very obviously did not want the stuff touching him. *What was his name again?*

Martha had her hands out, and her eyes closed as though she were praying. She embraced the dust-like dots as they gathered around her.

"Remember," Roxanne said. "We will need each of you to accept this . . . accept the essence . . . and then return it in order to bring it back. There will only be a few minutes for which this is possible."

The dots were inside Oscar. He could sense them—could sense Stephen Tell inside his body, moving toward his brain and thoughts.

You know my every secret. No broken dream or awful thing hides from you. Now you each have some of my knowledge. It's dissipated within each of you. When you shut your eyes you'll each know some of me. And some of you will gain knowledge untoward anything you've known previously. If you choose, you can all come together.

The folks who witnessed the act looked startled. *We are all locked in this small theater. This feels different. I feel different.* He felt the dots inside him; Oscar thought it was like the time he had morphine after getting his knee operation.

Soon, the dots seemed to dissipate. *It's inside all of us now.* Oscar looked to Martha and they exchanged a smile. *I don't know what it is, but this is wild.* In that moment, Oscar felt he could do anything in the world. He felt like the Universe was his for the understanding.

Roxanne broke the mood. "Mr. Tell has passed from this realm," she said. "We will need to come together to call him back."

The man—Stephen Tell—had passed. Oscar knew it. *There's something you feel and sense when something isn't alive anymore. He's not alive. Not here. Gone.*

The crowd murmured.

"I want each of you to reach down, now, and feel what's inside of you," Roxanne said. "It's important that you process Stephen's essence and then bring it back."

Oscar shut his eyes. He was somewhere he'd never been before; he looked out on an endless desert landscape. In his mind's eye he raised his hand, only it wasn't his hand, it was Stephen's. Near him, he saw an older man and knew instinctively it had to be Stephen's father. "Out here is the special place you will go when you need to be revived. You will gather yourself back here. Think about horses racing toward you across the plain, each carrying a part of you."

His heart raced. *If this is a magic trick, it's somehow gotten inside my head and planted this memory inside me. That's impossible.*

"Each of you should be connecting to Stephen now," Roxanne said, her voice the gentle timbre of a yoga teacher.

"I am," Martha said next to him. Others followed suit, as did Oscar.

In his mind, the vision continued. The horses gathered. The father spoke. "Each steed has a piece of you, carried in a saddlebag. We need each horse to come close. We need every part of your essence back . . . to bring you back."

The horses closed in. They formed a circle. Oscar felt nervous at first, but then felt calm as the first came and he sensed no threat, despite the size.

He guided Stephen's hand toward a saddle bag. As he opened the flap, he recognized the dots . . . the essence . . . float out and guide themselves toward Stephen's body . . . the body he seemed to be inhabiting.

Oscar lost control of the body as others gained it.

One after the other, a person went to a horse, opened a saddlebag, and let loose the essence. The dots floated back toward Stephen's body. Oscar felt Tell's body filling more with each arrival.

How much time is going by? This feels like it should be taking forever, but it's going fast. Weird.

Soon there were only three horses making their way toward Stephen. Then two. Then one. As the final horse strode up, it seemed different. There was something off about its gait.

He felt Stephen's power . . . he was close.

"My son, it is almost time to return to the land of the living," his father said.

Stephen's hand reached toward the saddlebag. He moved the flap up and away.

The essence did not float out as it had done so many times before.

Oscar felt Stephen panic.

"Where is it?" his father asked.

"What is happening?" Another voice. Oscar couldn't place it. Roxanne's? He couldn't be sure.

"We need all of it," his father said. "Every bit. Without it, there's no going back."

Stephen's hands searched the saddlebag again. Empty. There was no sign of it. "It's gone," he said, his voice disembodied in echo.

The sky grew dark. The horizon's colors shifted. Reds. Purples. Blues. Black. No stars in the sky. No clouds. Pure darkness.

Oscar felt nervous. *Get me out of here. Now. This is not good. Hope it's part of the act.*

A sound of a thousand hoofbeats thundered on the horizon. A lip of red opened over the hill, like a scalpel opening a wound across the sky.

Fire.

Riders coming for Stephen.

Come to take the unnatural to hell. Or somewhere worse.

"He's gone!" Roxanne yelled. "Where'd he go?"

Oscar opened his eyes. It took him a moment to snap out from the meditative state. In front of him, Stephen Tell looked pale. *He's dead. Holy hell.*

There was a commotion toward the back of the room, where the seat sat empty where the sweating man had been.

"Did anyone see him leave?" Roxanne asked. "I swear I was watching the entire time. How could I not have noticed?"

Others reaffirmed they hadn't seen him leave, either.

"We need to go look for him," another man said. "Before he gets too far."

Staring at the empty seat, Oscar knew it had to be too late. The sweating man had gone. It'd be too late to revive Stephen Tell.

Folks filed toward the door. Many left, spooked, without looking at the dead man.

Martha hurried up to him. "We should leave," she said as softly as possible.

Oscar nodded. She took his hand.

They went outside without looking back, slipping through the front door. Outside on Magnolia, the crowds hurried past.

As they walked toward their car, Oscar could have sworn he saw the sweating man ahead of them. When the man turned, Oscar realized he couldn't picture the man's face any longer. He second-guessed his memory.

"I keep thinking I'm seeing him everywhere," he said to Martha.

"Me, too," she said. "But I don't think it's him. He's long gone by now."

"Or right under our nose."

"How would we know?" he asked. "I don't remember him so well."

"Same here," she said. "I wonder what his piece looked like and where he's going to go with it now… what he's going to do."

And just like that, the man had vanished, his own magic act taking the last piece of Stephen Tell with him. The promise and proof of the miracle revival had gone, too, its secret buried and lost once more.

The End

Lost Little Girl

Christina Sng

Are you lost, little girl?

Come with me,
I'll take you to your mother.
Here, take my hand
And follow me.
Yes, it's this way
And not the other.

Down this corridor
And into the basement.
She is waiting for you
In that last room.
Wait, what are you doing?
Stop biting my hand!

She's in there, I said.
Let go now!
God! You got a chunk
Of my flesh.
Are you chewing it?
That's disgusting!

Blood is spilling!
Wait, I need to lean
Onto something. Dizzy now.
Let me get you to your mom.
There's the door.
She's… yeah she is tied up.

It is to keep her safe.
Hey, you don't have to bite me!
Get your hands out of my face.
Wait! Stop digging your fingers
Into my eyeballs!
Take this, you little…

Yeah, slam you against the wall
And smash in your head.
That'll make you stop, you sick…
Oh God, my guts…
They're spilling out…
I…

BREAKING NEWS:

5 year-old girl rescues mother
From multiple serial killer.
Hailed a hero. Awarded a medal.

IN OTHER NEWS:

Rumors that the serial killer
Was discovered eaten
Has been completely
Disproved by video footage
That recently surfaced.

Mr. Forget-Me-Not

Alexis Kirkpatrick

Call me a hopeless romantic, but I knew I would love Jonathan Moscowitz until the day I died from the very moment I first saw him. I met eyes with him over the top of a cardboard box of books that I had been carrying from the moving van. His eyes were so pale blue I could see them reflect the morning sunlight from twenty feet down the sidewalk. I don't know if it was the weight of the books I held between my hands, or if it was the way he caressed his hair out of his eyes as he regarded me, but I felt my knees buckle.

The dirty old box with its dozens of books tumbled from my grasp and onto my brand-new buckle shoes. I stood there for just a moment, staring down at my feet and the small library strewn across the fading grass, willing either one of us to disappear, so I would not have to see the interest leave his eyes when I glanced upward once more.

Imagine my surprise when out of the corner of my blurred vision, I saw a small pair of hands turn the box upright and begin placing the books carefully back into it. I wiped away my tears and gawked. He smiled in return. His eyes were blue. Pale blue. My shoes were old. Yes, that's it. I was embarrassed because my shoes were so filthy and worn. How silly to be embarrassed over such a thing! I suppose, though, when you're twelve years old, everything seems like the end of the world as we know it.

I was carrying boxes into the house when he rode by on his bicycle and said hello to me. I covered my shoes with the box in my arms when he came over to shake my hand.

"I'm Jonathan," he chirped.

"I'm Eleanor."

***

Jonathan would pass me notes during class. He never cared if the teachers glared at him, or if his classmates would prod and tease. He would fold each note into a tiny star shape and toss it over the heads of three other students to my desk. I would get such a thrill in my stomach when I saw those stars drop from the sky and into my hands.

Once, he wrote me an extra special note. It was folded into a perfect square, like all the other papers he sent me, but this one was different. 'Will you be my girlfriend?' It read. There were two boxes drawn at the bottom; one labeled 'yes' and the other 'no'.

There was sunlight that filtered through the dirty windows, sunlight that illuminated the dust in the air and warmed the room, but in that moment I felt warm enough to heat an entire building myself. I fidgeted and picked at my knee socks as though doing so would quell the delicious tingling I felt in my stomach. The birds were singing louder than usual, and if I breathed in deeply enough, I could smell the fresh, damp earth just outside the window and I could imagine the cool breeze that would turn my nose and cheeks pink as Jonathan and I would hold hands on our way home.

I picked up my pencil, prepared to make a tiny 'X' in the left box when I heard the slap of a ruler on the chalkboard.

"Miss Eleanor," the teacher called, "what have you got there? How about you give that to me and we can talk after class?"

I crumpled the paper and stuffed it into my mouth before the teacher could reach my desk. I saw Jonathan's eyes from across the room. They were so beautiful, so pale blue, and so inquisitive; pleading, even. Through the mouthful of paper, I smiled and nodded to him.

***

Jonathan always used to ask me why I never wanted to see the pictures he'd taken of us together. We were but fifteen years old, and I was so pretty back then, with chocolate brown hair that curled over my shoulders and long eyelashes. Still, I couldn't bear to look at the photographs, not after I saw the figure in the distance. I was perfectly aware of how far-fetched it must have sounded, but in each picture I beheld, the silhouette of a tall, thin man stood in the background, too distant to make out any specific features.

"Do you see him?" I asked Jonathan one day. We had taken a blanket to the public gardens for a picnic lunch, on a day so bright that his dark hair shone like a beacon, and so hot that the ice cubes we brought for our lemonade had long melted by the time we sat. It was summer, an innocent, playful time of cicadas buzzing and sticky fingers from the drippings of a vanishing popsicle.

There were forget-me-nots growing in that garden, pale blue as Jonathan's lovely eyes and dotting the ground like painted raindrops. It was summer. It had just begun to get warm once more, and he and I laid next to each other and breathed in the scent of dew.

"Did I see who?" Jonathan replied, staring dreamily into the sky. The particular cloud he was looking at was one that closely resembled a lamb. I placed the photograph I had been studying onto his lap. It was a wonderful picture; just the two of us, sitting on our blanket, hands and shoulders touching. We were both beaming; the forget-me-nots were blue. And there was the man. Just past the flowers, standing atop a hill cast in shadow by a captured cloud. Waiting. Watching. I needed Jonathan to see him desperately; I needed someone else to know. I gestured to the man.

"Right here. Who's this? I don't remember there being anyone else around when we took this." Jonathan glanced at me; his brow furrowed. He picked up the photograph and chuckled.

"You almost had me, Ellie. C'mon, quit messing around and come here." He tossed the picture to the side and patted the blanket next to him. I let him fold me into his arms and fall asleep underneath pale blue petals that matched the pale blue sky, but the man standing on the hill never left my mind. I glanced at the photo a few more times; the flowers, the figure, and our faces. I named the man Mr. Forget-Me-Not.

***

The day he and I graduated high school, Jonathan picked me up in a blue car that clashed horribly with his maroon cap and gown. My mother cried; my father handed her tissues from a box he had been carrying all morning, and told us that they would see us both at the ceremony. I smiled pleasantly through clenched teeth when he pulled out his camera, and smiled even more pleasantly still when it flashed and a four inch photo slid out. I felt my stomach churning to the rhythm of my father fanning the polaroid back and forth, back and forth. He gave Jonathan a hearty handshake, a pat on the back, and pressed the photograph into his hand. My father gave me a kiss on the cheek, and Jonathan and I left the house, the bottle-green grass tickling the soles of our feet as we walked to his car, our shoes slung over our shoulders. I remember thinking Jonathan's car would have been the exact shade of blue as his eyes if it had been painted just a fraction lighter. The seats smelled like pine-sol, and the wind that swept through Jonathan's dark hair as we drove smelt of clean linen and summertime. He tacked the picture my father had given him to his rear view mirror with a hastily chewed piece of gum and took my hand in his. His fingers laced in mine; I did my best to ignore the pit in my stomach that I felt deepen as I stared at the photo. I couldn't have been sure at the time, but it seemed almost as if Mr. Forget-Me-Not had moved closer. There he was; tall and willowy as ever, and slightly; almost imperceptibly nearer to where Jonathan and I stood smiling.

***

I began to make out the features of Mr. Forget-Me-Not's face around the time that Jonathan and I were married. Years after high school had breezed by in a whirlwind that flushed my cheeks and tasted of cheap chocolate on Valentine's day. Summer had fallen away with the leaves, leaving a crispness to the air that seeped through the windows of my bedroom as I got ready with my bridesmaids. There was a picture of Jonathan pasted to the floor mirror in which I gazed at myself as I adjusted my dress. The fabric felt like cold butter sliding over my skin, and looked glossier than the lacquer I had been nervously peeling off my nails.

"You look lovely," my mother whispered in my ear as she fastened the last button at the nape of my neck. She brushed wisps of hair out of my face and told me not to wear too much lipstick or else Jonathan's mouth would be stained red in front of the whole church. I blotted my lips with the tissue that my maid-of-honor, Alice, handed me. The soft sunlight peeking through the curtains streaked her golden hair and flashed off her pretty white teeth.

"You're so lucky," she gushed, taking the tissue now stained with pink. "You both are. I wish I were getting married, too."

I turned back to Jonathan's picture and smiled to quell the knots in my stomach. His bright blue eyes shone back at mine from the mirror. I closed my eyes and pictured his easy, crooked laugh, the way his ears stuck out from his sharp jaw. I pictured his tousled dark hair, the hair that hadn't grown any more tidy with his age. Jonathan's bright blue eyes shone back at mine. My bridesmaids and mother filed noisily out of the room, leaving me alone to stand in front of the mirror. I watched particles of dust drift through the sunlight like snowflakes when I brushed Jonathan's cheek with my thumb. I kissed my finger and pressed it to his grinning face, imagining the way his lips would taste underneath the rainbow of a stained glass window.

I was sitting on the banister of the staircase in the church when I heard my father call for me to come down.

"It's time," I heard him say. I could feel my body flush against the crystal snow of my dress; my hands imperceptibly shaking as I gathered the fabric into my hands and began to descend the stairs. The cloth of my dress felt like feathers and hay against my skin. I pushed open the door and stepped into an unfamiliar hallway. The doors had changed; looming cold and tall over my head as the bouquet of forget-me-nots went slack in my grip. I remember the fluttering in my stomach disappearing with each beat of my heart growing louder in my chest. I ran from door to door in this strange hallway, beating the unyielding wood with open palms. I called out for my father. I called out for Jonathan. I called out for anyone who would hear me as the hallways wound in circles to nowhere, swallowing me into them as my white shoes slapped against the linoleum.

"Ellie," my father called, suddenly next to me, holding me as I shook, stroking my hair. "What's wrong? What are you doing?"

"I got lost," I apologized quickly, "I haven't been on this floor before. I just was having a hard time finding my way."

My father's brow knit, just as Jonathan's had during our picnic so many years ago.

"We were here up here just yesterday for the rehearsal, Elle."

"I-"

"Nevermind. Come with me. It's time."

I let him take my arm and hold it against his until I stopped trembling. He walked me to Jonathan in front of a sea of pastel dresses and curled hair stiff with hairspray.

"I promise to love you always," Jonathan murmured. His eyes were bright blue. The priest's face was kindly and plump, red with rosacea that stained his cheeks like the blood of Christ.

"I do."

The photographer took a picture of me and Jonathan on the steps of the church as our friends threw handfuls of rice over our clothes and beaming faces. The camera gleamed; brilliant white light suddenly lit the winter air. I didn't realize what had happened until the warmth from the flash faded. My smile felt fragile all of a sudden; held together with glue that couldn't conceal the cracks. When the man with the camera handed me the shiny photograph during the second course of the reception dinner, I forced myself to thank him through gritted teeth. Captured in the picture, Jonathan and I were laughing, shielding ourselves from grains of rice falling like rain as we kissed on the bottom step. And there, standing in the shadow of the door was Mr. Forget-Me-Not. He was far nearer than I had last recalled; close enough that I could make out the shape of his hands and shine of his shoes. And his face. I could see the faintest outline of his thin, taut face. His eyes looked like shadows beneath the silhouette of his slicked, black hair. But the worst of him, far worse than the eyes that sunk into his head, was his grin. Mr. Forget-Me-Not smiled a smile too large for his face, far too wide for his thin frame. He smiled as though he knew something I did not, and though fearful, and beginning to hyperventilate over my raspberry sorbet, I couldn't help but wonder what it was.

***

The world seems to move more quickly when children are brought into the world. On the Tuesday that Grace entered our lives, Jonathan and I both cried until there was nothing left of us at all. The nurse laughed that she had never seen parents cry more than their newborn, and closed the door softly behind her as she left. The afternoon was quiet and calm when Grace finally slept for the first time; on that perfect Sunday when we welcomed her with open and unsteady arms. I twirled my fingers through her ginger curls as she slept. The three of us embraced each other on a bed meant for one and watched the world move quickly outside from a moment frozen in time. I felt something almost like sadness when we packed our car and returned home. I kept my eyes on Grace, and Jonathan laughed and told me as we put blankets into the backseat that I had called the nurse the wrong name for the fifth time that day. I flipped through the photographs of the three of us nestled together on the cot, and tried to ignore the shadow in the corner of the room.

***

When Grace's ginger hair was long enough to put into pigtails that brushed the tops of her small shoulders, Jonathan got a phone call that left his face thoughtful and sad. He looked like the grey clouds drifting over the snow, I thought; murky and drawn. I listened to Grace fumble through nursery rhymes on the piano in the living room and gazed out at the blankets of white spread across the yard, oblivious to the tears that stuck to my husband's eyelashes.

"Ellie," he muttered, "that was your mother. She asked me to pass along the news that Alice didn't make it."

"Didn't make it where?"

Jonathan blinked. "Out of the hospital. She passed away, Elle."

I glanced at him quizzically out of the corner of my eyes.

"Don't you mean Alicia?"

"Elle, I... no. I mean Alice. Your maid-of-honor? At our wedding?"

Alice. My head spun as I shut my eyes and tried to conjure an image. Golden hair. No, dark hair. Hair dark as night, that touched her waist and was streaked with auburn when the sunlight stroked it. Alice.

"Oh," I replied. "Oh."

***

The door talked to me every time I opened it at night. Every evening since Grace left for university, I found myself staring at the moon over my bed and wondering why it was that I couldn't sleep. When the moon hid behind the night sky, or when it rained, I'd stare at the back of Jonathan's head as he slept beside me. I'd admire the fine silver hairs that traced their way from his scalp and down his neck; the storm grey stubble that coated his chin. His lashes would caress his cheek, and I wished so often that I could see his eyes open in the sleepy darkness. His eyes were blue; bright blue. Instead, I slipped out from underneath the quilts and paced the hallway.

When I was a little girl, and I couldn't sleep, my mother always knew how to calm me. I grabbed a pair of moccasins from my closet, and the car keys from on top of the kitchen counter and tip-toed out the side door.

"Side door open," droned the door. It sounded bored, I thought. I let it close softly behind me and pulled my pajamas tighter about my body. The moon was brighter tonight, lighting the steps from the door to where the car rested in the driveway. I approached it as quietly as I could, wincing at the noise it made when I pressed the 'unlock' button on the keys.

"Side door open."

"Ellie, what are you doing?" Jonathan's voice sounded groggy; tainted ever so slightly with an aftertaste of panic that he did an excellent job of masking. I smiled.

"Go back to bed, love. I just couldn't sleep, so I'm going to pay mom a visit. I won't be gone long. Go on back upstairs."

Jonathan's eyes widened. He wrapped his robe around him and tied it tightly as he descended the steps and approached me. He pulled me to him, and I folded like paper into his familiar embrace. He smelt of listerine and clean linen. The gravel of the driveway was beginning to hurt my feet, and I wished I had remembered to take a pair of shoes outside with me. Taking my face into his hands, his eyes searched my face. Pleading.

"She won't be there, honey. It's late. Come back inside."

"What do you mean?" I laughed. "Of course she will."

Jonathan stroked my cheek with his soft, creased fingers. I melted into his eyes just as I had when I was a little girl. His eyes were blue; bright blue. As radiant as the moon, and as warm as the sun.

"Come back to bed with me. I'll stay awake with you until you sleep."

"But I-"

"Elle."

He wrapped his arm around my shoulders, guiding me back up the steps and into the house.

"Side door open."

He closed and locked the door behind us, then took my hand and led me to the staircase, where I paused for a moment. Immediately, I wished I hadn't.

I stared at the picture frames littering the wall of the hallway, too transfixed and horrified to say anything, much less turn away. From mere yards away, identical in every photo; Mr. Forget-Me-Not loomed and grinned his terrible grin. His eyes were so black; his teeth were too long. His height gave him the appearance of a sort of macabre statue in each picture. 'What do I know?' that too-wide smile taunted. His fingers looked more like claws; long and thin and pale and sharp. I tore myself from the frames after a long moment and followed Jonathan back to bed where, true to his word, he held me until at last I found sleep under the cold, white moon.

***

The floors of the hospital made the sun look brighter when it flooded through the window opposite my bed. There were drawings littering the windowsill; drawings of horses and smiling people with triangle dresses and long straight hair. The paper was colorful, and when it caught the light, it made the drawings illuminate like silhouettes on the sidewalk. There was a vase of small pale blue flowers next to the bed. They looked unassuming and kind;

delicate. Blue. They matched the color of the pillowcase. The room smelt of isopropyl alcohol.

I could hear hushed and harsh whispers from just outside the closed door. I was tempted to open it, to prop my head against the frame and listen to what was so important. Instead, I sat on my bed and looked at the trees outside.

I wished the windowsill weren't so bare; it would have been so lovely to have something to decorate such a blank room. The sunlight was beautiful and warm, but within the clean white walls, the only source of color was a vase of blue tulips next to the bed.

The whispers had grown in volume, and now sounded clipped and sharp. Like garden shears. Or kitchen knives.

"—abandoning her," someone said. "—needs you."

"Doesn't care enough to remember—" someone else spat in return.

"—ashamed of yourself," shouted the first voice, "—know that isn't true."

I stood and crept to the door, turning the silver handle as quietly as I could before peering slowly into the hall.

Jonathan stood with his back to me, his shoulders tense and square. He was bristling with agitation, I didn't need to see his face to see that. And there was a woman. Her face was blotchy and streaked with dark mascara that she swiped at viciously when her eyes met mine. Her hair fell gracefully about her shoulders; ginger curls that swept like waves over her cheekbones. A child no taller than her knee reached up and tugged on her dress, hand outstretched.

"I can't do this," the woman muttered. She swept the child into her arms and rushed down the hall. Her fiery hair flew in flames behind her as she ran. I could hear her sobs echo. I wondered what she was crying for.

"Go on back in, Ellie," Jonathan said.

We both sat on my bed, side by side, and Jonathan held my hand in his. He traced slow circles over the back of my hand, outlining the bright blue veins that snaked through my now-translucent skin. I looked at him and tried to smile. His eyes were so blue against the white of his hair. Jonathan reached into his coat and pulled out a small white envelope.

"Here. Grace gave this to me. She wanted you to have it."

I chuckled. "When is she going to finally make it out here and visit me?"

Jonathan cast his eyes to the floor and said nothing.

I opened the envelope gingerly and closed my fingers around the glossy photograph within, feeling a pang that reverberated through my chest. I slid it out as slowly as I could.

The picture was of me and Jonathan, our hands resting on the shoulders of the ginger-haired woman that had run down the hallway just minutes prior. She was not crying in this picture, her face brimmed with laughter that threatened to bubble over like a pot on the stove. Jonathan and I beamed smiles that creased our faces around our eyes and chins. There was someone else with us, though. Someone's hands rested on my shoulders; pale and long and sharp. Mr. Forget-Me-Not's limbs trailed from my sweater and shrank into his curled shoulders as he grinned from just above my head. He bared both rows of teeth in a snarl that stretched over his face like canvas paper, just barely reaching the hollows of his black eyes. The dark of his irises seemed almost to fill all the empty space; they were so sunken into sockets above his gaunt cheekbones that they looked like canyons in his skull. My breath caught in my throat, and I threw the picture to the side of my bed, scrambling away from the envelope as quickly as my limbs would allow.

"What's wrong?" Jonathan took my shoulders and held on tightly. "Elle, what happened?"

I was shaking like a leaf beneath his hands. I glanced warily at the photograph, now lying face-down on the floor.

"I... I saw—"

"Saw what?"

I looked at Jonathan, at the worn face that I had aged with my love, into his beautiful eyes, and lost the words I had been searching for.

***

There is a vase of small, pretty flowers on my bedside table. Forget-me-nots. They are pastel blue, just like my pillowcase. The rest of the room is white, and altogether too clean. There is a man sitting in a chair facing the window, his back to me. His head is in his hands, and his pure white hair makes his fingers look dark in comparison. His shoulders heave with quiet sobs he doesn't seem to want me to hear. I watch him until every possibility of things I might say to comfort him fades from my mind and I am left blank, in a blank room, with the sobbing man and the forget-me-nots.

There is a vase of small, pretty flowers on my bedside table. They are pastel blue. There is a man crying, and his back faces me. I watch the parking lot outside the window as I listen to the rhythm of his heavy breathing. I watch a woman carry a paper bag to her car. The bag splits at the bottom and oranges tumble to the pavement, rolling underneath the wheels and bursting on the ground. I imagine the way the juice becomes sticky in the sun; the smell of ripe fruit.

I watch a small boy teeter by the window on rollerblades. He stumbles over something, then catches himself. He staggers away and does not return.

I watch a woman in a surgeon's mask light a cigarette on the edge of the asphalt. She sits on the curb and slumps over; the life seems to go out of her. Smoke curls from her lips, partially obscuring her face in tendrils of grey. There are bags underneath her eyes. Her hand shakes as she takes another drag.

I lean backward onto the bedspread that I did not bother to straighten today. There is a vase of small, pretty flowers on my bedside table. Next to it, there is a porcelain frame. I reach for it and take it in my quivering fingertips, turning it over as I do.

I smile back at myself from the frame, sandwiched between two other people whom I cannot recognize. The man to my left looks happy, but tired.

His arm encircles me, frozen in time. His eyes are so beautiful. So beautiful, so bright, and so blue. His are eyes that look familiar, though I suppose with eyes like that, he must have seen a thousand lifetimes before the one in which he was captured in this photograph. I must have known him at some point.

To my right is a man much taller than the former. He towers over the two of us; thin and willowy and gaunt. He is dangerously thin, with a skeletal frame and face. His black hair is slicked back, and his black eyes seem to fill his skull. They burn through me, and I want to look away but I find I can't. His smile is unsettling; too wide and too sharp, baring both rows of teeth. I feel a coldness in me when I look at him, a sort of dark, deep dread that seizes my heart in a clenched fist and doesn't let go.

I tear myself away from the picture frame and set it facedown on the bedside table. There is a vase of small, pretty flowers next to the frame. I cannot remember what they're called. I feel certain they have a name. Across the room, the crying man has quieted. The only sound within the blank walls is that of his slow breath, and I realize that he has fallen asleep sitting up in his chair. I begin to watch the parking lot again. There is a couple; young and energetic. The boy swoops her up into his arms, swinging her about. Her dress is the color of lilacs, and it swirls about her as her feet are lifted from the ground, enveloping her in fabric that flutters and flies. The boy's dark hair falls into his eyes and he caresses it out of his face in a single, gentle movement. He reminds me of Jonathan. Jonathan should be coming to visit any day now. He forgot yesterday, but he'll be here tomorrow. We'll play slapjacks, and he'll joke that my hands are thinner than the playing cards. We'll eat swiss cake rolls that he brings from the convenience store, and we'll sit at the window and watch life pass by. Tomorrow.

A shadow stirs at the corner of my vision. I turn my head away from the window, away from the formerly-crying man in the chair and regard the figure at my bedside. His clothes are too dark, and his emaciated figure is swallowed up by them. His eyes are set too deep, his mouth stretches into a smile that is too wide. He stares, and says nothing. He grins at me as if there is a joke that he knows that I don't. Fear bubbles in my stomach, rage gurgles in my throat.

"Get the hell out," I growl. "I don't want to see you mocking me with that silly face of yours." I try to sound braver than I feel, but my voice wavers ever so slightly. The smiling man says nothing. Tears begin to well up in my eyes, and a lump burns in my chest like alcohol.

"Who are you?" I stammer. The smiling man's face does not change. He leans over, so his black eyes meet mine. They are so dark and so deep, like a ditch to fall into. Like asphalt. Like nighttime.

"It doesn't matter anymore." He rasps.

I glance at my bedside table just beyond his dark overcoat. There is a small vase of pretty flowers. Forget-me-nots. That's what they were called.

Forget-me-nots.

The End

Home Theater

Vince A. Liaguno

The gaping mouth of the antiquated machine swallowed the sealed rectangular units as a thousand spools whirred to life somewhere deep inside the contraption. Miles of black tape stretched taut with a screech, then snapped, filling the room and my ears with the sounds of tortured cats and breaking bones.

The instructions said the machine had been refurbished. And restoration in this day and age meant the infusion of technological soul, that mid-21st century invention in which mechanics and biology were infused. My great-grandfather once said that it was the natural progression of man's attachment to his worldly possessions—that the gadgets and gizmos man had come to rely on should anthropomorphize.

Still, refurbishes were strictly black market. Machines were under tighter government control than people, their personification having gotten ahead of man's ability to control it. My great-grandfather's fingerprints—or lack thereof, to be exact—gave testament to the Great Technological Uprising. His was only a jealous laptop that melted his fingertips to the keys when he spoke of upgrading to a newer model, but others had suffered far worse at the hands of unchecked mechanical emotions.

But I had grown weary of government sanctioned virtual reality and craved something new in a world in which the concept of modernism had long morphed into something taboo. With the proscription of ingenuity came the underground refurbishment movement that had led me to my latest purchase: The Celluloid Amalgamator.

The physical shell of the machine held little wonder, with its unremarkable dented metallic exterior and strange yawning mouth. But what it did with that mouth and in its unseen bio-mechanical guts beyond promised to impress those of us looking to ride the next virtual wave.

As the Amalgamator sucked the equally strange sealed units into its bowels, I half-heartedly noted the warning label that advised it be fed no more than a maximum of three items per experience.

I had lost count at ten.

***

The wireless currents of virtual interconnectivity permitted me access while my mind's eye parted the red velvet curtain. The sensations of bodiless play were familiar to me, and I quickly gained my virtual-world equilibrium. I glanced around and shivered.

First rule of home theater play was to take immediate inventory of your surroundings and quickly assess. I was outdoors. Snow whited out the landscape as far as the eye could see even in the encroaching dusk. I blinked to adjust to the grainy, grindhouse visuals, like cinematic floaters behind my retinas. I gauged the first scene to be late seventies or maybe early eighties.

Cool. A retro vibe.

The sound of a helicopter in the distance, but getting decidedly closer, was muffled by the thick blanket of snow all around me. There was movement in my peripheral vision. My head snapped to the right.

A dog. Siberian Husky.

The animal was lumbering purposefully through the deep snow, snout down, its breathing labored. Rounding the corner of what I now realized was a mountain range, the helicopter came into view, flying low to the ground and coming from the same direction as the dog. The helicopter appeared to be flying in near-parallel formation to the dog, both animal and machine lining up almost perfectly in my sights as they came toward me on the horizon.

Gunshots. Rifle. High-powered.

The helicopter was firing on the dog.

I turned and ran, keeping ahead of the hound. Up ahead, I could see the semi-circular roof of a barracks. Shots continued to ring out behind me, but I didn't dare stop to see if the dog had been hit. If those in the helicopter had seen the dog, they had seen me.

The barracks drew closer and my chest grew tighter with each increasingly difficult breath. The droning of the helicopter sounded louder and I could hear the high-powered bullets punch the snow behind me now.

As I crested the top of a snowbank, a camp came into view. A long section of ramshackle, weather-beaten barracks lay before me. I made a dash for the shelter, mindful of the deadly chase behind me. Virtual reality now carried with it certain perils as it had evolved; namely, the real-life risk of injury and even death. It was the ultimate high for adrenaline junkies who didn't want to move off their couches.

I leaped for the nearest door, diving in with my left shoulder and full body weight. Mercifully, the door gave easily and I spilled in to...

(a blinding flash of light...a fusion of harsh fluorescence and orange flame that left a lingering smell of charred flesh in my nostrils)

...what appeared to be a boiler room. I shook off the bumpy virtual segue and took stock of this new scene. A labyrinthine conduit of rusted pipes snaked through what appeared to be a cavernous structure. All around me were rows of large metal drums, water tanks maybe. Systematic rows of grated walkways above and below me, punctuated by ladders that granted access up or down, indicated that I was deep in the bowels of wherever the Celluloid Amalgamator had placed me. The temperature was stifling, steam rising up from down below through the grating on which I stood.

Suddenly, from below me—or maybe from above, it was hard to discern direction in this place of steel and steam—came the sound of metal scraping against metal. Like nails on a chalkboard, only sharper, the sound piercing and shrill on my eardrums. But there was something else filtering in through my peripheral hearing, something vaguely familiar. As the sound made its way from my subconscious to conscious self, it took on a childlike shape and numerical form, syrupy with a sing-song rhythm.

One, two, Freddy's coming for you...

Almost simultaneous with my mind's click of recognition, I saw an image taking shape as it emerged from a thick cloud of steam ahead of me on the grated walkway: the tattered, red-and-green striped sweater, brown fedora, the leather-gloved right hand with blades attached to the fingers. Fingers that were scraping against one of the metal drums and filling the subterranean boiler room with what sounded like metallic screams as the man came slowly, steadily towards me.

An old film villain. Freddy something-or-other. Killed kids in their nightmares.

Freddy the old film villain draws closer. This is surely to be the first confrontation of the game—one I need to win to move to the next level. I look to my left, then my right, then behind me.

Weird… there are no options for picking up weapons or supplies.

Inharmoniously, the sound of a phone ringing echoes loudly throughout the cave-like space.

"Aren't you going to answer that?" comes the gravelly voice of virtual Freddy. He's now close enough that I can see the stretched tendons and scarred musculature of his hideously burned face. I marvel at the realism of the graphics. He wiggles a bladed finger just down and to my right.

I look down to see an antiquated telephone—I vaguely remember that it's called a *rotary phone*—sitting atop a dainty, lace-edged doily on a small wooden table. The quaintness of the display is discordant with the industrial quality of the larger set piece. This whole gaming experience is taking on a bizarre, almost hallucinogenic vibe now that—despite being a little thrown by it—I'm really digging.

Virtual Freddy continues to advance, so I lift the handset, anticipating that this is a crucial interchange to advance in the game.

"Hello…"

(another fluorescent-flame fusion of blinding light and burned flesh smell, more intense this time)

…I said into the receiver. The transition was rougher this time causing my line of vision to jump and shake as if I was in an earthquake. Seconds later, it subsided. I found myself sitting on both my knees in between a couch and coffee table in a comfortable living room that I didn't recognize. The furnishings were (again) decidedly retro but stately, denoting an upper-class affluence.

An ominous male voice in tinny analog sound is coming through the phone receiver and asking me if I've checked the children.

"Huh?" I said into the receiver, pulling it away from my face and looking at it as if the beige plastic instrument would somehow clarify the caller's statement.

"Have you checked…?" The line broke into static before the caller finished, and then another male voice, this one more urgent, forceful, emerged through the white noise.

"The call is coming from inside the house," it said.

More static, with the two voices now surging and ebbing alternately through the white noise that grew louder, more cacophonous. I listened as the voice with the clipped British accent repeated its question about checking the status of some unseen children while the other continued to urgently inform me of the origination source for the phone call.

I slammed the receiver down in its plastic cradle, severing the weirdly disembodied voices.

The game was becoming stranger than any I'd ever participated in, the objectives of this particular session not clear at the outset as was the norm. There were no weapons or supplies but, then again, there were no real villains yet either—or at least none that had been programmed for any aggressive attack mode. Stranger still were the transitions between scenes, turbulent and permeated by that harsh light and odd smoldering smell.

This is what you sign up for when you buy on the black market, I thought.

Deciding that the game wouldn't advance sitting there on my knees waiting for the phone to ring again, I rose and walked across the smartly-furnished living room into the foyer where I opened the front door…

(again that choppy jump…like a poorly executed film splice…the accompanying sensory elements even stronger this time)

…and stepped out into a cool, autumnal night.

I looked around me. I was standing outside a nondescript home on what appeared to be a suburban block of equal nondescription. The few cars parked on the street spoke again of the mid to late 1970s, while the multihued leaves scattering across the front yard in the chilly breeze denoted it was fall, probably late October or early November.

A flickering across the street caught my eye. A pumpkin, on the porch of a home just like this this one, smiled at me. Dancing light emanated through its haphazardly carved mouth, triangular eyes, and nose from the candle that burned within its gut. Somewhere, off in the distance, the sound of giggling children.

Halloween.

It was that old holiday—banned now for a good twenty years—on which children donned costumes and traversed suburban streets collecting candy from strangers.

No one could have seen any problems with that, *now could they?* I marveled at the naiveté of people as I surveyed the landscape and contemplated on my next move.

Then, as if in silent answer to my mental deliberation, an answer came from the house with the illuminated jack-o'-lantern across the street: An upstairs light flicked on and off in rapid succession.

I jogged across the lawn and crossed the empty street. As I closed on the house, I noted an archaic passenger van parked in front. I made note of that for later, in case transportation was necessary. In my virtual gaming experience, nothing in these simulated set pieces was random.

I climbed the porch and cautiously opened the door, still nagged by the lack of available weaponry in this particular session. Despite my recurrent misgiving about the absence of routine cybernetic provisions, I dismissed this as a byproduct of the customized aspect of the Celluloid Amalgamator and continued on in the game.

I was in the foyer of a darkened house. I strained to discern a sound—any sound—but could hear only the ticking of a clock somewhere in the living room off to my left. Glancing around to take stock of details that could mean virtual life or death, I noticed a series of framed photos—five frames of varying shapes and sizes—on top of a tall, rectangular table set against the wall under a mirror and beside a coat rack. As I leaned in to take a closer look at the photos within the frames, my breath caught in my throat.

The photos were of my family—my parents' twenty-fifth wedding anniversary photo, my college graduation, my sister and her husband holding their firstborn son, the entire family gathered in front of that old log cabin we rented one summer eons ago, and...

(one more stronger burst of incandescent light accompanied by a nauseating whiff of singed skin...)

...then I was jolted forward, my neck snapping back as I felt myself propelling frontward. The pace and intensity of the session was picking up, disorienting me momentarily. I struggled to regain virtual equilibrium.

Concentrate, I told myself. I knew from countless hours of virtual gameplay that quick, calm assessment of one's simulated surroundings with a head clear and unencumbered by reactive emotion was the key to success. Game designers were in the business of throwing people off their game—both real and metaphorically speaking. There was no time in that virtual instant to reflect on the incongruity of my family photos within the game. I took a deep breath, concentrated.

It was dark. I was seated, held down by a metal bar lying across my lap and held back by a diagonal shoulder harness. I was in some kind of cart, rounded at the front. The jumble of clinks, clanks, and rattling gear sounds indicated that the cart was moving; the jerky movements informing me that the cart moved along some kind of crude track system.

Somewhere ahead of me in pitch blackness, a shrill scream followed by a flash of neon red light and an image of grotesquery—a chained woman, a deformed man, a meat cleaver. The light illuminating the macabre scene went out as fast as it had flared and there was another sound now, coming from the opposite side. Maniacal laughing, exaggeratingly evil. Another flash of neon—this time green—and the image of a trio of witches hunched over a cauldron. A little boy's face emerges from inside the giant pot and then descends, emerges and then descends again.

Rudimentary animatronics. Cheap Grand Guignol set pieces.

My mind worked overtime to connect the virtual dots as the cart suddenly whipped to the right. An eruption of neon yellow light straight ahead of me. A towering furry beast lurched at me, the reedy sound of artificial snarling blasting through speakers above. It jerked to a stop inches from the front of the cart, the beast—a werewolf—bobbing slightly in its sudden halt.

A carnival funhouse.

With that click of recognition, the yellow light flickered off and I could hear the mechanical sounds of the werewolf retreating back to his cubby to lie in wait for the next funhouse guest. My car rolled forward again, this time shuddering forcefully to the left. The speakers emitted the sound of torrential rain punctuated by loud claps of thunder. Ahead of me on the tracks, an overhead spotlight switched on and off, mimicking intermittent lightning flashes and bathing the tracks in alternating white light and blackness. Suddenly, a woman—middle-aged and nondescript—darted out from the darkness on my right. She stopped, panting and frightened, and looked behind her. Her eyes bulged in fear—and then she looked directly at me and screamed.

"Kevin! Help me! For God's sake… help me!"

The snap of recognition hit me like an aggressive slap to the face—hard, raw, and open-handed, the kind that left an angry, red palm-print welt.

The woman was my mother, and she was terrified. I blinked, furrowing my brow at the sheer incompatibly and impossibly of her being in the game with me…here in the virtual funhouse. I barely had time to register her anomalous appearance in the game when she turned and sprinted off across the tracks into the darkness to my left. The funhouse car lurched forward again, moved a few feet, and then sputtered violently to a stop, the attendant squally soundtrack grinding to a fading halt as if someone had switched the power button off. Only the faux flashes of lightning remained, the storm setting of this part of the ride now rendered eerily mute. From the right again came a new series of sounds: a ripcord being pulled, an engine catching and coughing to life, then revving.

A chainsaw.

I was still faintly aware of being restrained inside the funhouse car when the lumbering figure stepped out of the blackness and onto the tracks. The man was enormous in stature—tall, broad, heavy. The kind of physique my mother—the same mother who must have been running from this human beast—would have called *big-boned*. He wielded a grimy chainsaw in front of him, waving it wildly to and fro. His face was a hideous mask of dried, mottled skin—not his own—that only heightened the effect of menace and malevolence. The chainsaw-wielding monstrosity briefly looked my way—a tick of passing interest in my sitting-duck stance inside the funhouse car registering in his eyes behind the grotesque skin mask—before clumping off in the direction my mother had fled moments earlier.

I let the notion that I was inside a bootleg virtual reality game with my mother who was being chased by maniac with a chainsaw sink in. Something wasn't right…didn't add up. Those framed family photos, the weird transitions between scenes, that burning flesh smell. Implausible, incompatible with any gameplay in which I had ever engaged before.

I was now keenly aware that I was a prisoner inside the funhouse car, which remained unmoving on its tracks. I rattled the lap bar that held me to the seat and…

(*…another erratic jump, this one so strong my eyeballs seemed to joggle inside my head, accompanied by another silvery-gold surge of light and stench of rotting meat so putrid that I could feel myself heaving…*)

…and I was outdoors, blinking in bright sunshine, a welcoming summer breeze caressing my face and blowing the residual odor of rancidity out of reach of my senses. I quickly surveyed my surroundings—a backyard, a picnic table, a tall tree with a tire swing, adults standing and sitting, talking animatedly, children darting between these adults in a chorus of giggles and merriment, a chocolate lab giving chase, tail wagging…

A palpable sense of dread and unease was building in my chest before the images even locked into place in my mind. Comprehension slowly unveiled.

A family reunion, circa 2018. Mine.

Virtual reality melded with memory and swept over me in a wave of nostalgia rolled together with unsourced apprehension. There I was…my little boy-self running with my sister and cousins, our family dog—Chester, who lived to 16 and died when I was away at college—chasing us in happy canine oblivion. My grandparents, seated on lawn chairs under the huge sycamore that would come down a few years later during a hurricane, were watching us run—my grandmother smiling from ear to ear, my grandfather nursing a Coors Light. I scanned the yard and the assortment of relatives and neighbors for my parents, eventually spotting my father—tongue protruding slightly from his mouth in a typical gesture of concentration—tossing horseshoes with two of my uncles.

As the first thought of my mother's whereabouts inched its way to the forefront of my mind, a sound—off in the distance— rushed up behind it, cutting it off.

A scream—my mother's—and the angry funhouse chainsaw.

Panic overtook me. I whipped my head right, then left, scanning the horizon for the game's escape hatch—a compulsory module that functioned as an emergency exit built in to all virtual gameplay that allowed for safe debarkation.

Suddenly, screams from all around me. The reunion guests were all looking out in different directions, slowly backing toward the center of the yard, their mouths contorted in terrified shouts and cries. To the north, my mother running towards them, the hideous skin-mask man in pursuit with the chainsaw; to the east, the boiler room guy in the striped sweater with the finger-knives; to the south, a tall man in gray overalls and shapeless white mask I hadn't encountered yet, carrying a long butcher knife in one hand, a severed head carved out in ghoulish jack-o'-lantern caricature in the other; finally, to the south, the white Siberian husky, violently convulsing as it ran, bursts of blood and gore erupting from its hide, sinewy tendrils shooting out and flailing wildly in all directions.

Fuck this. Game over, I thought and grabbed for the VR headset. I'd gladly risk the likely post-game cybersickness from premature ejection than experience the next scene in this virtual horror show. As I yanked the apparatus away from my head—prepared for the typical postural instability or oculomotor disturbance—I was struck with searing pain at my temples and across my forehead. The smell of burning flesh now assaulted my nose with the accompanying sound of sizzling. I retched at the sickening corporeality: the virtual reality goggles were soldered to my head.

As the procession of game-character atrocities advanced on my horrified family and childhood self, I realized with sinking certainty that

I had loaded home movies into the Amalgamator, which had spliced my reality into fictional snippets from the myriad old horror movies I'd also stuffed into the infernal contraption without heed of warning. With none of the conventional industry safeguards embedded in this black-market machine, I was now an eternal player in this circuitous augmented reality—virtual damnation on a looping reel.

Unreality was my new reality. The new world order was one of chimera and cinematic chaos, an imaginary celluloid existence made up of grotesquely disparate parts and a strange, anachronistic timeline with an unending runtime.

The only thing left to do—to hope for—was to traverse this interactive world of motion picture images in search of some cybernetic Easter egg, a buried clue that might lead me to a hidden level or unlock a concealed room. Maybe the Amalgamator's twisted designer included interred graphic elements somewhere in this virtual freak show.

Something that would release me. Or torture me. Maybe both.

With my simulated family and little boy-self screaming behind me, I set out walking in rewind. Back through the funhouse, I'd go check the children, investigate the flickering upstairs light, take a ride in the retro passenger van. All roads lead to somewhere—and, now, nowhere.

After all, the only way out is through.

The End

The Case of the Wendigo

Tracy Cross

Have you ever been hungry but didn't know what you wanted to eat? I woke up from a deep sleep, hungry. I shuffled into the kitchen and stood in front of the open fridge. Even last night's bar-b-que leftovers were unappetizing. And the sauce was delicious. I closed the door and stood in the kitchen.

I walked down the hallway to the bathroom when I saw my stepson (everyone calls him Scooby) left the television on again. I mumbled to myself as I slid past the bed and started to turn it off. The whitish light from the television seemed to shine on his body. He looked like a long, lean piece of caramel.

I watched him shift around. My stomach lurched. My body morphed as I stared at him. My mouth filled with saliva as my legs stretched and transformed. I could feel my posture stoop forward as I scraped the ceiling with the hump in my back. I looked at my hands-which were now talons.

My talon scraped at his foot. He rolled around as I felt a primal part of my brain take over. I needed to eat him... I needed to eat him whole. I leaned forward over him. My nose transformed into a snout and puffed hot air. If I could get just a taste...

***

Scooby told us that he woke up because there was some kind of a wolf in his room. He pulled on his cutoffs and ran past it, to the living room. He almost didn't make it because the wolf grabbed his legs and tripped him up. He managed to get the door open to the porch.

"I jumped from the porch and I think I broke my leg." Scooby sat at my grandmother's kitchen table, explaining what happened.

"And where's the wolf thing?" My cousin Xavier (aka The Professor, because he was all about *X-Men* comic books and science) asked.

My grandmother kneeled in front of Scooby. She touched his leg, "You broke or snapped a bone. I have a little experience because I worked with doctors. You need to get this looked at before it swells."

"I called an ambulance. Since it's three a.m., Scooby, they should get here pretty quick. I mean, I can't take you to the hospital." My cousin, Tasha, yawned, "At least, I don't feel like it."

"Y'all believe me, right?" Scooby looked around at us, "I know you believe me, Dee, you always been my little homey."

"Sure, Scooby. I mean, why else would you jump off the second floor of your house? I mean, if a monster chased me, I don't know what I'd do." I shrugged.

"Well, I would get a bat and beat the crap out of it!" Tasha joked.

"No, you wouldn't. You got scared when you heard a noise in the attic," The Professor countered, "On the other hand, I would rig a device to…"

"Y'all talking like you would do something." Grandma laughed, "You guys would run, just like Scooby did. And we don't even know if it was a wolf he saw. I think it's ridiculous."

"I swear, y'all gotta believe me. I think it's…" Scooby started before the two annoying and tiny dogs my grandparents owned barked like crazy.

Tasha looked out the window, across from the dining room table. "No ambulance here yet. Somebody's at the door."

I ran to the front enclosed porch. I peeked around the side of the house and saw Scooby's mom and stepdad under the light, at the door.

"Up here!" I waved them in, "It's just Scooby's folks."

Scooby shifted in the chair. His mom breezed by me. His stepdad hung back. He made like he fixed his fro but I saw him stare at Scooby. Like a mean stare.

"We are so sorry he bothered you." Scooby's mom apologized, "I don't know what's wrong with him!"

"It's okay, I was up. It's time for Robert to go to work," my grandma said.

We heard Grandpa Bob shuffle down the stairs. He stood on the landing at the bottom of the stairs and looked into the kitchen, "What's this? A party?"

"Scooby said he saw a wolf and it tried to eat him." The Professor explained, "Although, the physics of a wolf eating a human…"

"Gag me!" Tasha waved the Professor off, "I mean, the wolf coulda broke Scoob into little chunks then ate him."

My grandmother and I stifled a laugh. The kitchen was filled with the colors of the sirens from the ambulance, "Go put the dogs in the basement!"

Tasha opened the door to the small room between the kitchen and outside. She yelled at the dogs, "Sammy! Lovie! Go downstairs!"

Someone banged on the door, "Somebody call for an ambulance?!"

Tasha opened the door, "I called! He's up there!"

Scooby's stepdad didn't move. He didn't speak. He just stood and stared.

"Donnell, get up and let's get you to the hospital." Scooby's mom grabbed him by the arm. "Let's go. These guys will help you down the stairs."

"Xavier, go get a shirt for this boy. He can't go to the hospital only wearing a pair of cutoff shorts." Grandma gestured for him to run upstairs.

"I'll get some socks, too. I'll get you a pair of clean ones that I just got for the dance. I want my socks back, Scoob. The rings match my outfit."

Meanwhile, Scooby had a fit and yelled, "Jerry can't go! I don't want him near me! You stay away from me!"

"Donnell, it's fine. He can meet us with the car. Now stop all this fidgeting. You shouldn't have jumped like a fool! And off the second floor..." Scooby's mother fussed as they struggled to get all six feet of Scooby out of a five-foot door.

"I'll meet you at University Hospital." Scooby's stepdad turned and walked out the front door.

"Hey! You okay?" I asked his stepdad.

He stopped, clearly bothered that I spoke to him.

"What?" he snapped.

"Your arm. You got a thing or something." I pointed to a huge black bruise on his forearm. The longer I looked, the more bruises and scratches I saw.

"Nothing! Fell on a hiking trip last week." He stomped to the porch, "I'll meet you at University!"

Strange.

***

My parents deposited me with my grandparents (her mom and stepdad) while they went to Oklahoma or somewhere. She trained to be an air traffic controller. My dad and my little sister went because it was free, and she was a baby. My cousins' parents were also traveling. They were deposited here like me. We were sprawled out in my grandparents' backyard on hammocks my grandfather strung up between some trees.

The Professor read comic book after comic book.

Scooby practiced his graffiti on his cast. "When I get this off, I'm going bombing. For real!"

Tasha practiced her moves for the Drum Corps camp she attended in the mornings.

My mind was torn between two books about vampires, "I can't decide."

Scooby looked over at the book. "Hm, DeeDee, I like the other one. Not the gold old gothic looking one."

"Yeah, me, too."

Tasha caught her flag in midair and pointed at the small paperback I held in front of me, "What's it called? *I Am Legend?*"

"Professor?" I asked.

"I go with the consensus." He didn't lift his eyes from the page.

My grandmother brought out watermelon cut into chunks and salt on the side. We all salted our watermelon and let the sticky juices run down our chins.

"Hey, is everything good between you and your dad?" Tasha asked Scooby.

"*Step*dad. And no. He's straight up bogus with all his lies and shit. I mean, my mom can't see that he's lying, but I'm telling you–he was trying to eat me!"

"Scoob, why would he try to do that? I don't think you'd taste very good. You just so skinny." I poked him.

"I was enough for him."

"Has he tried anything else?" Professor asked, "You know, severing limbs, possibly trying to eat your toes or something?"

"Lissen, Spock: I know what I saw and I'm being straight up. Ever since he came back from Canada, he's been acting weird. Like, not normal-weird, but weird-weird."

"Well, I've done some research and I don't think your stepfather is a wolf. He seems to be more of a wendigo." The Professor set his comic book down.

We all perked up.

"I mean, you said your stepdad came back from Canada not too long ago, right?"

"Yeah, he went up there for a job. He was fine before he left but when he came back, he was acting strange," Scooby said.

"Did you notice any marks on his body, like bites or bruises?" The Professor sat up and tented his hands in front of him.

"I ain't trying to get all up on my stepdad like that."

I remembered, "Hold up! I saw some stuff on his arm when he came over the other night. Like bruises or something."

"Anywhere else?"

"Professor, does it look like I had the time to check out his body? I mean, I said something about it, and he covered his arm and left. It was like, what, three or four in the morning?" I said.

"In all probability, he could have been bit by one. I mean, I'm reaching here, but that's my hypothesis…"

"Dumb it down, it's summer." Tasha twirled her flag overhead, "I ain't tryin' to think here."

"He got bit, came back and then the bite took hold of him and changed him." The Professor looked at his hands. "And the only thing that can kill it is silver."

Tasha caught the flag, out of breath, "We ain't got no silver."

Scooby popped up, "We don't need no silver. I'll beat him like Sugar Ray on Duran. He'll be all 'no mas'!"

Tasha and I rolled our eyes.

The Professor went back to reading his comic book, "When y'all are serious, let me know."

***

The girls across the street from us were celebrating someone's birthday. I sat on the porch, watching them bob up and down the stairs. They looked like little confections, wearing their frilly dresses and hair in ponytails.

Looks like they used gumballs to hold the hair together and the dresses were like the liners on cupcakes. All the best parts were in the middle. I even smelled them. They smelled sweet, like chocolate and butter. My stomach growled. I needed to wait until tonight.

Later, after sunset, I followed one of the girls home. Everyone knew everyone over here, so little Tafisha walking home was no big deal because she could run up to anyone's house and ring the doorbell. *Not today, Tafisha. I've got plans for you.*

She skipped beneath the streetlights, her dress flouncing around and smelling so sweet. I can imagine popping those ponytails in my mouth—the sweetness of the gumball holders. The chocolate and buttery tasting limbs. My grip on reality was slipping because I could see she was a little girl, but I could also see that she was my next meal.

I needed to make my move before she was close enough to home that she could scream. I hid on the porch of the old Jones place—the parents moved out and left the kids on their own. Then, the authorities took the kids away.

"Tafisha!" I whispered. I still had trouble with my mouth. The teeth were huge and pointed. I know it sounded like I whispered, "Tafeetha."

She stopped skipping and looked at the porch, "Who is it?"

"It's me, Scooby's dad. I dropped my wallet and I can't reach it."

"It's real late, Mister. I gotta get home." She whispered but she started down the walk towards me, "I mean, I really gotta go but if you need help…"

"Tafisha, I need a lot of help." I held my head back because drool poured out of my mouth in anticipation of feasting on a lovely chocolate cupcake with sweet topping.

"You really need help with your wallet?" Tafisha edged closer, almost in my grasp.

"Yeah, really. I'll even give you some money to go to the arcade if you help me find it." Sweetness radiated from the pores of her skin… cocoa butter mixed with sweat.

She reached the bottom step and I snatched her. She muffled a scream as I covered her mouth and took a succulent bite into her head. The blood gushed down my throat like cream filling. I used my talons to rip the dress off her arm before I pulled it out of the socket. She tasted sweeter than I ever imagined.

***

I was at Miss Cathy's house, when I heard the news. I heard it in the kitchen and straight from Miss Cathy's mouth. Tafisha's mom could barely speak through her tears, but I understood most of what she said. I ran out to the backyard where a game of "Hide and Go Seek" started.

"Y'all!! Hey! Tafisha didn't go home last night! The police ain't lookin' because they said she's a runaway!"

The group was a bunch of neighborhood kids and Miss Cathy's two boys in the backyard. "For real?"

"Yeah! That's what they said inside!" I put my hands on my hips.

"But she went home right after the party yesterday! I walked with her part of the way," one voice yelled.

"I don't understand why someone would take Tafisha! She's the nicest girl!" Another voice commented, "Your cousin babysits her. She gon' be mad."

"We should go look for her. We need to find her," someone said.

"Wait! Let's go get Scooby an' them at the arcade! The more kids, the better. And I know my cousins know some places we wouldn't think about looking."

We were a mob of kids running down the street. People waved. Some stopped and stared. Other kids joined us as we ran to the end of the block and across the main street. The video game arcade was two streets over. I went once with the Professor, but I kept losing my quarters. I preferred roller-skating with Tasha.

I ran into the arcade and grabbed Scooby and Tasha. "Where's the Professor?"

"He went to do 'research' or something." Scooby made air quotes when he said "research".

"Well, somebody go get him! Y'all come on!"

I gave them a short version of what happened. Scooby hobbled on his crutches in the doorway, looking out at the neighborhood kids. Tasha hung back.

The blip blip video game sounds and music playing in the arcade made me want to go play, but we needed to find Tafisha.

"Alright, y'all gotta chill while we come up with something!" Scooby raised one of his crutches and cleared the space. He hobbled down the two steps and headed towards the alley beside the arcade. "Everybody here wanna help?"

The kids mumbled.

The Professor ran towards us with books in his hand, "They got me at the library. What's up?"

"...and the police said they weren't gonna waste time looking for a runaway," I said.

He nodded and listened, "Look, I checked some books out about 'wendigos' and I think we need to—"

"Hey! Quiet, Scooby has a plan!" Tasha snapped.

"Okay, we all know Tafisha. I say we split into three teams. I think four to a team should be good. If something happens, go to my grandma's house or get Miss Sue next door to us." The Professor said as he pointed out each team,

"Now, you guys search on Miss Cathy's block and we can search the next block over."

"Why don't we call the police?" one of Miss Cathy's boys—I think his name was Alex—yelled.

"Because the police don't care about no little black kids. Remember Chris Jones and his little brother? How they came and took them away after their parents left them? We gotta take care of us!" I waited for Tasha to throw up a Black Power fist like I saw the dudes further down the block do when they preached on the corner. She looked mad.

"Alright. If we do this, we do this together y'all. And nobody call the police. We could get in trouble. We gotta get some sticks and stuff. You know, arm up, just in case." Scooby used his crutch to move some garbage in the alley. "Here's some sticks of wood with nails in it. Everybody grab one. If you don't get a stick, go find one or a branch. Anything."

"I'm gonna help but y'all gotta remember that I'm going to that 'Zapp Heartbreaker' party at the roller rink. DeeDee is coming with me." Tasha crossed her arms.

So much for militant Tasha.

"I know, I know. Let's look for an hour, then we can go. And I was the one going with DeeDee roller skating. Remember, Grandma was gonna drop us all off together? I mean, it's only logical because everything is close to each other." The Professor pushed up his glasses with a knuckle.

"Thanks, Spock." Scooby mumbled as we divided into groups, "I'll go with Tasha and 'em."

"Why you comin' with us?" Tasha asked.

"To prove somethin', Sherlock."

Everyone stopped talking. We went our separate ways, half hoping to find Tafisha and be heroes on the news. Tasha was right. The police didn't care about lost black kids. Even when Miss Cathy's sister was kidnapped and killed. The dude lived right around the corner from her. Plus, we heard that someone heard Miss Cathy's sister screaming and run out the dude's house buck naked.

Since then, we decided we can take care of our own.

We strutted down the block and checked the bushes. We called her name. We thought we were doing everything we could to find her. When we reached the old Jones house, where Chris and his brother lived until Family Services took them, Scooby slowed down.

"Looks about right," he said.

"Right about what?" The Professor stepped forward.

"Hold up, alright! Just... let me look." Scooby moved towards the steps before he stopped. He turned to face us. "Okay, y'all, I didn't tell y'all everything."

"What do you mean, *everything*?" Professor asked.

Scooby adjusted the crutches beneath his arms. He looked down at the ground and whispered, "He could either look like my stepdad or that hybrid thing you were talking about before."

"A wendigo?" the Professor asked.

"Yeah, Sherlock, we already went over all this." Tasha laughed.

"And I said we needed silver then everybody started whining and…" Professor began.

"Shut up!" Scooby raised his hand, "Anyway, we've got to be careful. He's got these long claws because he stuck me in my foot and it hurt."

"No way." Professor shook his head, "No way… I mean a wendigo is like a human wolf hybrid. Maybe he had long nails or something. Maybe you were still half asleep. I've got these books from the library. We should really go over what I found."

"Somedays, I wish you didn't talk so much," Tasha mumbled.

"Intelligence over beauty, dear cousin. You know, you could have gone out of town with your mother instead of staying with Grandma. Me and DeeDee would have been just fine," Professor countered.

Tasha opened her mouth to speak until she heard the sound of Scooby puking. We all ran towards him. He tried to wave us off. By the time we got to the porch, we realized why.

In the lingering daylight, we saw Tafisha. Or what was left of Tafisha, anyway. It looked like she was half eaten and ripped apart. We saw an arm or a leg here or there, but no head. Her dress was half soaked with blood. I tripped over a shoe and my lunch came right back up. So did everyone else's lunch.

Scooby wiped his mouth with the back of his hand. "I know this was my stepdad. Don't ask me how, but I know it."

"Duh, we not askin' shit." Tasha ran off the porch and puked until her stomach was empty.

***

"What the hell were all y'all thinking? Looking for that little girl! You leave the police to do that work!" Grandma yelled at all of us while the police put up yellow tape. They blocked off the whole corner and didn't even thank us.

"We did what they wouldn't do! I heard at Miss Cathy's they thought she was a runaway. Tafisha is too stupid to run away!" I snapped.

My grandma shot me the "If you don't shut up right now" look. I leaned over, pretending to pull up my tube socks. I heard Miss Cathy screaming and running towards us.

"Aw shit," Scooby mumbled.

His mom ran beside Miss Cathy, "Calm down, it could be something good. You know, at least they found her."

Miss Cathy yelled, "No! At least these kids found her! You racist bastards! Didn't even look!" She yelled into any news camera focused on her.

My grandmother gathered us up and took us home. Scooby stayed behind with his mom.

"Thanks for finding that baby. We know they weren't gonna look anyway. But don't do anything this stupid ever again," she chided us.

"Grandma, you gotta understand something… we gotta kill it," the Professor stated.

Tasha added, "Or it's gonna kill us!"

"Kill what?" Grandma asked.

"The wendigo!" we said in unison.

Grandma rolled her eyes, "Lord, help me."

"And I kinda don't wanna die because I made pom-poms for my skates." I added, "Plus, we don't wanna be next, considering it's Scooby's stepdad."

"None of this makes any sense." Grandma smacked her forehead, "Tell this to your grandfather. He needs something to do instead of getting on my nerves. I gotta go to work."

Grandma worked late nights at a nursing home. Grandpa was a carpenter and general fix it man. I thought he would understand us better. He'd believe us, I was sure.

***

He didn't believe us.

We explained everything we knew as he sat across the table from us in the dining room. Grandma had some mahogany furniture and red shaggy carpet that felt funny under my feet. The furniture reminded me of the Addams family because it was all so big.

The Professor pulled out all the books from the library and made a presentation. Even I was convinced when he showed us pictures of scratches and wendigo bites. I felt afraid for Scooby.

"So, that's why Scooby was over here when he broke his leg." Grandpa finally said.

"Yes!"

"And y'all ain't goin' roller skating tonight." He looked at each of us.

"Police put the block on lockdown. It's like a 'curfew' or something," the Professor said.

Grandpa sat and stewed for a few minutes, which felt like forever. "Okay, let's say I believe you."

Our eyes widened as I asked, "What? Grandpa, you believe us?"

"I said, what if I *said* I believed you. Now what? What's the plan?"

"I guess we haven't gotten that far yet." The Professor walked around the table to let Scooby in. We all heard him banging on the door.

"Can I hang here? My mom is still with Miss Cathy. I think she's gonna spend the night over there. And I… uh… don't wanna go home, you know." Scooby set his crutches against the wall and joined us at the table.

"What about your stepdad?" Grandpa asked.

"I'm calling him 'Marcus' now. He's not my stepdad. He's just some crazy dude my mom married." Scooby paused, "And now he's trying to eat the neighborhood."

Grandpa held his hand up to stop Scooby from talking. Grandpa said, "You don't even realize how ridiculous this sounds. I can't say there's no such thing as were...wendi...whatever. I'm gonna need some time to really think about all this."

"A wendigo in the hood is highly probable *because* no one would believe us." The Professor rubbed the three hairs on his chin he called a goatee.

"Makes sense. Nobody ever believes us." I flopped into a chair.

"Totally." Scooby nodded, "Buncha black kids talkin' about wolves runnin' around...I'm so sure *everyone* would believe us."

"For once, Professor, you've got a good point." Tasha spoke up from the back of the room, "All this stuff is makin' us sound crazy anyway. I mean, even I'm on the fence."

"Tasha, girl, please. It really happened." Scooby plead his case, "I couldn't make this up even if I wanted to."

"I'm sayin' that's exactly the point. No one believes us, even Grandpa. And we were sure he'd be in our corner," Tasha added.

"Now, wait a minute! I never said I didn't believe you," Grandpa said.

"But you didn't say you believed us." Tasha smirked.

"I said I wanted some time to think."

"Grandpa, time is something we don't have. You didn't see Tafisha. I mean, seriously, we all gagged and not like them 'Valley Girl-gag me with a spoon' gag. I saw my lunch." I hoped my argument convinced him.

"We need silver. Like silver bullets. They kill werewolves or hybrids!" The Professor snapped his fingers.

"Where we gonna get silver? Wait! I'll just go out back and get some from the silver mine!" Tasha snapped.

"Now, calm down." Grandpa clapped his hands together, "Get something to eat and watch the movie of the week. I need to think."

He patted the table before he pulled on his painter's cap and headed down to the basement. We heard him clicking and sawing while we ate our dinner—fried catfish and home fries. Grandma left us some peach cobbler for dessert.

We watched *V* on the big TV in the living room. Scooby fell asleep on the couch. I slept in Tasha's room—with her boombox playing all the music I hated—while The Professor worked on his book. I don't know what it's about, but it's huge.

Grandpa called us down to the basement a few days later. The news was still talking about Tafisha. Scooby's mom finally went home. Marcus, Scooby's stepdad, picked up some night work as security or something. He mumbled when he told us.

"As long as he's out of the house."

"You do realize when he's out of the house, we don't know where he is. We can't track him. It's better when he stays home," the Professor said.

We all looked at him before Tasha said, "Thanks for making us feel safe."

"You guys made a convincing argument. It was everyone believing in something so much, I actually pulled out my old silver necklace and put it on. Not to mention the presentation The Professor made."

The Professor's ego filled the room when he smiled. He pushed his glasses up with a knuckle. Then, he pretended to fix his fro.

"Anyway, for when you guys go out, I made some things for you to take. Just don't get caught." Grandpa laid some modified baseball bats on the table. He also made some interesting things for Tasha and Scooby. "I put this machete on the end of this bat for stabbing. I added straps for you guys."

"I guess this means you believe us?" Tasha smirked.

"I like this!" The Professor picked up a bat and swung it in a circle.

"Can I wear my roller skates, since I didn't get to go last week?"

Grandpa raised his hand, "Now, we gotta have a plan."

***

"Man, Scooby is pissed he has to sleep at home." I laced my roller skates up with my new black and white pom poms.

"How else are we supposed to know if he's home?" The Professor tossed some popcorn in his mouth.

We watched another episode of *V* and waited. Scooby had a walkie talkie and we had the other one. When Marcus went out, we were going to hear three long beeps.

"Hopefully, he won't jump over and break his other damned leg." Tasha laughed.

I grabbed some popcorn. "His cast should be coming off soon, at least."

The walkie beeped three times and we were off. Grandpa got into his station wagon. We followed. Scooby moved across the yard pretty fast for someone on crutches. He slipped into the way back of the station wagon.

"Where is he going?" Grandpa asked.

"Took him long enough. We've been waiting for a while since the two kids after Tafisha went missing. And we still couldn't catch him." The Professor looked out the window.

***

Those stupid kids won't stop following me. They don't know that I know they are following me. Tonight, I have a surprise for them. I can't wait to strip the cast off Scooby's leg and eat it like a drumstick.

The chubby one, Tasha, looks like a big ol' caramel covered apple with that stupid bat. The other two look like Slo Pokes. I plan on taking my time with the last two: peeling the clothes off while they scream and start from the bottom up.

I crouch in the alley and watch the station wagon drive by. I need to get their attention.

I walk to the middle of the street and howl.

***

"He's behind us!" Tasha yelled.

We turned to look at the thing in the street. It was in shadow and ran upright, then on all fours towards the station wagon. The Professor jumped then let out a small yelp.

Grandpa crossed himself, "Y'all get right with God. I ain't never seen nothing like this."

"This is it!" Scooby yelled.

Tasha stuck the machete edge of her bat out the window. Scooby pulled himself over the seat. I was squeezed in the middle between Scooby and Tasha. I held my bat between my legs. Once he settled, Scooby stuck his bat/bayonet out the other window.

It dropped low and ran towards us. Grandpa sped up and tried to hit it before it jumped over the station wagon. It raked its talons across the roof.

Grandpa stopped in the middle of the street. I heard him rev the engine before Tasha said, "Pull over, we can get out and kick its ass!"

"Let me follow it to see where it's going," Grandpa grumbled.

The wendigo ran for a bit before it veered off into the front yard of an abandoned house. Grandpa pulled up in front as we piled out. The Professor held up a hand signaling for us to stop.

"He's on the porch."

Scooby limped in front of us. He tossed the crutches aside.

I looked around. He'd led us to the worst part of the hood. The part where all the houses were abandoned or crack houses. This was the part of town no one cared about because the people were too focused on drugs.

We heard a low growl. Scooby limped up to the porch. Tasha ran to the left side of the porch and the Professor ran to the other side. I stood in the front on the dead grass.

The abandoned house was a two-family house. It was painted green. Little bushes were planted in front of the porch. I imagine at one point in time, it looked really pretty. Tonight, it looked like the most desolate place I ever imagined. Streetlights didn't help it look any better because it cast some eerie shadows.

The windows were broken out and looked like eyes. Dirty white curtains hung halfway inside and outside. The door hung on for dear life. The screen door was tossed on the porch. The upstairs porch had huge holes in it. If you looked up, you could see the second apartment.

The wendigo lunged at Scooby before Tasha brought her bat down hard on his back. Scooby stabbed him and the Professor ran up behind him. He tried to take out his legs but was kicked. He flew backwards. I ran over to help him up. We ran over and started to beat this thing with our bats while Scooby and Tasha did as much damage as they could.

The wendigo bared its teeth and snarled. He swiped at each of us. I was the closest and felt his claw on my arm. I yelled a swear word I was never supposed to say.

"Get down!" Grandpa yelled as he aimed his shotgun at the wendigo.

It ran towards Grandpa. Scooby yelled, "No!"

Scooby and Tasha stabbed at the legs. Grandpa shot and it missed. The wendigo laid on the ground. I ran up behind it and smashed it on the head. I smashed it a few times before the Professor pulled me back.

"Wait, cuz," he whispered.

Scooby managed to stand over him. He stabbed the wendigo in the back of the head. It swiped those long claws around trying to grab at him. Somehow, between stabs, it flipped on its back and reached up for Scooby.

Grandpa stood over it, "I'm not gonna miss this time."

He fired twice and it was all over.

I thought I heard the wendigo mutter something that sounded like, "Sorry."

"He's trying to say something," I said.

"Do any of us look stupid enough to lean down and listen?" Tasha snapped.

The wendigo's hand grabbed Scooby's free leg and pulled him on the ground.

"What the...?!" the Professor asked.

Tasha lurched forward and bashed what was left of his head in with her bat. She didn't stop, even when the bat broke. She picked up the machete and stabbed him until we managed to pull her back.

"Not gonna hurt nobody else," she whispered.

I discovered later that Tasha babysat Tafisha during the school year. She was like her little sister. She loved that girl.

We stood in a semi-circle around the body. The yellow street lights shined down on us, casting shadows across our faces. Grandpa looked at each of us and nodded, "Y'all done good."

"Grandpa, I ain't know you were Catholic!" I gasped.

"When something like this is in front of the car, I will be whatever religion I need to be to protect you kids. Besides, it was the first thing I remembered."

We watched Scooby's stepdad change back into a man. The snout disappeared. The claws made a weird sucking sound. It kinda looked a little like in the movies but it smelled awful. We argued about what to do with the body until Grandpa stepped up.

"Let's put this on a tarp and take it around back." He tossed something plastic on the ground.

We rolled the body over and dragged it as best we could. We left it in the middle of the dead yard.

"Go wait for me by the car." He waved us away.

We walked down the alley between the houses. The sound of a shovel hitting the ground echoed around us. We wondered what he was going to do with the body of the wendigo.

"If he buries it, it may heal," the Professor said as he tossed his weapon in the back of the station wagon.

We looked back and saw the whoosh of a flame. Grandpa shuffled between the houses, holding a shovel and an empty jar.

"Guess he didn't bury him," I said.

"Get in the car. We don't talk about this again." He didn't look at any of us as he started the ignition. "It will burn itself out. It'll be fine."

Scooby stared at the flame for the longest time before he sighed, "What about my mom?"

"Boy, let her think he left. Don't say nothing, understand?" Grandpa's tone was firm.

We rode back to Grandma's house in silence.

I looked down and saw blood on my sock. I peeled it down. I knew what was there—a dark scratch that broke the skin. It was about four or five inches long. It was in a diagonal above my ankle. Then, I saw the scratch on my arm. The more I looked, the more I saw. My heart sank as I listened to Scooby, the Professor and Tasha talk in the back seat.

After the wendigo misadventure, I stood in the bathroom at my grandma's house. I looked at the bleeding scratch on my ankle. I had a scratch on my back and the one on my arm. I mean, they were just scratches. I can't change with a scratch. I mean, in the movies, they get bit or something. The Professor said that we needed to get bitten to change.

I filled the tub with water. The scratches burned as I slid in and under the water. My hair was gonna be a mess, but Tasha can cornrow it again tomorrow or even later. I held my breath. I needed to think because if I asked anyone anything, they would be suspicious.

Under the sink were some bandages. I wrapped it around my ankle. I wrapped one around my right arm where the scratch broke the skin. I knew I would have to lie and say I did it on accident or ran into something. They were too excited to really care or believe me.

Besides, if they found out... that scared me even more.

Next week, Scooby went back to the hospital. They cut the cast off and he almost jumped out the window when his mom pulled up in the car.

"Get ready! I'm about to wipe all y'all out on all the new games at the arcade—Donkey Kong, Pac-Man, Asteroids, and everything else up the street!" Scooby half hung out the window and yelled.

"Scoob!" we yelled and ran across the front yard.

"Grandma got some fresh boysenberries from her sister. We were celebrating." Tasha leaned on the station wagon as Scooby maneuvered out with his crutches.

"Only gotta use these for a little bit longer." Scooby shrugged.

"Because the muscles in your leg may have atrophied." The Professor began, "You haven't used them for most of the summer..."

We all stared at the Professor. He shut his mouth. "What? I thought you guys would want to know!"

"Professor, we don't need to know everything about everything. Duh!" I said.

Scooby's mom waved to us as she grabbed her things out of the station wagon. "I can't thank you guys enough. I knew the police wouldn't do much. They don't like to come out to this hood and help us. The neighbors are all thankful, too."

"You may need to exercise more precaution when selecting a mate," the Professor said.

"Yes, more precaution and judgment. I didn't think he would leave like he did." She smiled and walked over to him. "Maybe I should wait for you to grow up a bit and snatch you up!"

The Professor nudged his glasses with his knuckles and blushed. "I think you'll be too old for me, ma'am. I have the utmost resp..."

Scooby's mom kissed the Professor on the cheek. "It's okay, I'll wait."

"Ma! That's gross!" Scooby yelled.

Tasha turned away and pretended to stick a finger down her throat.

I swirled in circles on my roller skates. They felt good on my feet until a strange odor wafted beneath my nose. It was sweet, maybe vanilla?

I heard them all talking while I looked around the neighborhood. The house across the street from my grandmother's was pink. Pink like fluffy frosting pink. A little girl bounced down the front steps wearing a white fluffy dress and white ankle socks.

My stomach growled. My mouth filled with drool. I scratched at the scratch I covered on my arm. I didn't realize how hungry I felt until I looked at her. Then, I realized she looked like a fluffy piece of birthday cake.

I dropped to one knee, like a sprinter, before I realized it. I rotated my neck until I heard several small cracks. My body transformed as I tried to skate across the street. My feet burst from my skates. I felt them flap as they hit the ground. I heard voices behind me, but I was hyper focused on her.

She was going to taste really good.

The End

Don't Ask Jack

Neil Gaiman

Nobody knew where the toy had come from, which great-grandparent or distant aunt had owned it before it was given to the nursery.

It was a box, carved and painted in gold and red. It was undoubtedly attractive and, or so the grownups maintained, quite valuable—perhaps even an antique. The latch, unfortunately, was rusted shut, and the key had been lost, so the Jack could not be released from his box. Still, it was a remarkable box, heavy and carved and gilt.

The children did not play with it. It sat at the bottom of the huge old wooden toy box, which was the same size and age as a pirate's treasure chest, or so the children thought. The Jack-in-the-Box was buried beneath dolls and trains, clowns and paper stars and old conjuring tricks, and crippled marionettes with their strings irrevocably tangled, with dressing-up clothes (here the tatters of a long-ago wedding dress, there a black silk hat crusted with age and time) and costume jewelry, broken hoops and tops and hobbyhorses. Under them all was Jack's box.

The children did not play with it. They whispered among themselves, alone in the attic nursery. On gray days when the wind howled about the house and rain rattled the slates and pattered down the eaves they told each other stories about Jack, although they had never seen him. One claimed that Jack was an evil wizard, placed in the box as punishment for crimes too awful to describe; another (I am certain that it must have been one of the girls) maintained that Jack's box was Pandora's box, and he had been placed in the box as guardian to prevent the bad things inside it from coming out once more. They would not even touch the box, if they could help it, although when, as happened from time to time, an adult would comment on the absence of that sweet old Jack-in-the-Box, and retrieve it from the chest, and place it in a position of honor on the mantelpiece, then the children would pluck up their courage and, later, hide it away once more in the darkness.

The children did not play with the Jack-in-the-Box. And when they grew up and left the great house, the attic nursery was closed up and almost forgotten.

Almost, but not entirely. For each of the children, separately, remembered walking alone in the moon's blue light, on his or her own bare feet, up to the nursery. It was almost like sleepwalking, feet soundless on the wood of the stairs, on the threadbare nursery carpet. Remembered opening the treasure chest, pawing through the dolls and the clothes and pulling out the box.

And then the child would touch the catch, and the lid would open, slow as a sunset, and the music would begin to play, and Jack came out. Not with a pop and a bounce: he was no spring-heeled Jack. But deliberately, intently, he would rise from the box and motion to the child to come closer, closer, and smile. And there in the moonlight, he told them each things they could never quite remember, things they were never able entirely to forget.

The oldest boy died in the Great War. The youngest, after their parents died, inherited the house, although it was taken from him when he was found in the cellar one night with cloths and paraffin and matches, trying to burn the great house to the ground. They took him to the madhouse, and perhaps he is there still.

The other children, who had once been girls and now were women, declined, each and every one, to return to the house in which they had grown up; and the windows of the house were boarded up, and the doors were all locked with huge iron keys, and the sisters visited it as often as they visited their eldest brother's grave, or the sad thing that had once been their younger brother, which is to say, never.

Years have passed, and the girls are old women, and owls and bats have made their homes in the old attic nursery; rats build their nests among the forgotten toys. The creatures gaze uncuriously at the faded prints on the wall, and stain the remnants of the carpet with their droppings.

And deep within the box within the box, Jack waits and smiles, holding his secrets. He is waiting for the children. He can wait forever.

The End

Our Tragic Heroine

Matthew R. Davis

Quarter of an hour after walking off stage, alone in his dressing room, Narcisse leans on his tattooed hands and stares into the bulb-framed mirror. A mild tremor galvanises his body, and it's not from the adrenaline release of rocking out to ten thousand people. His phone lies on the counter before him, its face turned away as if ashamed.

When he can pull his wet eyes free from their doubles in the mirror, he sees his figure framed by the ephemeral opulence of the room behind him. Lilies sprawl from glass vases, funereal white and raw-flesh pink, virulent yellow and ominous black; their heady fragrance is underpinned by notes of cinnamon from the incense that burns in three brass holders, sending curls of smoke dancing through the leaves, and an acoustic guitar sits upon its stand like an upstart prince on his throne, awaiting the caress of restless fingers. Everything is just the way he wants it, a life-long dream come true—but now, at the height of Our Tragic Heroine's burgeoning career, Narcisse has good cause to question the cost of such dreams.

The man standing before the mirror is known to friends and family as Jason Partridge, but long has he sought to leave that persona behind. Staring back at him is the star he always knew he could be: a lean, sculpted torso beautified by scrolls and loops of black ink, pink feather boa draped around hard shoulders and reaching down to brush at the waist of leather trousers, stylish bottle-black hair dripping a fringe over kohl-rimmed azure eyes and a sensuous yoni-split of lips. Jason has often gazed into mirrors and marvelled at Narcisse staring back at him, but tonight that wonder has taken on a sharp and melancholy edge. The eyeliner, having survived seventy-five minutes of stage-born sweat, is now running down shapely cheeks to the corners of his mouth, and salt tangs his tongue as if he'd licked his own pungent skin.

Tonight's gig was their biggest yet, the first date of Our Tragic Heroine's national tour in support of their wildly successful debut album—the kind of show he's been dreaming of since he turned thirteen and formed his first triumphant E-major chord on a second-hand Yamaha guitar. He and his best friends have worked so hard to reach this pinnacle, spent countless hours in rehearsal rooms and studios plotting their ascent towards this lofty goal. And now that the rush is wearing off, he's wondering: *was it all worth it?*

The dressing room door cracks open, and the near-telepathy he's developed with his band tells him the identity of his visitor even before Simon Khachaturian–known to the world at large as Sigh–slips into the corner of his eye and closes the door behind him. Narcisse watches as his singer's reflection enters the frame of the mirror and leans against the back of a chair, black lilies draping their heads at his shoulder like mourners seeking consolation. Our Tragic Heroine's vocalist fits neatly into the décor of the room, his rangy figure wrapped in a deep burgundy velvet suit over a paisley waistcoat, his narrow face–equally expressive as his four-octave voice–half-hidden behind long, sweat-dampened locks as dark as Narcisse's own. He stares at the floor as if waiting for his cue, then lets out a melancholy breath that echoes his stage name.

"You got the message, too."

Not a question; Sigh needed only a single look to confirm it.

"What have we done?" Narcisse asks quietly, either of his friend behind or the rock star crying in the mirror before him.

"Us?" Sigh looks confounded by the question. "What *could* we have done?"

Does he not understand? Narcisse closes his eyes for a moment, blocking out his desperate reflection, and now all he can see is the screen of his phone–the terrible message it had been waiting to share with him since he and his brothers led the crowd through a rousing rendition of their debut album's acoustic finale.

Guys, I'm so sorry. Narcisse had wondered what Patrice could possibly be apologising for, even as his eyes had taken in the answer. *It's fucked up, I can't even find the words–but you need to know–*

"This was a long time coming, man," Sigh says, cutting into his thoughts. "Decadence always brings a reckoning. We *all* knew that. And we did what we could to stave it off–we helped in every way we knew. But some things are just...inevitable."

Narcisse wonders if his singer understands the ambiguous nature of his words. He must; the man's a brilliant lyricist, erudite and eloquent and *knowing*. Every line he commits to the page, to the stage, is layered with subtle strata of meaning. He must realise, then, that the reckoning of which he speaks has come not only for another, but for them, too.

"We need to talk about this," he says, and right on cue–as if kicking in on the first beat of a verse after a guitar and vocal intro–the rhythm section enters.

Ansh is still shirtless, because he likes the freedom it allows him when attacking his drum kit and because he's proud of his stringy brown body, but the stick-twirling exuberance he displays whilst playing is nowhere to be seen now. His eyes are huge, disbelieving, and Narcisse can tell that Ansh Kapoor–

known to the fans and the media as The Captain—has yet to shed a tear, still struggling to comprehend what has happened. His wiry arms hang lifeless like the long black hair that reaches down to them, and it's a sure sign of shock that his fingers aren't tapping out restless rhythms against the thighs of his red tartan punk trousers.

He's been guided into the room by the sure hands of their bassist, who looks less stunned and more resigned to their mutual revelation. Pickman—legally known as Paul O'Donnelly—is the only member of the band not to have black hair due to dye or ancestry, his rust-red locks tamed into a severe and stylish short cut that accentuates the androgyny of his fine-boned face, and he, too, has yet to change out of his stage gear: a long black skirt over heavy goth boots and a purple T-shirt that bears the glitter-speckled words NOBLE HERO, the name of the fictional band from their album's conceptual storyline. He wears as much make-up as Narcisse, but it has not run, because Pickman is also yet to weep over the terrible news.

The Captain lingers near the door, lost in his numb and unexpressed grief, as Pickman crosses to the table near Sigh and prepares himself a glass of the absinthe Narcisse had requested as part of their rider. The guitarist's thoughts flash to the group photo from the centrefold of their album sleeve, where they sit like Wildean decadents in a gothic Victorian parlour around a silver service dominated by a bottle of the green stuff, and again wonders at how far they've come since their days in the run-down Jacoby Apartments, where weeknights would often find the four of them gathered at a card table with one wonky leg as they passed around bottles of cheap red and plotted their eventual rise to stardom.

The five *of us,* Narcisse thinks as he turns away from the mirror, remembering that they'd used to share intoxicants more dangerous than mere wine, and sees another kind of red blossoming in the plastic barrel of a syringe.

"I can't believe it," The Captain mutters, his head twitching in denial. "Not now. Nah, man. No way. Not like this."

"I was just telling Narcisse that this was always going to happen," Sigh says. "It's awful, I know. It's so fucking tragic. But for all that, we can't honestly say it comes as a surprise."

"*Some* of it did," Pickman murmurs, throwing a glance at his guitarist, and Narcisse *knows*—he saw it, too. "And that makes me wonder how much of it is ours to own."

"None of it!" Sigh holds out his hands, beseeching. "I know what you're thinking—that we took advantage of a bad situation, that we wouldn't be here right now if we hadn't. But remember, what we did, we did out of love, with blessing and support. We weren't the only ones who wanted this success."

"Bit of a double-edged sword, that, isn't it?" Pickman takes a seat and sips at his absinthe. "We were blessed, yes—but at what cost?"

"All swords are double-edged," Sigh points out, and then the dressing room door bursts open for the third time in as many minutes. But this time, the entrance is as loud and happy as it is unwelcome.

"There you are!" cries Rhiannon Lloyd, toting a popped bottle of champagne in one hand. She's still wearing her stage costume, too, though hers, as befits a dancer, leaves a lot more leg and cleavage on display. "What a fuckin' show! You were great, the fans were great—I was great! Who's having a drink with me?"

She glances around, her ebullience undented by their morose silence. Looking at her silver hair and dark-rimmed eyes, the sepia and black dimity outfit that makes her look like a sexy goth moth, Narcisse can't help but feel irritation—it's not her fault, she's playing the role they made for her, but she's inauthentic in a way that reveals the artifice of everything that surrounds their heartfelt songs. Rhiannon's just starting to cotton on to the mood of the room when he lifts one hand to her and says, "Get out, please."

She looks cut by his words, his low and defeated tone, and the champagne wavers in her grip. Sigh is quick to cross the room and place a conciliatory hand on her shoulder.

"Sorry, Rhi, no offence. Look, we've just had some really bad news, and we need a little time together to process it, okay?"

The dancer stares at him, at all of them, belatedly taking in the shattered expression they share. "Oh. Shit. Um, I'm sorry, guys."

"It's okay," Narcisse says, and throws her a tired smile to show there are no hard feelings—she's blameless in this, after all. "We'll join you for a drink later."

"Sure." Rhiannon sends each of them a look that vacillates between confused and sympathetic, allows Sigh to direct her back out the door. When she's gone, the rest of the band can hear him calling to Nudge, their amiable but very capable security guy. Pickman reaches out with one hand and plucks anxiously at the low E string of Narcisse's backstage acoustic; The Captain finally moves his fingers, using them to grasp the soft petals of a nearby lily as if only now realising how fragile beauty can be; Narcisse turns back to the mirror and stares at himself, blames himself, trying to ignore the black rectangle of his phone like that could repudiate the news it bears.

Sigh is soon back, closing the door. "I've asked Nudge to keep everyone away from the room for a while. There won't be any more interruptions."

"Something's been interrupted, all right," Pickman says, "and permanently. So, what are we going to do about it?"

"What *can* we do?"

"We can start by actually saying her name," The Captain snaps, and all eyes flick to him. "All this pussyfooting around, and for what? She's dead, man. Dimity's *dead.*"

And there it is, out in the air at last.

Guys, I'm so sorry. Patrice's message, still ringing through their minds like a brutal blow to the head. *It's fucked up, I can't even find the words — but you need to know. Dimity died tonight. The centre just called. She's gone. Twenty minutes ago, just like that. I'm so sorry.*

"We wouldn't be here if it wasn't for her, and we all know it." Pickman drains his drink and returns to the table, lines up another three glasses. "We just finished celebrating her life, or a version thereof. Now, we need to celebrate her memory. Come on."

Our Tragic Heroine gathers around the table as Pickman prepares them each a glass of absinthe, melting in sugar cubes with spring water through a slotted spoon; Narcisse is sure he's not the only one thinking of their album shoot, the parlour, the creation of an image they strive to uphold even now when there is no one around to see. The Captain sniffs back impending tears, and Sigh drapes a comforting arm around his shoulders, gives him a comradely squeeze. Then Pickman is passing the glasses around, and together they raise them, looking as always to Sigh to be their voice.

"To Dimity Hardacre," the singer declares, closing his eyes. "Our beloved muse, our dearest friend—our tragic heroine."

They sip at their absinthe, pensive, and Narcisse thinks back to the lounge of that dingy Jacoby apartment where it had all come together, the four of them swilling cheap red wine as they sat around the card table and told Dimity the name they'd decided on for their band.

"You're calling it *what?*" she asked, pausing in her preparations, holding the rubber tubing taut around her arm. Her eyes probed each of them, but it wasn't long before they dropped back to the table and the loaded needle waiting to get her off. "Bit close to the bone, don't you think?"

"It's honest, and it's evocative, and in a way, it's a tribute," Simon said, his gaze flicking away from her as she lined the needle up with a raw hole in the crook of her elbow. "You brought us together, Dim. We would never have all met if it wasn't for you. You lent your hands to fate, guided the four of us to where we needed to be."

"And your tribute is to tell the whole world that I'm a fucking wretch?"

Dimity ignored any answers that may have been forthcoming and sank the plunger down. Her eyelids fluttered and she slumped in her seat, sighing as though she'd just relieved herself of some painful wind. A loop of purple hair caught in the corner of her lax lips, but she didn't seem to notice; beside her, Ansh reached up and gently untucked the errant strand. The four of them watched her, waiting for their friend to surface from her momentary rapture—a shared ritual common in its observation. She only roused when Jason leaned over the table to cook up his own tar-brown shot, and she assumed control of the process with well-practiced hands that, as always, bore traces of paint around the chewed-down nails. He let her fix him up, and in that moment, he was as close to her as he could ever be, closer than if they'd been lovers. They shared the needle, shared their blood. The act was sacred, a pact sealed with trust.

"Like Pick pointed out, the blessing was a mixed one," Narcisse says now. "Dim was flattered to be our muse, but it forced her to see herself in a different light. She saw herself through our eyes–the ugly weakness of her condition and the fucked-up romance we saw in that. We glamorized her suffering, and she didn't feel comfortable with that."

"But what we did was truthful," Sigh argues. "I certainly didn't make her problems sound *desirable*. The album is a paean to the beauty of her soul, and yeah, I can see how it romanticizes trouble and addiction, but it's also a clear warning about the consequences. If anyone ends up shooting smack because of it, they've not paid any attention to what I'm saying."

"Fair call," Pickman concedes, "but that's not what I meant. True, we're not responsible for our audience in that way–just *her*."

"But, like you said, she saw herself anew because of us, and she changed for the better," Sigh argues. "She got off the horse. She would've been out of that place in another week, home and sober. Patrice didn't say, but I'd bet anything she didn't die from an overdose."

"She was clean, man." The Captain nods, fervent. The youngest of the group, he's always looked up to Dimity like a big sister, always been the quickest to believe both her earnest truths and her junkie lies. "I know it."

"I believe that, too." Narcisse finishes his absinthe, realizing that none of them could know for sure–what with rehearsals and press commitments and everything that came along with playing in a professional band on the rise, they hadn't seen Dimity in months. They'd relied on her cousin Patrice to keep them updated on her progress in rehab, to pass on news of their own, always thinking that soon there would be time enough to see their old neighbour and good friend. They'd regarded it as a break while she got better and they got famous, but was that the truth? Now, he can't help but feel that they'd abandoned her when she needed them most.

"There's another thing," he says. "The moment she died. You can work it out closely enough from what Patrice said, from when he sent that text. I think it was while we were on stage, playing our last song."

Pickman nods, getting it. "Oh, yes. Of all our songs, it would have to be *that* one that sees her off."

Sigh frowns, not liking where that train of thought is headed. The last number they're playing at these big theatre gigs is also the last track on their debut record–the record that wouldn't exist if it wasn't for Dimity. It's a showstopping acoustic ballad that may well, in time, prove to be their signature song: "Dorian's Last Dance".

Narcisse remembers Dimity's face as they played her that song for the first time in the lounge of her shabby apartment, sitting on the floor amongst Indian cushions and curls of cinnamon incense smoke like a troupe of derelict hippies: he and Paul strumming acoustic guitars, Ansh rapping his sticks on a pizza box, Simon too nervous to pull his eyes from the lyrics penned in the exercise book before him. Dimity looked like she was watching as all her secrets and shames were pulled out and paraded before her, each one buffed to a melodic shine that made them seem almost beautiful. Oh, none of the lyrics were directly about anything she'd done, and no one outside their inner circle of friends would ever know that Dimity was the inspiration–but *she* knew, and couldn't decide whether to be flattered, appalled, or both.

"What do you think?" Simon asked her, finally able to meet her eyes, biting his lip at the ambivalence he saw there.

Dimity shook her head as if rousing from a nod-off, but she couldn't help a smile from touching her lips. "If that song was about anyone else, I'd think it was the best fucking thing I'd ever heard."

Ansh frowned, desperate as ever for her approval. "You don't like it, Dim?"

"Oh, I do!" she assured him. "It's an amazing song, it really is. But…knowing it's *me* in those lyrics…it's like you're celebrating everything about me that I hate."

Simon grimaced. "Oh, man. I'm sorry, Dim. It's…I'm not trying to be funny here, you know, but it's supposed to be a love song."

"I know, sweetheart." She leaned forward to touch one paint-flecked hand to the back of his. "And I love that you guys made the gesture. But it makes me wonder…is this how the world sees me? Is this all I'm good for–a song that will make total strangers feel *sorry* for me? I mean, I know I'm just another dumb junkie loser with aspirations to Great Art, but…I want to *make* that art. I don't want it to be made *of* me."

"And you will," Jason said, "We're going places, I just know it. And you're coming with us, Dim. We love you and we love your work. We were thinking that, you know, you could help us out with the visuals. Design gig posters, T-shirts. Maybe paint the album cover."

Dimity stared at each of them, and they didn't understand at the time. They didn't realise that, to her, it seemed like she was being asked to become complicit in her own backhanded apotheosis–to aid and abet their characterisation of her as a damaged angel with track marks on her broken wings.

"We'll see," is all she said then. "I wish you all the luck in the world, boys, and no one wants to see you succeed more than me. But do you really need to go picking through my poor bones for inspiration? I mean, *fuck*. What's the album cover going to be, a pair of my dirty undies?"

The image on the front of their first record is of Rhiannon-as-Dorian, with streams of stars pouring from her kohl-lined eyes as void-black darkness yawns open behind her, a ravenous gulf whose unending appetite will not be denied. The album is called *To Dorian, with Love*.

"What are you telling me here?" Sigh wants to know now, fingers clenched tight around his glass of absinthe. "That you think our song somehow killed her?"

"No, of course not," Pickman murmurs. "But the timing…"

"Come on. That track's a *celebration*, man."

"Sorry, but no, it's not. Call it what it is, my brother. It's a requiem."

Sigh's mouth drops open to frame a retort, then snaps shut again. He labours over his lyrics and concepts, every word and image chosen with precision, so he looks utterly thrown to realise that he's missed such an obvious distinction. Pickman nods sadly, then turns to Narcisse.

"You saw it too, didn't you?"

Oh, he had.

The final song brought the four of them to the front of the stage, as close as they can get to the clutching hands of ardent fans, lined up on chairs of rich wood and crimson velvet–Narcisse and Pickman toting acoustic guitars, The Captain manipulating mellow beats from a Kaoss Pad, Sigh crooning some of his best and most heartfelt lyrics. Rhiannon performed an emotive dance behind the band, acting out Dorian's swansong, and warm lights fanned out across the crowd as glittering tinsel confetti streamed down from overhead like silver rain. The large video screen above the abandoned drum kit would now play a short film wherein Rhiannon performed the same dance as seen below, intercut with poignant scenes of Dorian accepting her destiny and giving way to an encroaching darkness that would flare, so bright and possibly hopeful, to a brilliant sepia corona over the last chord.

Halfway through the second verse, Narcisse leaned back, exulting in the ceremonial symbiosis of audience and band, and spun halfway around on his chair to watch the screen. What he saw was almost enough to throw him off the beat. Only muscle memory and musician's instinct kept his hands moving through the simple chords.

He'd watched the film that was to accompany "Dorian's Last Dance", and this was not it. Not at all. What he saw instead was a procession of clips that seem to have been shot in the familiar saturated tones of a Super-8 camera, and the woman dancing and smiling and shooting up and crying and staring intently out of the screen was not Rhiannon Lloyd. It was Dimity, of course, horsing around in the small yard of the Jacoby in a summer dress as the sun flared and washed out a dreamy afternoon–dragging broken nails down the inside of her forearm to open up the syringe-stab scabs as she sprawled naked and bruised on the dirty tiles of her bathroom–gazing solemnly into the lens with her eyes full of sorrow and love and condemnation.

Narcisse stared at this vision for the rest of the verse, only turning when the professional voice in the back of his mind prodded him to face the crowd for the big chorus. He tried to put the film from his mind, to focus on the peak of this amazing show, and he just about managed it. That professional voice assured him that someone had lined up the wrong video, that someone was pranking them with the reality behind their sheen of drama. But there was another voice singing back-up inside his skull, and it told him that such clips could not possibly exist. *Look closer*, it seemed to croon, and when he focused on the masses of people clapping and chanting along before him, he understood why.

Spotted throughout the crowd were hundreds of fans wearing tour T-shirts emblazoned with the album cover, hundreds of chests bearing the image of

Dorian weeping stars before the widening abyss…but now that stylised image had been replaced by the earthly one that inspired it. Dimity stared back at him hundreds of times over from within the audience, one face replicated time and time again amongst the infinite variations of diversity around it, and the effect was delirious, maddening. Narcisse blinked and blurred the crowd, stared down at his fretboard, and by the time he stood to take a bow along with his brothers, those shirts showed only the familiar design he loved enough to have had it tattooed on his bicep.

He leaves that surreal detail untold for the moment and explains what he saw on the video screen to Sigh and The Captain, who turn to Pickman for corroboration. The bassist gives a grave nod, and The Captain immediately produces his phone to search through fan-shot footage of the show that's already been posted online. Clips of "Dorian's Last Dance" confirm that what his brothers say is true.

"How the hell could that happen?" Sigh wants to know, bewildered. Narcisse doesn't have an answer for that, so he shrugs—but he knows it was no simple substitution by a mutual friend, jealous of their first true moment in the sun. They'd have known about any such film had it been shot—hell, they'd have been in it, cavorting with her—and besides, no one could have gotten into the theatre and fiddled with the video projector without the crew knowing.

"She wanted to tell the truth," The Captain says. "We turned her life into a lie, didn't we? All this time, we thought we were doing her a favour—but Dim never wanted to be put up on a pedestal. She was a simple soul. She just wanted to be accepted for who she was."

They fall silent, thinking of their friend. Narcisse is remembering a hundred mental snapshots of Dimity Hardacre, and they all reflect what his drummer has just said. Dimity was always about careless fun, uncomplicated enjoyment—he's always thought of her as a young soul, wide-eyed and open to the world. Perhaps that's why none of the band ever tried to sleep with her, youthful and horny as they were then and now; despite her vices, she'd always somehow come across as an innocent, sensual rather than sexual, sisterly rather than seductive. They'd all kissed her from time to time, a playful dance of lips and tongue, but that had felt more like a drunken act of sharing, of trust and friendship, than a prelude to anything carnal.

"I really thought we'd done a good thing," Sigh says eventually, his eyes haunted, and then quotes from Gilbert & Sullivan: "*Pray observe the magnanimity we display to lace and dimity.*"

"We all did," Narcisse says. "But for all that we tried to help her with toxic exes and fair-weather friends, with her dramas and her addiction… how are we any better? We begged her to get clean, but then we'd shoot up with her sometimes, anyway, like we were *encouraging* her to keep fucking up. And it was easy for us to drop that shit, since we were just experimenting—we weren't going to get hooked, because we had the perfect cautionary example of where that would lead sitting right there in front of us."

"We've always called Dimity our muse, but that's being too generous–to *us*. She's our fucking meal ticket, isn't she? We observed her life from the outside and then we *stole* it right in front of her, and we turned it into a fantasy, and we built our name on her misery."

"We *used* her," The Captain whispers, and bursts into tears at last. Pickman draws him into a hug, his own eyes finally unleashing the flood he's been holding back ever since the news came in. Narcisse remembers Simon once telling them all that Dimity means *twice-warped* in Ancient Greek, and now he sees the truth of it–warped once by fate and circumstance into a perpetual victim and hopeless addict, and again by her best friends into an insidious icon for troubled teenagers the world over.

"Did we ever really see her at all," Sigh muses, his voice thin with sorrow, "or did we just see what we *wanted* to see?"

Then, sudden and unwelcome–a series of four knocks on the dressing room door.

Unless some emergency has come up, Nudge has failed in his duty. A rush of irritation overtakes Narcisse, for this grief and guilt is private.

"Go away!" he barks.

The only response is another four knocks–one for each of them, he thinks, before anger takes over. He glances at himself in the mirror and sees furious sparks in those electric blue eyes. Reaching the door in a half-dozen quick strides, he pulls it open to confront the interloper.

"Rhiannon? I told you—"

The words die in his mouth. His hand falls from the door handle and slaps loosely against the thigh of his leather pants. His abrupt change in mood is noted by the rest of the band, and he can distantly hear them rallying behind him.

She stands in the doorway, dressed in that stage outfit, swaying gently on the spot; no champagne bottle dangles from her limp hand, but for a moment, Narcisse thinks her drunk. She's staring at him with wide, intense eyes, and as soon as he thinks of the way Dimity had gazed out of the video screen during "Dorian's Last Dance", he understands what he's seeing. He hears The Captain gasp at his shoulder and knows that he's not alone in this strange revelation.

Sour sores open in the pale bare flesh of her forearms, and streaks of tainted blood run down to her wrists. Bruises appear on her legs and throat like faces on photographic paper dipped in developing fluid, shit-brown and piss-yellow, and the Dorian costume fades away in just the same manner. The stage make-up disappears from her face as those features become sallow, sunken-eyed, so familiar–as those long silver locks darken to a tumble of messy purple–as firm feminine curves soften and grow less defined, professional pulchritude turning to everyday eroticism. In moments, Dorian is gone and Rhiannon is gone and *she* stands before them, naked in every way, detailed in every last particular, unvarnished and unveiled. She's beautiful and plain and deep and disastrous, her ragged lips trembling with curses even as her wet eyes widen with love.

And then she seems to blur as if draped in gauze, reduced to basic expressions of her complex self. The intense reality of her, every pore of her skin and every strand of violet hair reproduced in absolute clarity, is swiftly replaced by an abstracted representation—the woman before them is now rendered in strokes of paint, her outline marked in thin slashes of black and her pale skin stippled with brush marks, her nipples dabs of darker pink and her belly button a single stab of sable, and the style is instantly recognisable to all four men because they've seen dozens of canvases by this same hand.

"Dim," The Captain whimpers, and as if she takes this as a request, she begins to fade away right there in the doorway, the white wall of the theatre corridor appearing through the rough but knowing strokes of paint that comprise this impossible self-portrait. But before the vision vanishes completely, Narcisse sees her brush-struck mouth move five times. A blown kiss, and four syllables. And somehow, he understands them perfectly.

Now, you see me.

Then she is gone, and the corridor itself now begins to dissolve as Jason's tears return, hotter and harder than before. Behind him, he hears Ansh's anguish deepen, and Paul utters a low bark of agony, and now Simon, too, succumbs to the sorrow. He turns and embraces his brothers, and together they cry for their lost friend, their manipulated muse. They weep in regret and guilt, in loss and love. And when Rhiannon Lloyd ventures back down the corridor, drawn by all this noise and still clutching champagne to her chest, she's as disturbed as she is pleased to find herself pulled into the group hug and greeted like a long-lost sister.

"Oof! Are you guys okay?" she asks with a hesitant smile, remembering how they'd sent her packing just minutes before.

"I think we will be," Sigh says through swallowed tears, speaking as always for all of them. "But we need to make a change to the show. Just a little one, but it's very important."

Narcisse slaps his back in support, their band-born telepathy ensuring that he already knows what his singer is saying. "That wasn't your video for 'Dorian's Last Dance' that played tonight. It was a… a tribute to our dear friend. We owe her so much, and we want the world to know that. So if we can, we're going to show that tribute at every gig from now on."

"Oh, but I put so much work into my video!" Rhiannon protests, before softening at the tears she sees shimmering in the band's eyes. "Still, never mind. You've got to remember what's most important. And it's your story in the end, so you're forgiven."

Narcisse stares at her as if she's said something quite profound, then lifts his lips in a sad smile and plants an affectionate kiss on her forehead.

"That's what we're hoping."

The End

October

Lucy A. Snyder

Thirteen years on, and still
I miss you more than anything.

If you were here, Henry,
October would be a limitless
expanse of pre-teen Halloween.
I'd help you pick out fat pumpkins
for a messy jack-o'-lantern massacre,
our yard a garish Styrofoam graveyard,
a different monster movie every night:
mostly cheese, but the occasional fright.

But you're not here. You're nowhere
but in what's left of my imagination.
I'm the sorriest unmother anyone's seen:
pushing fifty, binging Count Chocula,
ugly crying to "Dear Winter" on Pandora,
wondering who both of us would have been.

Unforeseen

Greg Chapman

Eric awoke to find their bedsheets flecked with blood.

He followed the trail of droplets on the carpet to the bathroom door, the problem of how to get the blood out of the carpet briefly crossing his mind.

His fiancé's sobbing came from the other side of the door.

"Jane?" His voice reverberated, creating a strange echo that mingled with his fiancé's cries. "Jane, is everything alright?"

Her keening beckoned him, but when he tried to turn the doorknob he found it locked.

"Is something wrong–are you sick?"

Moments passed and a new series of thoughts surfaced, but they were severed when Jane unlocked the door and fell into his arms. Her thin body shook in his grasp–he'd never seen her so upset. The night before had been routine. They'd had dinner, and fallen asleep watching TV.

"What's wrong?" He eased a damp strand of dark hair from her cheek. "I saw blood…"

She looked deep into his eyes and there was a moment of doubt before her words came. "We were going to have a baby…" she said. "But I lost it."

***

He didn't know why, but Jane's revelations had angered him.

He'd readied himself for the day in solitude, aggressively scrubbing his skin in the shower, brushing his teeth so roughly his gums bled. Even his necktie he saw as a tool to punish himself. He chose such thoughts over consoling her.

Why had she kept it a secret from him, only to take it away in the revealing? It would have made him happy, wouldn't it?

Silence and selfishness lingered throughout breakfast, the coffee tasting significantly more bitter. Their gazes had lost any semblance of warmth. Something inside begged him to take Jane's hand, to share in her grief, but one thought repressed all the others:

Did I even want a baby?

***

Signing up for life insurance in case of the unforeseen. He used to see the unforeseen as something that happened to other people. He sat in his cubicle, headset on, realizing that the unforeseen was nothing anyone could prepare for—no matter how many dollars they threw at it.

"Hello?" the woman's voice oozed through his earphones.

Eric stared at the photo of him and Jane atop Mt Fuji from their vacation a few years before....Before the unforeseen.

"Hello, are you still there?" the woman said again.

Eric shuddered and coughed. "Yes, sorry Mrs. Jorgensen—"

"It's *Miss* Jorgensen."

"Sorry…what was I saying?"

She sighed. "You were about to update my policy."

"Uh, right, yes."

He clicked a few computer keys and brought up Mrs.–Miss Jorgensen's file: Elaine Jorgensen, forty-eight-years-old, mother to three, non-smoker.

"Are you sure you want to upgrade your hospital cover, ma'am?"

"Uh, yeah–that's why I called you."

He glanced at Jane's beaming face again. Mt Fuji rising gloriously into the early morning sky. He knew he would have failed her and the baby. He was not father material, his own father had been a failure, so why would he be any different?

"What I mean is–do you really need this particular level of cover? You're already covered for non-essential hospital admission and surgery," he said.

"I know, but I'm not covered for emergency treatment–what if I have a stroke, or one of my kids gets in a car accident, or really sick—"

"Or you have a miscarriage…" Eric interjected.

"Excuse me?"

He swallowed hard. "Oh, I'm sorry, Mrs. Jensen – I didn't mean to imply—"

"I can't believe you! I'm unable to have children which is why I had to adopt. That's very personal to me. Why would you bring that up? And it's Miss Jor-gen-sen!"

Eric tugged at his necktie which felt more like a noose.

"You… you were talking about being prepared… for the unforeseen."

"The *unfor*-what? What the hell is wrong with you? You can't even get my name right, for Christ's sake!"

"I'm sorry Miss Jorgensen," Eric said. "I just don't want you to make any rash decisions. Nothing is set in stone."

"For someone whose job it is to sell insurance, you're really bad at it, mister. I think I need to speak to your supervisor, right now!"

***

Eric knew his cubicle was a cage and that his supervisor, Mr. Donaldson, had the biggest cage of all. He could feel the man's disdain–his judgement from across the desk.

"What in God's name were you thinking, speaking to a customer like that, Eric?"

Eric sat silently, taking his punishment.

"I mean, you've been here nearly ten years," Donaldson continued, smoothing down his pale grey silk suit jacket. "You've got a solid track record here with this firm and now you almost blow it all away."

Eric imagined Jane at home, scrubbing her own blood from the shag pile. Her baby's blood.

Donaldson walked to sit beside him. "Is everything alright at home, Eric? How are you and Jane? You two are supposed to be getting married in a few months, right? She must be driving you nuts with all the wedding planning?"

"Everything's fine."

Donaldson frowned as if he'd confirmed Eric was actually insane. "Maybe you need to take some time off–get away with Jane for the weekend."

Where would they go, Eric thought. Where could they go where their newfound resentment wouldn't follow them?

"Eric, are you listening to me?" his supervisor said.

He turned to Donaldson. "Have you ever lost anything important, Bill?"

Donaldson frowned again. "*Lost anything important*–what are you talking about?"

Eric swiveled his chair to face his boss. "You must have lost something important: a friend, or a relative?"

Donaldson placed a hand on Eric's shoulder. "Did you...lose someone?"

Eric turned away to a window overlooking the city. "I didn't even get a chance to meet them."

The man stood and slowly backed away from him. "Okay, I don't know what's gotten into you, but I think you need to take the rest of the day off. We'll talk on Monday, alright?"

Eric was compelled to follow him, to know his answer, whether he'd experienced the unforeseen.

"Tell me!" Eric said. "What have you lost!?"

Eric watched himself grab hold of Donaldson and push him into the glass doors of the display case near his desk. A shard of glass sliced open the man's scalp, and his pale grey suit flooded with blood.

As Eric ran from the room of cubicle cages, he knew that Donaldson understood the true meaning of the 'unforeseen'.

***

Eric was a victim of circumstance, an unwilling agent of chaos.

He sat in the park, fumbling with his phone as the rest of the world sailed by. He knew he needed to call Jane, but how could he give her two pieces of devastating news in one day? How could he ever speak to her again after everything? He wondered how long it would be before she called him…or how long before the police came to arrest him for assaulting his boss? All he had now was time.

The phone buzzed in his hand, but it was his mother's name which flashed up on the screen, not his fiancé's.

The unforeseen.

"Hi, Mum," Eric said.

Her voice was broken, blubbering, not unlike Miss Jorgensen, the forty-eight-year-old mother of three who couldn't have children of her own.

"Your father…" she said, between sobs. "He had…he had a massive coronary. We lost him about an hour ago…"

Eric felt his pulse quicken at his mother's words, but something else gripped his attention. Across the street from the park, he saw a homeless woman taping a poster to one of the light poles. Hand-written black bold text that read: LOST sat above a familiar name. The homeless woman scurried away up the street with a bundle of identical posters in her grimy hands.

"Eric…" his mother said. "Are you still there? Did you hear me?"

He thought of his father, of his absent parenting, of his criticisms of Eric's choice of partner and career. A massive heart attack was the easy way out.

"I bet Dad never saw it coming," Eric replied.

He ended the call and ran out into the late afternoon traffic, narrowly avoiding being struck by a yellow cab. He made it to the other side of the street and ripped the poster down.

It was indeed a LOST poster, but the name on it was his.

***

Eric ran through the crowds after the woman, but she always seemed to be a block ahead.

Every pole, every street sign carried his LOST poster, some even littered the gutters. No one else seemed to notice them, but Eric saw his name over and over, an incessant mocking. He grabbed a handful of them, but every block there were always more, so he gave up tearing them down.

How did this woman know about his misfortunes? Had she been stalking him?

He had to know.

Eric saw the woman turn down a blind alley and, as the shadows of the skyscrapers began to dominate and darken, he willingly followed her in. A trail of his LOST posters led him to a grubby and tattered tent at the end of the alley.

Was she lurking inside, laughing while he suffered?

He approached the tent carefully.

"Come out of there," he said. He held up his poster. "Come out of there and tell me what this means and how you know about me!"

He pulled back the crumbling tent cover and glimpsed the confines within. Hundreds of names looked back at him. Countless LOST posters, depicting all manner of individuals, of all nationalities.

"What the fuck?" he whispered.

A scraping of shoes pulled him from the macabre shrine of lost souls.

"Well, that didn't take you long."

The woman sneered at him with a toothless mouth. Her eyes were blank, the colour of curdled milk. She was clearly blind but moved in a manner which suggested she could still see. Her dark hair clung to the faux fur of her oversized coat.

"Usually it takes you people a lot longer to figure it out," she told him. "You must be one of the really smart ones."

Bile rising in his throat, Eric threw a crumpled LOST poster at her. It bounced off her chest onto the ground.

"What the fuck is this—some sort of sick joke!?" he said.

The woman scooped it up and unfurled it in her filthy hands.

"Oh, it's no joke. It's more of a...sign. The name's Cassie, by the way."

"A sign? A sign of what? How could you possibly know what I've lost today?"

"Your baby, your job, and your old man, right?" She counted them off on one hand.

Eric swallowed. "How can you know that—have you been following me?"

"I sort of...see it happen."

"How...you're blind? And why are you living here on the streets?"

She leaned up against a chain-link fence and put her hands behind her head, as if this had been the part in the conversation she'd been waiting for.

"Yeah, I lost my sight to a tumour about a year ago. My house and my job too." She tapped her temple. "But what I lost, I gained in here. When they took out the tumour a switch was turned on, or something. I started to see people's misfortunes and a chance to show them. I put out the LOST posters to warn people. To show them what could happen, if they don't do anything to change it. I figure if I help enough people, maybe I'll get my actual sight back. I choose to keep a low profile and let you folks come to me. Plus, it's easy to put up signs in the street when you live there."

Eric felt his heart slamming against his ribs. "So, you're trying to tell me that everything that's happened hasn't happened yet? It's just some sort of sick showreel? And you show it to people in the hope that you'll be able to see again?"

She shrugged. "That's it, in a nutshell. Hey, the way I see it, people have two choices–they either let it play out, or they can change it. Like I said, it's meant to be a warning."

Eric clenched the leftover posters in his fist. "How many people have you done this to?"

"You mean how many people have I helped? Hundreds. Some people don't always choose wisely, though." She chuckled to herself. "Look, friend, I'm genuinely trying to help you here–you just have to go for one of those choices. But you gotta do it before it's too late."

Eric stared at the ground, the LOST posters floating about his feet, the grit and grime beneath them and the trash and squalor. Squalor she chose to live in while she turned people's lives upside down. *Did he really want that baby, or that cubicle cage job, or a father who didn't agree with his life choices?*

Then he saw the brick.

"You're giving me just two choices," Eric asked.

She nodded. "Yep, two choices."

He bent to pick up the brick. "What if there was a third option–one that was unforeseen?"

Her blank eyes narrowed. "Say again?"

He brought the brick down across her face. As her blood sprayed across his, a wave of relief washed through his entire body. He'd finally found a way to completely lose himself.

The End

The Deals We Make

Lisa Morton

There's a man who comes in through my window at night. Sometimes he crawls into my bed. Sometimes he sleeps in a dresser drawer. I made a deal with him.

No…no, that's not right. He's not the one I made the deal with. I don't think…is he? Did I…

I need to think. My thoughts are…piled up, like dishes in a sink, the stack's going to crash…

The beginning. I need to go to the beginning. Move forward instead of up, sideways, around.

Forward, from the beginning.

***

The beginning: two years ago, I think.

My mom was complaining; her knees. She had painful arthritis in her knees, and I told her that wasn't unusual for someone who was seventy-four.

"Seventy-four?" she said. "But I'm a hundred."

I probably laughed, but she wasn't smiling. "You're not a hundred," I said, still waiting for the joke.

"I'm not? I thought I was."

Mom had been having more trouble remembering lately, but I just figured it was normal old age forgetfulness. Is it really so strange to not remember what you had for lunch, or what movie you saw last night?

It soon became clear, though, that this was more than just regular aging. Soon she couldn't remember what year it was, or the name of her next-door neighbor. She couldn't drive anymore because operating a car requires concentration she was no longer capable of. All she had was me–I'm the only child of divorced parents–so I took her to doctors.

The good news was that she didn't have Alzheimer's. The bad news was that she'd probably had a number of TIAs (transient ischemic attacks, also quaintly known as mini-strokes) and she had vascular dementia. Alzheimer's comes with an expiration date for the patient; vascular dementia... well, it goes on. And on. And on.

Mom was my best friend, my closest advisor, my role model, my icon. When I was growing up, other kids wanted to play at my house because of her. When she divorced my dad (I was 12), she refused alimony because she said she was just as able to work as he was. My dad was heartbroken over the split, but it was low-key and quick. He at least re-married. Mom didn't.

Now she couldn't remember her first and only marriage at all. Pictures of Dad just brought a puzzled look to her face.

The forgetfulness was soon compounded by delusions and abrupt mood shifts. The same strong woman who had always said it was up to us to make ourselves happy would burst into tears for no reason.

When it became clear that she could no longer live alone, I sold my condo and moved into her house to become her caregiver. I was only 38, not ready to give up my job (IT support for a museum), so I found a wonderful hired caregiver to look after her while I was at work.

When we were both younger, we'd often talked about this future, about how one day I would take care of her just as she'd once taken care of me. I had imagined waking her up in the mornings, bringing her breakfast on a little tray, both of us drinking tea as we laughed and talked about news or the day ahead.

The reality was: panic when I left the room for even seconds, followed by tantrums. Refusal to eat anything but ice cream. Adult diapers and daily loads of laundry. Being awakened at four in the morning to find her standing over my bed, asking about "those people living in the hallway closet." The dementia came with somniloquy, meaning I might be awakened by her wailing, bellowing, laughing, or screaming in her sleep.

And the doctor visits; dozens a year. A never ending stream of medications, new ones sometimes conflicting with old, none of it helping, eating through the budget, months to wean her off some of them.

I heard recently that caregiving is the single most hazardous job, and I believe it. I staggered through my days on three or four broken hours of sleep; I wrenched muscles getting her in and out of chairs and bed, I put on weight since she wouldn't eat unless I did. I silently endured the fits when I refused to take her to another doctor, or wouldn't let her drive. Every evening, after I'd sat in traffic for an hour coming home from work, I'd turn onto our street and feel a weight settle onto my shoulders like a boulder made of duty.

Lurking behind all of it like one of Mom's shadowy figures was the fear: that this was my future as well, that I would give away what might be the best years of my own life to her care, only to turn around and find myself in the grip of this genetically-bestowed nightmare.

This went on for nearly two years. I struggled to tell myself it was the disease, that it wasn't her; but my own memories–the ones of the best friend I'd laughed with and shopped with and traveled with and hugged and kissed–receded into the past.

Finally, she developed an infection; it proved resistant to antibiotics. The doctors threw different strains at it, but she got sicker and sicker. One morning I woke up and found her standing in the middle of her bedroom, gripping her walker, her expression frozen.

"Mom...?"

She didn't respond. She didn't move, except a slight tremble. I tried to take her elbow, to guide her. There was nothing behind her eyes. I called 911. As soon as I hung up, she crumpled. I caught her (she weighed nothing, but I still felt something give in my back), lowered her gently onto the bedroom carpet and waited.

The EMTs arrived, started treating her for a stroke. But at the hospital the doctors said it wasn't a stroke; it was the infection. They said she'd be in the hospital for at least a few days. They kept quiet on her chances.

I stayed at the hospital until a nurse with tired eyes and a kind smile told me to go home. I moved around the house–her house–turning on the lights, turning on music, setting my phone within easy reach.

Then I poured myself a too-big glass of tequila and celebrated.

Does that sound cruel? Should I have been ashamed? Maybe...but all I knew then was that for the first night in years I was unburdened, free to do what I wanted. I could watch a movie I'd wanted to see that I knew Mom wouldn't be able to follow, leaving her irritated. I could listen to music, or read. I could go out, or I could stay in. I could drink.

I opted for the latter.

At some point in the evening, exhausted and very drunk, I cried. I cried because I realized that it wasn't that I resented Mom and the life she'd forced me to take on, but because I resented what the disease had taken from her. I cried because I wanted back the person she'd once been, or even the person I'd once thought she'd be at this age. I cried because I felt like we'd both gotten raw deals.

That word–"deal"–swam around me with the rest of the room, borne on waves of tequila-fueled loss. Nothing seemed quite real.

Not even the man who stepped out of the front closet.

I'm sure I laughed. I'm sure I figured he was some drunk fantasy.

That's all I'm sure about.

I don't clearly remember anything else from that night. In my alcohol-imbued state, I thought he had stubby little horns and smelled like charcoal; he told me I already knew his name, and that he was here to "make a deal". I have an even vaguer memory of saying, "Sure."

The next morning I woke up with a terrible headache, a half-empty bottle of tequila that had been new twenty-four hours ago, and a foggy recollection of something with horns and an offer.

I was just stepping out of the shower when the phone rang. On the caller ID I saw a doctor's name; I recognized it from the ER. Heart hammering, head throbbing, I answered it.

It was about Mom.

She was doing much better and had asked for me. The doctor, whose name was Nguyen, sounded surprised. An hour later at the hospital, he told me he frankly wouldn't have believed this was possible and couldn't explain it.

Mom was awake and sitting up when I kissed her and then sat beside her. She asked me what happened. I told her we weren't sure. She said I looked haggard. I told her it'd been a long night for me.

"Oh, honey, I'm sorry to put you through that," she said.

I almost started crying again. One of the things I'd hated most about her dementia was how it had robbed her of empathy; I got that it was difficult for her to voice even her own problems, but sometimes I wished she would ask about me from time to time.

"Hey, are you okay?" she said, reaching out.

I took her hand. "I'm okay, just...I'm happy to see how okay you are."

There was something about her that was new, or rather old: a brightness to her eyes, a steadiness to her gaze; her attention didn't wander as it had over the last two years, her brow wasn't creased in perpetual confusion. "I have a strange question," I said.

"It can't be much stranger than some of the things these doctors have been asking me."

"Do you know what year it is?"

She looked at me strangely, laughed a little, and named the year. The right year. She hadn't been able to do that since the dementia.

The doctors kept her, filling her with fluids, running some tests, but they sent her home the next day.

On the first morning after she was home, I brought her breakfast in bed on a little tray. We laughed together, drank tea, watched an insipid morning talk show. I hadn't been so happy in years.

When her caregiver arrived just before I left for work, I told her everything that had happened. She looked uncertain until she checked in on Mom, and then she saw the change, too. She turned to stare at me with her mouth half-open in a smile. It wasn't just me. The change was real.

The doctors chalked it up to a chronic infection that had cleared up with the intravenous antibiotics they'd given her at the hospital. Of course they took credit for it. But that explanation made as much sense as anything.

Except...except for something that nagged at the back of my head, something about being drunk and a man and a deal.

Something I couldn't remember.

***

Mom continued to improve. My best friend was back. She got stronger and steadier. We took her off more medications. Soon she was down to zero.

We did things again that we'd loved long ago, like stay up late watching old movies. We especially adored old thrillers, the ones in black-and-white, like *The Postman Always Rings Once* and the one with Ingrid Bergman...what was it called? Where her husband is trying to drive insane? Oh, right: *Gaslight*. How could I forget that?

I no longer had to make all of Mom's meals; she started cooking again. She'd make me my favorites, like grilled cheese sandwiches, with my favorite cheese, providence.

No, wait...that's not right. It's another name, isn't it?

I started to get warnings at work; I made basic errors that even a rookie would've caught. Soon it didn't matter anymore, though, because I got in the car one day and couldn't remember why I was there, or where I was going.

I wasn't sleeping well, my dreams full of shadowy figures in corners, waiting for me to turn and see them. Then I'd blink and realize I wasn't asleep.

I stopped going to work, and could no longer drive. Mom got her driver's license again, though, so she got me to doctors.

They were baffled. None of the tests showed anything like strokes or any other evidence of early onset dementia. They started to put me on drugs. I thought they were the same things Mom had taken in the past—before her recovery—but I wasn't really sure. I dug some of the old medication bottles out from her bathroom cabinet, but I couldn't read the names on them, the letters were just odd lines and swirls that made no sense to me.

But through it all...I was happy. My Mom was back, taking care of me. It was almost like we'd gone back in time thirty years.

They put me on a sleeping pill that helps me get through the nights, but even my days are strange now. Our house is set next to a lake that holds awful creatures...

No, that's right—we're in the middle of a suburban street. Why did I think there was a lake here?

I love my mom.

She made me something good for breakfast.

Our next-door neighbor is a movie star; sometimes she acts out scenes for me.

And there's that thing in the back of my brain that I get flashes of: a deal-maker. Something about balances in the universe, about how you can't take away something, you can only move it. I don't remember saying "yes", but I think I did. I think I saved my mom, so it was worth it.

If that's right...I'd make that deal again.

The End

A Hole in the World

Christopher Golden & Tim Lebbon

Vasily Glazkov was warm. He reveled in the feeling, because he had not been truly warm for a long time. His fingers and toes tingled with returning circulation, and he could feel a pleasant stinging sensation across his nose and cheeks. Beyond the open doorway Anna held a steaming mug out to him. She was grinning. Around her was the paraphernalia of their mission—sample cases, laboratory equipment, tools and implements for excavating, survival equipment and clothing. As he entered the room the door slammed shut behind him, the window shades lowered, and they were alone in the luxurious warmth. Nothing mattered except the two of them. He took the mug and sipped, the coffee's heat coursing through him and reaching even those deepest, coldest parts that he'd believed would never be warm again.

Anna started unclipping her belt and straps, popping her buttons. She dropped her rifle and pistol, her knife, shrugging out of her uniform to reveal her toned, muscled body. He felt the heat of her. He craved her familiar warmth and scent, her safety, but he still took time to finish the coffee. Anticipation was the greatest comforter.

"Vasily!" A hand grasped his arm and turned him around. He frowned, stretching to look back at his almost-naked lover. But however far he turned she remained out of sight.

"Vasily, wake up!"

Glazkov's eyes snapped open. His breath misted the air before him, and he sat up quickly, gasping in shock as his dream froze and shattered beneath gray reality.

"Amanda?"

Amanda Hart stood in his small room, bulked out in her heavy coat. There was ice on her eyelashes and excitement in her eyes.

"Vasily, you've got to come."

"Where?"

"Down into the valley. It's stopped snowing, the sun's out, and you have to come. Hans is getting ready."

Glazkov looked around and tried to deny the sinking feeling in his gut. His room was small and sparse, containing his small supply of grubby clothing, a few books, and a single window heavily iced on the inside.

"You've been out alone again?" he asked. They had all been warned about venturing beyond the camp boundary on their own. It was dangerous and irresponsible, and put all of them at risk. But Amanda was headstrong and confident, not a woman used to obeying orders. He wondered if all Americans were like that.

"That doesn't matter!" She waved away his concerns.

"So, what's down in the valley?" Glazkov asked. The cold was already creeping across his skin and seeping into his bones. He wondered whether he would ever be warm again, even when he and Anna were together once more. It was only twelve weeks since they'd last seen each other, but the inimical landscape stretched time and distance, and the sense of isolation was intense. In this damned place the cold was a living, breathing thing.

"Come and see," Hart said, and she grinned again. "Something's happened."

Outside, the great white silence was a weight he could almost feel. It always took Glazkov's breath away—not only the cold, but the staggering landscape, and the sense that they might be the only people alive in the whole world. There were no airplane trails to prove otherwise, no other columns of smoke from fires or chimneys. No evidence at all that anyone else had ever been there. Old footprints and snowcat trails were buried beneath the recent blizzard. The three interconnected buildings that formed their camp—living quarters, lab and equipment hall, and garage—were half-buried, roofs and upper windows protruding valiantly above the white snowscape.

"We taking the snowcat?" Hans Brune asked.

"It's only a mile," Amanda replied.

The German tutted and rolled his eyes. His teeth were already clacking, his body shivering, even though he was encased in so much clothing he was barely identifiable as human.

"Come on, Hans," Amanda said. "I've already been down there once this morning."

"Stupid," Brune said. "You know the rules."

"You going to report me?"

Hans shook his head, then smiled. The expression was hardly visible behind his snow goggles.

"So if we're going to walk, let's walk," he said. "I'm freezing my balls off already."

"You still have balls?" Amanda asked.

"Big. Heavy. Hairy."

"Like a bear's."

They started walking, and Glazkov listened to the banter between his two companions. He knew there was more than friendship between them—he'd seen creeping shadows in the night, and sometimes he heard their gasps and groans when the wind was calmer and the silence beyond the cabins amplified every noise inside. None of them had mentioned it, and he was grateful to them for that. On their first day here they had all agreed that any relationship beyond the professional or collegial might be detrimental to their situation. While they weren't truly cut off, and their location was less isolated than it usually felt, there were no scheduled visits to their scientific station for the next six months. Hart and Brune probably knew that he knew, but there was comfort in their combined feigned ignorance.

He knew Amanda had a husband back home in America. Hans, he knew little about. But Glazkov had never been one to judge. At almost fifty he was the most experienced among them. This was his fifteenth camp, and the fourth in Siberia. He'd been to Alaska, St Georgia, Antarctica, Greenland, and many other remote corners of the world. In such places, ties to home were often strengthened by isolation, but sometimes they were weakened as well. Almost as if such distances, and the effects of desolate and deserted landscapes, made the idea of home seem vague and nebulous. He had seen people strengthened by their sojourns to these places, and he had seen them broken. He knew the signs of both. Most of the time, he knew better than to interfere.

Amanda led them away from the research station and toward the steep descent into the valley. The trees grew close here, hulking evergreens heavy with snow, and beneath their canopy the long days turned to twilight. But once they were into the thick of the forest the snow was not so deep, and the going was easier.

Glazkov, Hart, and Brune were here as part of an international coalition pulled together to study the effects of climate change. While politics continued to throw up obstacles to meaningful action, true science knew no politics, and neither did the scientists who practiced it. Sometimes he believed that if left to real people, human relations would settle and improve within a generation. Sport, music, art, science, they all spanned the globe, taking little notice of politics or religions, or the often more dangerous combination of the two. So it was with their studies into climate change. Deniers denied, but Glazkov had seen enough evidence over the past decade to terrify him.

"So what were you doing out here on your own?" Brune asked.

"Couldn't sleep," Hart said. "And I heard a noise. Felt something. Didn't either of you?"

"No," Brune said.

"Not me," Glazkov said. "What was it?"

"A distant rumble. And something like… a vibration."

"Avalanche," Brune said.

"It's possible," Glazkov agreed. "Temperatures are six degrees higher than average for the time of year. The snowfalls've been less severe, and there's a lot of loose snow up in the mountains."

"No, no, it wasn't that," Hart said. "I've seen what it was."

"What?" Glazkov asked. He was starting to lose his temper with her teasing.

"Best for you to see," she said. They trudged on, passing across a frozen stream and skirting several fallen trees, walking in silence for a while. "I thought it *was* an avalanche," Hart said, quieter now. "Wish it was. But the mountains are ten miles away. This thing… much closer."

Glazkov frowned. For the first time since she'd woken him, she sounded nervous.

"Should we call this in?" he asked.

"Yeah, soon," she said. "But we need photos."

"We can do that afterward."

"Not if it goes away."

They walked on through the snow, emerging from the forest into a deeper layer, grateful for their snowshoes. Brune shrugged the rifle higher on his shoulder, and Glazkov glanced around, looking for any signs of bears. There was nothing. In fact…

"It's quiet," he said.

"It's always fucking quiet out here," Brune replied.

"No, I mean… *too* quiet." He almost laughed at the cliché, but Hart's and Brune's expressions stole his breath. Heads tilted, tugging their hoods aside so they could listen, he could see realization dawning in both of them.

Far out on the desolate Yamal Peninsula, three hundred miles north of the Arctic Circle, there were few people, but they were used to hearing the calls, cries and roars of wildlife. Brown bears were common in the forests, and in more sparsely wooded areas there were elk. Musk deer were hunted by wolves. Bird species were also varied, with the great eagle owl ruling the skies. Some wildlife was dangerous, hence the rifle. Yet after twelve weeks here, not a shot had been fired.

"Nothing," Brune said. He slipped the rifle from his shoulder, as if the silence itself might attack them.

"I didn't notice before," Hart said. "Come on. Not far now, and we'll see it from the ridge."

"See what?" Glazkov demanded. Hart stared at him, all the fun vanished from her expression.

"The hole," she said. "The hole in the world."

***

Oh my God, she's right, Glazkov thought. *It really is a hole in the world. But what's at the bottom?*

"I didn't go any farther than this," Hart said.

"I don't blame you," Brune said. "Vasily?"

"Sinkhole," Glazkov said.

"Really?" Hart asked. "It's huge!"

"It's inevitable. Come on."

They started down the steep slope into the valley and the new feature it now contained. Glazkov thought it might have been over five hundred feet across. With the sun lying low, the hole was deep and dark, only a small spread of the far wall touched by sunlight. At first glance he'd had doubts, but there was no other explanation for what they were now walking toward.

A melting of the permafrost—an occurrence being seen all around the globe—was releasing vast, stored quantities of methane gas. Not only a consequence of global warming, but also a contributing factor. In some places such large quantities were released that these sinkholes formed overnight, dropping millions of tons of rock into vented caverns hundreds of feet beneath the surface.

"We'll need our instruments," he said. "Methane detectors. Remote camera. Everything."

"So, let's go back and get it all," Brune said. "And we need to call this in. We really do."

"Yes," Glazkov said.

"Yeah," Hart said.

But they kept walking toward the hole, hurrying now, excitement biting at their heels.

It took fifteen minutes to descend to the valley floor. It would take a lot longer to climb back up, but Glazkov didn't care. He could already detect the eggy trace of methane on the air, but it didn't smell too strong for now. It started snowing again, and as they followed a stream across the valley floor toward the amazing new feature, visibility lessened. The stream should have been frozen at this time of year, and much of it still was. But a good portion of the water flowed. Approaching the hole's edge, Glazkov heard the unmistakable sound of water pouring down a rock face.

"What was that?" Brune asked. He was frozen behind them, head tilted.

"Waterfall," Hart said.

"No, not that. Something else."

They listened. Nothing.

"We should head back," Brune said. "We need breathing equipment, cameras."

"Not far now," Glazkov said. He was unsettled to see that Brune had slipped the rifle from his shoulder.

"What are you going to shoot?" Hart asked, laughing. "Monsters from the deep?"

Three minutes later, as they emerged from a copse of trees only a hundred feet from the hole's edge and saw what waited for them there—the crawling, tentacled, slick things pulling themselves up out of the darkness, skin pale from lack of pigment, wet mouths gasping in new air–Amanda Hart was the first to fall.

***

Captain Anna Demidov and her team were ready. Fully equipped, comprehensively briefed, fired up, she was confident it would be a straightforward search and retrieval without the need for any aggressive contact. But if the separatists *did* attempt to intervene, Demidov's small Spetsnaz squad was more than ready for a fight. Either way, they would return with the stolen information. In this day and age a printed file seemed almost prehistoric, but the habits of some of Russia's top intelligence operatives never ceased to amaze her.

With her squad milling in the helicopter hangar, she took the opportunity to assess them one last time. Her corporal, Vladimir Zhukov, often teased her about being over-cautious and paranoid about every small detail. Demidov's reply was that she had never lost a soldier in action, nor had she ever failed in a mission. It was something he could not argue with. Yet the banter continued, and she welcomed it. The good relationships between members of her five-person unit was one of the most important factors contributing to success.

"All set, Corporal?" she asked.

Zhukov rolled his eyes. "Yes, Captain. All set, all ready, boots shined and underwear clean, weapons oiled, mission details memorized, just as they all were five minutes ago."

Demidov appraised the corporal from head to toe and up again. A full foot taller than she, and a hundred pounds heavier, some knew him by the nickname *Mountain*. But no one in their unit called him that. He didn't like the name, and none of them would ever want to piss him off.

"A button's undone," she said, pointing to his tunic before moving on. She heard his muttered curse and allowed herself a small smile.

Private Kristina Yelagin was next. Tall, thin, athletic, grim-faced, she was one of the quietest, calmest people Demidov had ever met. She had once seen Yelagin slit a man's throat with a broken metal mug.

"Good?" Demidov asked. The woman nodded once in reply.

"I don't like helicopters," Private Vasnev said. "They make me feel sick."

"And when have you ever been sick during a helicopter trip, Vasnev?" Demidov asked.

"I didn't say they *make* me sick, Captain. I said they make me *feel* sick."

"Feel sick in silence," she said.

"It's okay for you, Captain," Private Budanov said. He was sitting on a supply crate carefully rolling a cigarette. "You don't have to sit next to him. He's always complaining."

"You have my permission to stab him to death if he so much as whispers," Demidov said.

Budanov looked up at her, his scarred face pale as ever, even in the hangar's shadow. "Thank you," he said. "You all heard that? All bore witness?"

"See, now even my friends are against me!" Vasnev said. "I feel sick. I don't want to go on this mission. I think I have mumps."

A movement caught Demidov's eye and she saw the helicopter pilot gesture through the cockpit's open side window.

"That's us," Demidov said. "Let's mount up."

Professional as ever, her four companions ceased their banter for a while as they left the shadow of the hangar, boarded the helicopter, stowed their weapons, and cross-checked each other's safety harnesses. Demidov waited to board last. As she settled herself and clipped on her headset, and the ground crew closed and secured the cabin door, the crackle of a voice came through from the cockpit.

"We've got clearance," the pilot said. "Three minutes and we'll be away."

"Roger," Demidov acknowledged.

"Sorry to hear about Vasily, Captain," the pilot said.

Demidov froze. The rest of her squad, all wearing headsets, looked at her. Corporal Zhukov raised his eyebrows, and Vasnev shrugged: *Don't know what he's on about.*

Demidov's mind raced. If something had happened to Vasily and she hadn't been informed, there must be a reason for that. Perhaps the general would assume that such a distraction would affect her current mission, and he'd inform her of any news upon her return in six hours.

But after the pilot's comment, her distraction was even greater.

"What's that about Vasily?" she asked.

The comms remained quiet. A loaded silence, perhaps. Then a whisper, and the helicopter's turbines ramped up, the noise increased, and the green 'prepare for takeoff' light illuminated the cabin.

Demidov hesitated, ready to throw off her straps and slip through to the cockpit. But she felt a hand on her arm. Budanov. He shook his head, then lifted what he held in his other hand.

Without pause, Demidov nodded, giving silent assent.

Private Budanov was their communications and tech guy. Just as heavily armed as the rest of them, he also carried a bewildering array of hi-tech equipment, some of which Demidov barely understood. There were the usual satellite phones and radios, but also web-based communication systems and other gadgetry, all designed to aid their mission and help them in case of trouble. He'd saved their skins more than once, and now he was promising something else.

Sorry to hear about Vasily, Captain.

As the helicopter lifted off and drifted north, Budanov opened a palmtop tablet and started tapping and scrolling. Three minutes later he handed it to Demidov, a map on the screen. He motioned for her to place her lover's last known position on the map, which she did—the scientific research base on the

Yamal Peninsula. He took the tablet back, nursing a satellite phone in his other hand, and four minutes later he paused.

None of them had spoken since taking off. When Budanov raised his eyes and looked at his Captain, none of them needed to.

Demidov took the tablet from his lap and looked at what he'd found.

***

"This is all on me," Captain Demidov said. Her heart was beating fast, and a sickness throbbed heavy in her gut. Part of that was understanding what she was doing–disobeying orders and going AWOL whilst on a highly sensitive mission, as well as hijacking a Russian army helicopter. But most of the sickness came from the dread she felt about Vasily's doom.

Science team missing... seismic readings from the area...

"Captain, I can't alter course," the pilot said. She could see his nervousness. He and his co-pilot were sitting tense in their flight seats, and she could sense their doubts, their inner debates. They wore pistols, true. But they also knew who they carried.

"I'm ordering you to," she said.

"Captain, my orders—"

"I'm not pulling rank," Demidov cut in. "This isn't about that. But I *will* pull my gun if you don't do what I say."

"And then what?" the pilot asked. "You'll shoot me?"

...drastic landscape alteration... entire region quarantined...

"Let's not discover the answer to that question. Yelagin, here with me." Private Yelagin squeezed through into the cockpit beside Demidov and behind the two pilots. "You know what to do," Demidov said.

Yelagin leaned forward and started flicking switches. She'd been a pilot before being recruited into Spetsnaz, and she knew how to disable tracking devices and transponders, and where any emergency beacons might be.

"Keep an eye on them," Demidov said. "I'm going to speak to the others. And Kristina... thanks."

Yelagin nodded once, then settled against the bulkhead behind the pilots.

Back in the cabin Demidov looked around at the others. She saw no dissent. She hadn't expected any–they'd been together as a solid core group for over four years, had seen and done many terrible things, and she knew their trust and sense of kinship went way beyond family. Yet, she still felt a burning sensation behind her eyes as she met their gaze.

"You know what we've done," she said, a statement more than a question. Of course they knew.

"We're just following your orders," Zhukov said.

"I can't order you to do this."

"You don't need to," Vasnev said. "Vasily Glazkov is your friend, so he's our friend too. We all help our friends."

166

"There'll be repercussions."

Vasnev shrugged. Budanov examined his fingernails.

"Right," Demidov said, sighing softly. "It's only an hour's detour. Our original target isn't going anywhere, and we'll finish our mission as soon as possible."

"That's if the Major doesn't send a jet to blow us from the sky," Zhukov said. His voice was matter-of-fact, but none of them dismissed the notion. They were on dangerous, unknown ground now, and no one knew exactly what the future might hold.

We're coming for you, Vasily, Demidov thought.

***

Anna will come for me, Vasily Glazkov thought. *She'll hear about this, put her team together, and come to find out what happened.*

He could see nothing around him in the darkness. But he could feel them there, sense them, and whenever they moved he could smell them–rotting meat, and grim intent.

If only I could warn her to stay away.

***

"Captain, you need to see this." The pilot sounded scared, and as Demidov pushed through into the cockpit she fully expected to find them facing off against two MI-35s. That would be the end of their brief mutiny.

But the airspace around them was clear, and she saw from Yelagin's shocked expression that this was something worse.

"What is it?" Demidov asked.

"Down there." The co-pilot pointed, and the pilot swung the helicopter in a gentle circle so they could all see.

There was a hole in the valley. Hundreds of feet across, so deep that it contained only blackness, it had swallowed trees and snow, ground and rocks. Two streams flowed into it, the waters tumbling in spreading sprays before being swallowed into the dark void. It was almost perfectly circular.

It looked so out of place that Demidov had to blink several times to ensure her eyes were not deceiving her.

"What the hell *is* that?" Yelagin said.

"How far's the scientific station?" Demidov asked, ignoring her.

"Just over a mile, north and over the valley ridge," the pilot said.

"Take us there."

She heard his sigh, but beneath that was a groan of fear from the co-pilot.

"Don't worry," Demidov said. "We can take care of ourselves." She knew that was true. She commanded the biggest bad-asses the Russian army could produce, and they'd seen each other through many treacherous and violent

167

situations. They had all killed people. Sometimes the people they killed were unarmed, more often than not it was a case of kill or be killed.

They could definitely look after themselves.

But none of them had ever seen anything like this.

"Get ready," she said back in the cabin. The others were all huddled at the cabin windows, looking down at the strange sight retreating behind them. "We're going in."

***

Where the hell are you, Vasily?

Demidov stood in the main recreational space of the research base and stared at the half-drunk cup of coffee that sat on the edge of a table. Somebody'd walked away from that cup. Maybe the coffee was shit, or maybe they'd been in a hurry.

"Captain?"

She turned to see Corporal Zhukov filling the doorway. His face told the story, but she asked anyway.

"Any sign?"

"Nothing," he confirmed. "All three of them. Budanov and Yelagin are checking logs to see if there's any record of what drew them out of here, but there's no question they're gone. Vasnev found nothing in the lab to give us any clue."

"They went to the hole," Demidov said, thinking of Vasily Glazkov. Not her husband, but he might as well have been. Would be, someday, if he hadn't fallen into that fucking hole.

"Would they all have gone?" Zhukov said. "That doesn't seem logical."

"Scientists. Every discovery's an adventure. They know better, and protocol demands certain procedures, but it's easy to get carried away when something new presents itself. Like ravens seeing something shiny."

Zhukov shifted his massive frame, his shadow withdrawing from the room. "I take it we're going out there."

It wasn't a question. He didn't have to ask, and she didn't have to tell him.

***

Vasnev moaned about the cold every step of the way. To be fair, it was cold enough to kill, given time. So cold that the snow refused to fall, despite the gray sky stretching out for eternity overhead. It was as if the sun had never existed at all.

"My balls have crawled up inside my body for warmth," Vasnev whined.

"You're confused," Yelagin muttered. "They never dropped to begin with."

Demidov tried to ignore them. The wind slashed across the hard-packed snow and the bare rock and cut right down to the bone. They had heavy jackets on, thick uniforms, balaclavas and gloves. Their mission had been meant to take place an hour's chopper flight from here, where it would still have been damned cold, but they'd never have been this exposed for this long.

"This is idiotic," Vasnev groaned. "They kept this from us for a reason. They've got to be sending a team. And you know damn well the pilots have probably already called it in...probably reported us the second we set off. We should just wait for someone else to arrive, someone with better gear—"

Budanov slapped the back of his head. Vasnev whipped around to glare at him, and for the first time Demidov worried real violence might flare amongst them. They'd had their share of hostilities over the years—any team does, given time—but this moment had venom. It had teeth.

"If we wait," Budanov sneered, "do you really think they'll let us help look for Vasily and his science friends? We'll be hauled out of here, original mission scrubbed and this one along with it. We'll be slammed into a room and made to wait while they decide on our punishment, and meanwhile someone else will be looking for Vasily and we won't know how long they'll take or how much effort they'll go to."

Demidov stared at him. They were about the most words she'd ever heard Budanov say at any one time. His ugly face had twisted into something even uglier, but his eyes glinted with fierce loyalty, and she wanted to hug him. Instead, she trudged onward as if nothing had happened.

Vasnev mumbled something else as they all started walking again. Demidov did not turn when she heard the sound of a rifle being racked, but she knew it had to be Zhukov. The Mountain.

"Don't think I won't shoot you just for the quiet," Zhukov said.

Vasnev kept silent for a whole four minutes after that. It was a brief but blessed miracle.

They reached the ridge above the valley and took a breather, staring down at the hole. The sky gave no hint as to the time, not up here in the frozen fuck-you end of the world, a place the world knew people had once been sent when they'd screwed up worse than anyone. Yet, Vasily had been so excited to come here with his two research partners, to live in a prefabricated base smaller than a Soviet-era city apartment and freeze his ass off, all to prove what the world refused to believe. Yes, the planetary climate was changing. But Siberia was still cold enough to kill you.

They slid and climbed and scrambled their way down into the valley. Demidov checked her radio. "Wolf to Eagle. You still reading me?"

A crackle of static on her comms, but then she heard the pilot's voice. "Eagle here. Still tracking."

"You might need to make a pick up in the valley later."

"At this point, why not?" the pilot said. Just as she'd expected. He might have called in their diversion from the mission already, but until someone came to shut them down, Eagle wasn't going to abandon Wolf. Not a chance.

They started across the hard-packed snow toward the hole. Even from a distance, the darkness of it yawned, as if it had a gravity all its own, drawing them in.

"I'm going to be moaning along with Vasnev in a moment," Yelagin said. "I don't know I've ever been this cold." Her teeth chattered.

"Kristina, you're Spetsnaz," Demidov said curtly. But they both knew she meant something else. It wasn't about their training, their elite status, their special operations. It was about being a woman in a field dominated by testosterone-fueled men who waved their guns around like they were showing off their cocks. They had to be tougher, she and Yelagin did. Especially Demidov, the woman running the show.

"I'll bear your disappointment," Yelagin said. "My nipples are going to snap off like icicles."

That got a laugh, breaking the tension, and suddenly Demidov felt grateful to her. Their closeness had started to fray a little, but now they were a team again.

"Captain," Vasnev said cautiously, lagging behind.

"I swear I will fucking shoot you," Budanov reminded him.

Then Corporal Zhukov echoed Vasnev. "Captain."

His voice gave her pause and made her turn. Vasnev had knelt in the snow. Zhukov stood over him, face as gray as the Siberian sky.

Vasnev looked up. "We've been moving parallel to some markings I couldn't make out, like someone dragged branches through here to obscure animal tracks."

"You didn't mention the tracks themselves," Zhukov said.

"Bear," Vasnev said. "And I saw some wolf tracks, too, up on the ridge. Same weird markings there, brushing the snow. But something happened right here, on this spot."

Demidov didn't like the hesitation in his voice. It sounded a bit like fear. Vasnev might have been a malingerer and a moaner, but he'd never been a coward.

"What 'something?'"

Zhukov answered for him. "The bear tracks stop. Whatever made those brush marks, it picked up the bear. Carried it off."

Vasnev stood, pointed at the hole. "It goes that way."

***

Demidov stood at the edge of the hole, a few feet back, not trusting the rim to hold her up. Sinkholes had appeared in many places in the area but she didn't think any of those on record had ever been this big. The hole seemed carved down into the permafrost and the rock and earth below. No telling how deep it went without doing a sounding. They had nothing to gauge the depth except two long coils of rope they'd found in the science team's base. That seemed unlikely to help them.

"Do you not just want to shout down, see if you get a response?" Kristina Yelagin said, standing at her shoulder.

Budanov snickered. "Yes, let's do that."

Yelagin shot him a death stare, but he ignored her, wrapped up in his own efforts. He had taken out the comm unit attached to his belt and begun searching through channels for any kind of beacon or signal. On each frequency, he'd broadcast the same message. "Research Unit one-one-three, please come in. Research Unit one-one-three, do you read me?" A few seconds, then again. With no answer, he'd move on.

They were getting nowhere. Vasnev had stopped whining, but the cold had gotten down into Demidov's bones. *Come here, Anna, I'll warm you,* Vasily would have said. And she'd have let him. As she had so many times before. *Where are you, my darling?* The loving part of her felt lost, but Demidov had spent a lifetime training to charge forward when anyone else would flee.

Zhukov glanced around, nervous and on guard. He'd been more unsettled than any of them, and that concerned Demidov. If the Mountain worried, they all should.

"I don't hear a thing but the wind." Zhukov shifted, boots crunching snow. "Don't see a thing. Not so much as a bird."

"Enough," Demidov said. "Private Yelagin, get those ropes out. There were a few pitons with them."

"We don't have enough climbing gear for all of us," Yelagin said. "Shall I radio Eagle, have them bring more equipment from the base?"

Demidov wanted to tell her to follow orders. Do what she was fucking told. The woman made sense, but the problem was that it would delay their descent, and a delay would be costly if Eagle had really radioed the situation back to command.

"I'll do it," she said. "Meanwhile, get those ropes out and—"

"Captain," Zhukov said.

"Fuck me, what the hell is that?" Vasnev whispered.

Demidov narrowed her eyes. Her balaclava had slipped a bit and she tugged it away from her eyes. The others had begun swearing, lifting their weapons, taking aim. Demidov blinked to clear her vision, thinking somehow in spite of her team's reactions she must just be seeing something. Spots in her eyes. The things moving across the valley toward them couldn't possibly be real.

But they were moving nearer, coming into focus, and in moments she could no longer doubt. They weren't spots in her eyes or her imagination. They moved like some strange combination of tumbleweed and sea anemone, their flesh such a pale nothing hue that they blended almost too well against the snowy ground. Had they only stopped and kept still, they'd have been almost invisible at a distance. But they weren't stopping.

"Holy shit," someone said. Demidov thought she recognized her own voice. Maybe she'd said it.

They weren't stopping at all. They came from all directions, perhaps ten or twelve in all, rolling or slithering or some combination thereof, and they did not come without burden. They seemed nothing but a mass of tendrils, but each of them dragged something else behind them—something more familiar. Animals, some struggling and some limp, some broken, some bleeding. A musk deer, some squirrels, a leopard. One of the things had wrapped itself around a wolf. The beast could not extricate itself but it continued to fight, clawing, attempting to escape. It snarled and howled, as if trapped between the sister urges to fight and to scream in sorrow.

"Captain," Zhukov said, his voice gone cold. That was when the Mountain turned most dangerous. The more dead his voice, the more she knew he must be feeling. The Mountain didn't like to be made to feel. "Give me an order please, Captain."

In the distance, Demidov saw something big and brown in the midst of a squalling twist of those white tendrils. Three or four of the things had surrounded a moose—a fucking moose—and were dragging it back toward the hole. A knot of dread twisted in her gut as it finally hit Demidov. *Stupid,* she thought. *So goddamn stupid. Should have seen it instantly, should have understood.* If they could drag down a moose, a trio of curious, unarmed scientists would be no problem at all.

Feeling sick and jittery and wanting to roar out her fear for her mate, Demidov clicked off the safety on her Kalashnikov AK-12.

"Weapons free. Don't let these things get anywhere near us."

"Weapons free," Zhukov confirmed.

Instinctively they spread into a defensive circle, edging thirty yards away from the hole and using trees and rocks as cover. Demidov glanced around at her squad, already knowing what she'd see—professionalism, preparedness, calm in the face of these strange, unknown odds. Her senses were alert and alight, sharpened on the fear she felt for Vasily.

Whatever the hell these things were—

"Incoming, my eleven," Yelagin said.

The creature carrying the wolf had diverted from its route towards the hole and now moved towards them. The wolf still whined and howled, snapping at tendrils that seemed to arc easily away from its teeth. The creature seemed almost unaware of its burden.

It paused twenty meters away, half-hidden behind a tree.

Almost as if it was looking at them.

"Another this side," Zhukov said. "They're paused, as if—"

The creature holding the wolf slipped past the tree and came towards them across the snow, leaping rocks, compressing beneath a fallen tree and dragging the wolf through the narrow gap.

Demidov's finger caressed the trigger, and she experienced a moment of doubt.

Then Vasnev opened fire. He shot the struggling, crying wolf from sixty yards out. The wolf's blood spattered the snow and bits of fur and flesh scattered across the stark whiteness. The tumbleweed creature twitched and whipped backward, bullets tearing at its tendrils as it dropped the dead wolf. But then it drew itself up and began to slide toward them once more, skimming the surface of the snow, moving quicker as it came on.

"It's not...the bullets aren't..." Vasnev couldn't get the words out.

"Don't just stand there!" Yelagin moved up next to him and unleashed a barrage from her AK-12, took the tumbler mid-center, and blew it apart. It splashed across the snow a dozen steps from them, insides steaming as they sank into a drift. "Keep shooting till it's dead."

"Center mass!" Demidov said. "Blow them to hell."

Hunkered down behind a rock she braced her AK-12 against her shoulder and zeroed in on the thing dragging the musk deer. Then she opened up. Bullets ripped it up, stitching the dead deer and scattering the tumbler's twisted, pale tendrils across the snow. Several of them slapped against a tree and remained there, held in place by the sticky goo that must have been its blood. The fear that had coiled into her heart calmed itself. They could be stopped. They could be killed.

The feel of the recoil, the stench of gunpowder, the reports smashing into her ears were all familiar to her, and she kept her calm amid the chaos. They all did. That was why they made a good team, and why they had never faced a situation they could not handle.

Not ever.

Budanov and Zhukov were on her immediate right and they were both better marksmen. They twitched their weapons left and right, letting off short bursts and then adjusting their aim, anticipating the creatures' movements. All around them, bullets impacted trees and showers of snow drifted down. Visibility was reduced. The creatures took advantage and rushed them, but the soldiers chose their targets and kept firing.

"Ammo!" Zhukov shouted, and the others covered his field of fire as he reloaded.

"How many?" Yelagin shouted.

"Don't know," Demidov replied. She saw movement ahead of her, a pale shape slinking from cover behind a rock, and she concentrated a burst of fire. The shape thrashed and spun, tendrils or tentacles whipping up a snowstorm. One more burst and it grew still. "One less."

For a few more long seconds, the hills all around them threw back brutal gunfire echoes. And then it was done.

Demidov's eardrums throbbed in the silent aftermath. She breathed in, let it out, finger still on the trigger.

"Clear," she breathed, and the others repeated the word in turn. She stood slowly from behind her covering rock and stood in the center of their defensive circle, turning slowly to survey the scene. It couldn't have been more than a minute, but the area around them had taken on the appearance of a bloody battlefield.

Trees were scarred and splintered from the gunfire. The animals being carried by the tumblers were all dead, their demise signed across the snow in blood, bodies steaming, one or two still twitching their last. The other creatures—*Whatever the fuck they are*, Demidov thought—also lay dead, tendrils splayed across the snow's crispy surface and, here and there, melting down into it where their sickly pale blood had been spilled.

Hot-blooded, she thought. Hot enough to melt snow. But what the fuck has blood that color?

"Holy shit," Vasnev said. "What just happened?"

"Something from down there," Zhukov said. "Subterranean. Pale skin, no eyes…"

"What do we do, Captain?" Budanov said. "You want me to call this in?"

"Call it in," she agreed. "But I'm not waiting. We all know Vasily and the others must be down there. Somebody's got to stay up here and wait, but I'm—"

Zhukov and Yelagin called out that there was movement, the two of them shouting almost in the same voice. Demidov swore and lifted her weapon again, scanning the landscape all around. Between them and the sheer drop into that vast hole she saw motion down close to the ground, a slithering undulation, perfectly camouflaged but moving in.

"How many?" she asked.

"Can't tell," Zhukov said. "They're moving differently."

"Almost like they're under the snow," Yelagin said.

"Watch your ammo!" she shouted, then they opened fire again.

Snow flicked up and bullets ricocheted from scattered rocks. One creature erupted from a deep snowdrift and came apart beneath a sustained burst of fire, innards spattered down, those thin, tendril limbs whipping through the air.

Demidov's weapon clicked on an empty magazine. She ejected the empty, reached inside her jacket to grab another, smashed it into place and raised the AK-12 again—

—just as Budanov screamed to her right.

She turned just in time to see his head jerked hard to one side, tendrils across his face, skin stretching where they touched, tugged by some adhesive on those tendrils, or by octopus-like suckers. Even as she brought her gun to bear, blood sprayed from Budanov's mouth. He fell to the ground and the tumbler flowed onto his back, tendrils wrapping tight around his neck and skull.

"No!" Zhukov shouted, as he and the others opened fire. Their onslaught blew the creature apart. The thick white paste, its blood, splashed down across Budanov's back, mixing with his own in a sickly pink hue.

"Form up!" Demidov shouted. "Close in! We've got to get back to the base."

"Up that hill?" Yelagin asked. And she was right. They'd descended into the valley down a steep slope, almost climbing at times. To retreat up there with these things on their tail would be suicide.

They had to hold out down here.

"Mark your targets!" she said. The matter of ammunition was already worrying her. They'd come equipped for a simple in-and-out, an extraction that might not even have involved a firefight. As such, they'd come light, bringing only the bare minimum of spare ammunition. Four mags each, if that, and she was already on her second. Three more shots and—

She ejected, reloaded, marked a new target and fired.

The chaos of battle had always remained outside for Demidov. Inside, her mind worked quick and calm, always able to place an enemy and work out the various strategies and logistics that would enable their success.

Now, everything was different. This was like no fight she'd ever fought, and already she could see its terrible, eventual conclusion.

"Grenade!" Yelagin said, lobbing a grenade and ducking down. The detonation was dulled by the deep snow, the gray sky made momentarily light by sprayed snow and pale body parts.

More came. More and more, and as she loaded her final magazine, Zhukov was taken down.

Three of them wrapped around the big man's legs, throat, and right arm, and a wave of tentacles ripped the weapon from his hands. Demidov twisted around and took aim, but she was thinking the same as the others—*Do I pull the trigger?* They could not fire without hitting Zhukov.

The decision was snatched from them. Tendrils punched in through Zhukov's eyes, he screamed, a creature leapt onto his back and plunged its limbs around and into his open mouth. His throat bulged with the pressures inside, and as he fell he was already dead.

Demidov felt a surge of unreality wash over her. Zhukov had saved her life several times, and years ago before Vasily, the two of them had enjoyed a brief, passionate affair. It had ended quickly, because involvement like that would have put their squad in jeopardy. But the affection for each other had remained.

"No," she whispered, and she started shooting. Her bullets ripped through the fallen man and the thing on his back, tearing them both apart.

"Too many!" Vasnev shouted, turning as his machine-gun ran out of ammo, swinging it like a club, falling beneath a couple of tumblers as they surged from the snow.

Yelagin dashed to Demidov's side and turned back to back with her captain, and both of them continued firing for as long as they could.

When Demidov's weapon ran out she drew her sidearm with her left hand. But too late.

Yelagin was plucked from behind her and thrown against a tree, several of the pale, grotesque creatures surging across her and driving her down into the snow.

By then Demidov understood.

They weren't coming from across the valley anymore. A fresh wave had come up from the sinkhole. Dozens of them.

As they crawled over her, wrapped around her throat, tore the useless Kalashnikov from her hands, she raised her pistol. Too late. Her legs were tugged out from under her. Tendrils covered her mouth, pulled her arms wide, and she thought they might just rip her apart, that she'd be drawn and quartered by these impossible things, these tumbleweeds.

But whatever they intended for her, it wasn't instant death.

She felt herself sliding through the snow as they dragged her back toward the hole. They were warm where they touched her, and they smelled something like cut grass on a summer day. It was a curious, jarring scent. She tried to raise her head to see what was happening and whether she was alone. *Am I the only one left alive?* she wondered. But the tumblers were strong, and for the first time she sensed something in them other than animalistic fury.

There was intelligence. They kept her head back so that she couldn't see, and when she struggled she felt a slick, warm tentacle drape itself across her eyes, then pull tight.

Seconds later she felt the world drop from beneath her. She gasped in a breath and prepared for the fall, but she felt herself jerked up and down as the creatures descended into the hole. They must have been using their strange limbs to grab onto the sheer sides. Maybe they stuck like flies, or crawled like spiders.

Coolness became cold. She didn't notice the gentle kiss of weak daylight until it vanished entirely. The thing carrying her must have needed all its other limbs to descend, and her eyes were uncovered again. She could look up and see the circle of pale grey sky vanishing above. Around her, a strange luminescence seemed to accompany their descent. To begin with she thought it came from the walls, and that perhaps there was strange algae growing there, issuing a pale light through some chemical process. But then she saw a tumbler's limbs working before her as they rapidly descended into the hole, and they glowed.

A procession of terrors crossed her mind. Poisonous! Acidic! Radioactive! But she suspected she would be long-dead before any of those potential hazards caused her harm.

She caught a glimpse of Yelagin being carried by other things further along the sheer rocky wall, and then she heard Vasnev screaming. Three of them were still alive, but Budanov and Zhukov were dead. Perhaps soon she would have reason to envy them.

***

Amanda Hart was screaming.

Quiet, Glazkov wanted to say. *Stupid American, keep silent. Can't you hear?* He liked Hart, had no real issue with Americans in general, but they had a tendency toward hysterics. Now was not the time for hysterics. In the dim glow of the creatures' luminescence he could see Hart hanging from the ceiling like a forgotten marionette, but of course that was an illusion. Her limbs were not dangling, they were restricted. She screamed his name–*Vasily, Vasily, Vasily*–until he wished his mother had chosen another for him at birth.

Yes, Hans Brune might be dead. Given the way his ears had leaked after his skull had struck the wall, he pretty much had to be dead.

But we're alive, Glazkov wanted to say. *We're alive.*

His eyes blurred. It might have been tears obscuring his vision, or it might've been the blows he himself had taken to the head. He blinked and tried to focus. Glazkov hung upside down, so it might have been the head-rush contributing to his blurry vision.

No, he thought, looking at Hart. *That's not it.*

She cried out his name again.

His vision wasn't blurry after all. There were things moving on her face and body–things much like those that had carried them down into the hole, but so much smaller. Tiny things, like spiny creatures he might've found at the ocean bottom, but they were not underwater now. There must have been hundreds of them on her, perhaps thousands of the little things, moving around her with the industry of an anthill or a beehive, all of them producing that sickly glow. They moved with purpose, as Hart screamed.

As loudly as he could manage, Glazkov shushed her. Screaming wouldn't help anyone.

It occurred to him that it was strange, how calm he was. So strange.

But then he felt a little tug on his right forearm and he tried to crane his neck ever so slightly to get a glimpse of it, to see what might have caused that tug, and he saw that they were all over him as well. The tiny ones. *Babies,* he thought. But something told him that despite the size differential, the tiny ones were not the babies of the larger ones. Not at all. No assumptions ought to be made. Particularly not when the tiny ones were so busy, so full of intent.

He felt that tug again and cocked his head, managed a glimpse. They were there, skittering all over him, but now he understood something else.

He understood why Hart kept screaming.

They weren't just all over him, those little ones. They were *inside him,* too. Under the skin. Moving, and busy. So very busy.

Glazkov blinked, and for the first time he understood one other thing. Perhaps the most important thing. They weren't just moving inside him.

They were also speaking to him.

***

177

Budanov's whole world was pain and cold. He could hardly see. His head throbbed, his neck hurt, and his skull felt like something was tied around it so tightly that the slightest movement would cause it to burst. He'd spill his brains across the frozen ground. At least the pain would be gone.

No, Budanov thought. *No, I won't let that happen.* He never had given up in anything, and he wasn't about to start now.

He tried moving his limbs. They seemed to shift without any significant pain. Nothing broken. He rolled onto his right hand side and felt a heavy weight slip from his back, wet and still warm. He ran his hand up his front to his neck, checking for wounds. Nothing split open. He spat blood, and a tooth came out, too. His lip was split, and he'd bitten his tongue.

"Fuck," he whispered. *Good. I can still talk.*

Everything was silent.

Still lying on his side, he scanned his immediate surroundings until he saw his gun. It was down by his feet. He leaned down, head swimming, pulsing, and snagged the weapon with one finger. Straightening, hugging the rifle to his chest and checking that it was undamaged, he felt more in control.

He feared that everyone else was dead. His last memory was of one of those things coming at him, tendrils spread wide like a squid about to attack. He'd felt the impact of its warm, wet body upon him, then the sickly sensation of the limbs tightening around his neck and head… and then nothing.

He glanced behind him and saw the torn ruin of the creature, limbs split, body holed by bullets. A stinking fluid had leaked and melted into the snow.

Budanov sat up slowly and looked around.

Zhukov was to his right, dead. There was so much blood. Budanov's heart stuttered, then he calmed himself and brought his weapon to bear. His head swam. He'd known Zhukov for almost ten years, and they'd fought well together.

"Sorry, brother," he whispered. The words seemed too loud, as if a whisper could echo across the landscape.

He realized how silent everything was. How still. Groaning, biting his lip to prevent dizziness from spilling him to the ground, Budanov stood and looked around. He staggered a few paces from the mess of Zhukov's body and leaned against a tree.

Nothing moved or spoke, growled or sang. The whole valley was deathly silent, and he wondered whether he was actually dead and this was what came after—desolation and loneliness.

Then he heard something in the distance. A buzzing, far away, so faint that he thought it might be inside his head. He tilted his head left and right, trying to triangulate the sound, but it came from everywhere.

There were many of those alien creatures lying dead all around, and trees and rocks bore scarred testament to the strength of the firefight he'd missed. But other than Zhukov's corpse, there was no sign of his comrades.

Except...

Drag marks in the snow.

"Oh, no," Budanov breathed. They'd seen the animals being gathered by the tumblers and hauled towards the hole, before those things had switched their attention to the Spetsnaz unit.

He checked his weapon, switched magazines for a full one, wiped blood from his face, and started toward the hole. He would not leave his people, not while there was even the smallest chance they were still alive.

The buzzing grew louder. Close to the edge of the abyss he frowned and hunkered, still stunned by its size but now terrified by what might be down there. He turned left and right, trying to pinpoint the sound, but did not identify it until moments before the first helicopter swept into view.

The big Mi24 attack aircraft and troop carrier appeared above the ridge line across the valley, closely followed by two KA-52s in escort formation. Help had arrived, and he hadn't even had a chance to call it in.

Their helicopter pilots must have reported the forced change of destination the moment his unit left the aircraft back at the scientific station. Budanov didn't know how long had passed—he guessed little more than an hour—but that was plenty of time for this new unit to be scrambled and sent their way.

He knew how much trouble they were all in for disobeying orders and scrapping an important mission, but right then he didn't care. Something amazing and terrible had happened here. But for now his main concern, his *only* concern, was for the surviving members of his unit.

Budanov popped a flare and waved it back and forth several times, then tossed it onto a pile of rocks close by. He was ten meters from the hole's edge.

As the three aircraft circled the valley and hovered for a while above the massive hole in its floor, Budanov edged closer. He kept his weapon ready, convinced that at any moment one of those tentacled things would surge up from the depths and come at him.

If it does, I'll blow it apart.

But nothing came. He reached the edge, leaned over and looked down, and saw only darkness in that intimidating pit. The walls seemed sheer, and there was no sign of life. He thought of lighting another flare and dropping it over the edge... but he was afraid of what he'd see.

"Hold tight," he said, but there was no one to hear his words.

As the helicopters swung around and came in to land in a clearing three hundred meters away, Budanov jogged toward them, ignoring his aches and wounds. He wondered how long it would take to make them believe.

***

Their descent into the pit seemed to take forever.

Vasnev's screaming faded to a whimper, and Yelagin might well have been dead. Demidov tried to keep tabs on them both, alerted to where they were by the strange, shimmering luminescence emanating from the tumblers bearing them. Their bodies glowed, reminding Demidov of deep sea creatures—just as compelling, equally mysterious and alien. She couldn't help seeing beauty in their flowing movements, even though the tumbler held her with painfully tight tentacles clasped around her stomach, left arm, and both legs. It was pointless struggling or attempting to escape, but as they descended deeper and deeper, she had time to plan.

She could not simply submit to whatever was to come. Vasily and his companions were likely dead, but while there was even the slightest chance they were still alive, Demidov and the remainder of her unit had to fight.

She had a knife in her boot and a grenade still hanging from her belt.

"Oh, my God," Yelagin said from over to her left. "Look down."

Demidov was glad to hear her friend's voice, but when she twisted and followed her advice, cold fear slithered through her veins. Down beneath them, far down, a faint glow was growing in size as they continued their descent. To begin with, it might have been just one more tumbler, but as they drew closer she could see many separate points of illumination. It wasn't one. It was hundreds.

"Yelagin," Demidov said. "Vasnev. We need to get away."

"Captain, there are tunnels in the walls," Yelagin said.

"You're sure?"

"I just passed one. The glow of this thing lit it, just for a second. I don't know how far it went but…"

"But that's enough," Demidov said. "Vasnev? You alive?"

"I can't…" Vasnev said. "I can't believe…"

"You don't have to believe," Demidov said. "Do you still have your knife?"

A grunt that might have been an affirmative.

"We can't let them get us down there," Demidov said, wondering all the time what these things heard of their voices, what they thought, and whether there was any way they might comprehend. She guessed not. *Hoped* not. They were something no one had ever seen or heard of before, how in the hell could they know Russian? "If they get us all the way down, we're finished. Look down, scan the rock face, and when you see—"

"There!" Yelagin said. "Just below us. A ledge."

"Right," Demidov said. She'd seen it. A narrow ledge like a slash across the wall, similar to many they might already have been carried past. But this one was where they would make their stand.

As the creature carrying her flowed down the wall, limbs reaching and grasping, sticking and moving, Demidov slid her hand down her hip and thigh, bending slightly, to reach the knife in her boot.

This is when it stops me, she thought. *It'll know what I'm doing, sense the violence, and one wrench of those limbs will tear me in half.*

But the creature seemed unaware of the weapon now grasped in Demidov's hand. The ledge was close; they were running out of time. Without trying to make out whether Yelagin and Vasnev were ready, she slashed at the tentacles pulled tight across her throat.

The creature squealed. It sounded like a baby in pain, but Demidov was committed now. She cut again, then grasped the thing's body with her left hand–soft, fleshy, wet–and stabbed with her right. She felt the blade penetrate deep into the thing's hide and the squeal turned into an agonized scream. Working the blade hard to the left and right, she gutted the beast.

From a little further away she heard other screams. She hoped they weren't human.

Demidov fought, slashed, thrashed, cutting limbs and seeing them drop away into the darkness like exclamations of pain. A gush of warm fluid pulsed across her throat and face. She tried to close her mouth but wasn't fast enough. She tasted the dying thing, its rank spice, its hot sour blood, and as it dropped her and she fell, she puked into the darkness.

She slammed onto the ledge and the breath was knocked from her. Spitting, wiping a mess of gore and puke from her face, she rolled back against the wall and looked up.

Glowing like a ghost from the gore covering her, Yelagin was climbing down the rock face just a couple of meters above. She dropped and crouched beside Demidov.

"Captain!"

"I'm fine. Vasnev?"

"Vasnev fell. I saw him go, still fighting the thing that had him."

Demidov rolled again until she could look down... and wished she hadn't. She guessed they were fifty meters above the hole's base, and it was pulsing with the glowing things, all of them shoving forward to congregate around one place at the foot of the sheer side. Vasnev was plain to see, splayed across rock, broken, splashed with luminous gore. If the fall hadn't killed him, they soon would.

"We should go," Yelagin said.

"Go where?"

"A cavern. Just past the end of the ledge, I think we can make it. I saw it as I watched Vasnev fall."

Demidov stood, the two remaining soldiers holding onto each other to protect themselves from the dark, the fall, and the terrible glowing, monstrous things that lived in the depths. They moved carefully along the ledge, and just where it petered out was a crack in the rock wall. Standing before it, a waft of surprisingly warm air breathed out at them, as if this whole place were a living thing.

"What the hell was that?" Yelagin whispered.

"Doesn't matter," Demidov said. She had already heard the sounds from below, and a quick glance confirmed her fears. The things were climbing again. Coming for them, ready to avenge their dead. "We've got no choice."

Yelagin tucked her pistol into her belt and climbed away from the ledge toward the crack. Demidov followed. She had never been great with heights.

Inside an aircraft or tall building was fine, but if she was on the outside, then the great drop below always seemed to lure her with the promise of an endless, painful fall. Knowing what was coming for her from below only made matters worse.

"Here," Yelagin said. She was braced in the crack, back against one side and feet against the other, and reaching for Demidov with her left hand. Demidov grabbed her gratefully, scrambled, and soon they were inside.

It opened into more of a tunnel, relatively flat and leading directly away from the great hole. The wet, stinking remnants of the things they had killed still provided a low luminescence on their clothing and hair, and Demidov hoped the effect would last. They both carried flares, but they would burn harsh and quick. She couldn't imagine anything worse than being trapped down here in smothering, total darkness.

She tugged the grenade from her belt.

"Are you fucking crazy?" Yelagin asked.

"What choice do we have? They're coming!"

Yelagin drew her sidearm again and put it into Demidov's hand. "With respect, Captain, you blow the mouth of this tunnel, you could kill us quicker than those things out there. You'll trap us in here, if you don't bring the ceiling down on us. Hold them off as long as you can. I'll see if the tunnel leads to something other than a dead end."

Demidov nodded, switched the gun to her right hand and the grenade to her left. The bullets wouldn't last very long.

She heard Yelagin move away behind her, using the luminescence from the tumblers' blood to see. As the footfalls faded, fine tendrils whipped up over the ledge, and the first tumbler spilled into the mouth of the tunnel. Demidov took aim, dead center, and pulled the trigger.

***

"We're to place you under arrest and take you back to base," the Lieutenant said. He hadn't given Budanov his name. He hadn't even seemed keen to give the private any medical aid, but his medic had come forward and started tending Budanov's wounds anyway. While she cleaned and dressed his wounds, another man—a civilian—took careful photographs of the injuries. Two others had disappeared into the snowy woodlands, each of them guarded by a heavily-armed soldier.

Budanov had warned them, but they didn't seem to believe a thing he said. All but the civilians, who looked terrified and excited at the same time. *More fucking scientists*, Budanov thought. *That's why we're here in the first place.*

"But my captain and the rest of my unit might still be down there," he said. "The things took them down, and perhaps—"

"Your fault," the lieutenant said. He seemed eager to move, shifting from foot to foot and scanning the snowscape. One of the men had thrown

Budanov a thick coat, and he was eager for the medic to finish so that he could cover himself. All he wanted now was somewhere warm.

Demidov and the others aren't warm, he thought. They're down there. Cold, afraid. Maybe dead. But I have to know for sure.

"Can't you at least look?" he asked. "Get one of the KA-52s to hover over the hole, shine a light down?"

"We're not staying long enough for that," the lieutenant said. He was a tall, brash man, young for his rank, but Budanov sensed a good military mind behind his iciness. He knew what he was doing.

"You were coming here anyway," Budanov said. "Before you heard from our pilots. Isn't that right?"

"Not for long," the lieutenant said again, staring him in the eye for the first time. "Just long enough for these white-coats to get what they want, then we're getting the fuck out. You're lucky we're taking you with us. Your pilots left an hour ago when they heard."

"Heard what?"

The lieutenant glanced aside. Frowned. One of his soldiers ran across and stood close, muttering something into his ear.

"Everyone, back to the chopper!" the lieutenant shouted.

"But we're—" one of the scientists said. He was hunched closer to the hole, examining something hidden in the snow. *One of them,* Budanov thought, and he wondered whether it was one he'd shot himself.

"Do as I fucking say!" the lieutenant said. He looked rattled.

"What is it?" Budanov asked. Bullets were his only answer.

The KA-52 that had been circling the site dropped low over the hole and opened up with its big cannons, tracer rounds flashing into the darkness and impacting the wall. The explosions were so powerful that Budanov felt their vibrations through the solid ground, and snow drifted down from trees as if startled awake.

"But we don't know—" one of the civilians shouted.

"We *do* know," Budanov said. He stood, and just for a moment he fought every instinct that was telling him to flee.

I can't just run, he thought. *I have to help. They'd do the same for me.*

He turned his back on the helicopter and sprinted into the trees. No one called him back; either they didn't see him going, or they didn't really care. That lieutenant had been scared, and he'd had more on his mind than capturing an AWOL soldier.

Skirting around where Zhukov's body had been marked with a red flag, he saw a heavy white rucksack, dropped by one of the civilians. Coiled around its handles was a thin nylon climbing rope. He ripped it open, and inside were various devices and sample jars, and a radio.

As the cacophony of gunfire from the KA-52 ceased, the radio hissed into life.

"...leaving in three minutes!" It was the lieutenant's voice. "Ground Cleanse commencing eight minutes after that. You do *not* want to be here when the MiGs arrive."

Oh Jesus, they're going to blast the hole to hell!

Budanov crouched and ran closer to the wound in the land, tied the rope around a sturdy tree, and wondered just what the fuck he was doing as he threw the coiled mass over the edge and started to abseil into the darkness.

He descended nearly a hundred feet before he paused on a ledge, taking advantage of the glow from far below. From his pack he drew a couple of pitons and hammered one into the rock face as quickly as possible. Tying it off, he set his heels at the corner of the ledge and prepared to drop deeper. The seconds were ticking by in his head. How long since he'd heard the transmission? How many minutes remaining before MIGs started bombing the shit out of this hole in the frozen heart of the world?

The smell of methane lingered and he wondered if he was being slowly poisoned to death. Funny way to go, with bombs on the way.

To hell with it, he thought, and kicked off the ledge, shooting downward at reckless speed.

As he swung toward the wall again, boots shoving off for another rapid descent, he heard gunshots echoing up to him from below. He kicked off again, glanced down into the darkness...only it wasn't *truly* dark at all. Far below, a pale white glow rippled and undulated like a strange ocean. Closer, on the opposite wall, the same glow shifted and crawled and slid along the rock, and now he saw them on his side as well. Slowing his descent, Budanov's breath caught in his throat.

He hung on the rope and saw the glowing, many tendriled-creatures coming for him, racing up the rock wall of the hole. He shot a single glance skyward, calculated how long it would take him to reach the top from here, and realized he would be dead soon. In reality, Budanov had known this from the moment he had snatched the coils of rope and run for the methane-cored hole, but now he truly understood what he had done.

Down was his only chance.

"Captain!" he screamed. "Kristina! Vasnev!"

Budanov kicked away from the wall and let the rope slide through his hands, nearly in free-fall. He rocketed downward, and the tumblers raced up at him. All of his choices had been made, now. From this point onward, there were only consequences.

***

Demidov slid backward, the jagged rock floor of the tunnel snagging at her pants. The blood of two tumblers cast a ghostly pale illumination in the tunnel mouth. The pistol was warm in her hand as she waited, heart pounding. One of the tumblers she'd killed had fallen backward off the ledge but the other lay twitching just a few feet from the soles of her boots. She dug her heel into the rock and shoved backward again, gaining a few more inches of distance from the dead thing and the ledge beyond it.

It hissed as it bled. That might've been the sound of it dying or just the noise of its warm blood staining the cool rock floor of the tunnel, like the ticking of a car engine after it's been shut down. She whispered small prayers, her voice echoing in that cramped space, and she listened for Yelagin's return. How would they get back to the surface? If they kept themselves alive long enough, help might come, but what about Vasily and his science team? The hard little bitch she thought of as her conscience told her the man she loved had to be dead, but Demidov wouldn't listen. She told herself Vasily had to be alive.

Though maybe it would have been better if she could imagine him dead. If she could imagine he no longer needed her, that she could simply surrender to fate, give herself over to the death that even now crawled toward her.

The dead tumbler twitched and Demidov jerked backward, taking aim. She blinked, staring as she realized it was not the dead thing that moved but a new arrival. Behind the cooling, dimming corpse, another tumbler had crept over the ledge and slithered toward her, camouflaged behind its dead brother. They were getting sneaky now, and that terrified her more than anything.

They weren't just cruel, they were clever.

"I see you," she whispered.

It froze, as if it understood.

Demidov lifted the gun, still clutching the grenade in her left hand. The tumbler whipped to the right, raced along the wall and then onto the ceiling, clinging to the bare rock. Tendrils whipped toward her face and Demidov back-pedaled hard, sliding backward along the tunnel as she pulled the trigger. Bullets pinged and cracked and ricocheted off the walls, sending shards of rock flying. Two caught the tumbler at its core, splashing luminescent blood across the tunnel floor. Tendrils snagged her ankles from above, others tangled in her hair, and she screamed as one of them curled around her left hand—where she held the grenade.

Should have pulled the pin. Should have just thrown it. Should have—

She shot it again, center mass. Three more bullets and the gun clicked empty.

The tumbler dangled from the ceiling, its tendrils still sticking to the rock overhead. Demidov tried to catch her breath, to calm her thundering heart. Setting the grenade into the cloth nest of the crotch of her pants, she patted her pockets and checked her belt. Still had her knife, but she needed ammunition...and found it. One magazine. She ejected the spent one and jammed the fresh magazine home.

Something moved out on the ledge, slithering, rolling.

Demidov didn't even look up at it. She knew. They weren't coming one at a time anymore.

Gun still in her right hand, she snatched up the grenade again, pulled the pin with her teeth and held on tightly. The second she let it go, the countdown would begin.

Taking a breath, she looked up.

The tumbler dangling from the ceiling dropped to the floor of the tunnel, dead, just as the others rushed in. She saw two, then realized there were three, maybe even four, their glowing tendrils churning together and filling the tunnel mouth. Demidov fired half a dozen shots, bullets punching through the roiling mass, but she knew her time had come.

She dropped the grenade, turned, and bolted to her feet.

Bent over, she hurtled down the tunnel, firing blindly back the way she'd come. The countdown ticked by in her head as she ran. In the dimming light offered by the blood soaked into her clothing, she saw the tunnel turning and followed it around a corner. The ceiling dropped and the walls closed in and she feared that she'd found a dead end, except there was no sign of—

"Kristina!" she screamed. "Take cover, if you're here! Take—"

The grenade blew, the sound funneling toward her, pounding her eardrums as the blast threw her forward. She crashed to the floor, skidding along rough stone as bits of the ceiling showered down onto her, dust and rock chips. A crack splintered across the stone overhead and she stared up at it, lying there bruised and bloody, and waited for it to fall.

Nothing.

She took a dust-laden breath and realized she was alive. She'd dropped the gun when the grenade blew her off her feet. She looked around, ears pounding, but in that near darkness the weapon was lost.

She heard footfalls coming her way, reached for her knife, realized that the tumblers had no feet. The narrow beam of Yelagin's flashlight appeared, along with the remaining glow of the tumblers' blood on the woman's uniform.

"You're alive!" Yelagin said, more in relief than surprise. She didn't want to be alone, and Demidov didn't blame her.

"Seems we both are," Demidov said, sitting up and brushing dust off her clothes. "For all the good it will do us. We'll starve to death in here, if we don't suffocate first."

Yelagin knelt beside her. "We may die yet," she said, "but it won't be in this tunnel."

Demidov frowned, glancing at her, refusing to hope.

"Come on," Yelagin said, helping her to stand. "There's a way out."

"A way up?" Demidov asked.

Yelagin would not meet her gaze. "A way *out*," she repeated. "That's all I can promise for now."

A fresh spark of hope ignited inside Demidov and once again she allowed herself to think of Vasily. Maybe it wasn't too late. Maybe he was still alive.

All she and Yelagin had were knives, but for the moment they were still alive. They would fight to stay that way.

***

The tunnel sloped downward. Demidov's ears were still ringing, all sounds muffled thanks to her proximity to the grenade's explosion. Her head pounded but she took deep breaths and kept her arms outstretched, tracing her fingers along the tunnels walls as she tried to keep her wits about her. There were ridges and striations along the rock that were quite different from what she'd been able to make out on the side of the massive hole. If that sinkhole had been bored up from below by an enormous methane explosion, as Vasily and his team believed, then this side tunnel had been created by some other means.

Something had carved it out.

Several minutes passed in relative silence, with Demidov following Yelagin, the two women doing their best not to slip. The twists in the tunnel often led to a sudden steep section, and a wrong step might have led to a broken neck.

The luminescent blood they'd been splashed with faded with each passing minute, and soon Yelagin's flashlight was their primary source of illumination. The air moved gently around them, not so much a breeze as a kind of subterranean respiration, the tunnels breathing, evidence there were openings somewhere ahead and below.

Noises came to them, quiet whispers of motion followed by what sounded like thousands of tons of rock and earth shifting, but they remained very much alone in the tunnel. Demidov exhaled in relief when the tunnel flattened out and she found she could stand fully upright. Yelagin picked up their pace, and soon they were hustling along in a quick jog. The thumping of her heart, the familiar cadence of their steps, lent Demidov calm and confidence that allowed her to gather her thoughts. *Find the source of the air flow*, she told herself. *See if we can climb. Track down the tumblers and try to ascertain the status of the science team—dead or alive?*

"There's a glow—" Yelagin started to say.

Then she swore, stumbled, and hurled herself forward in the tunnel. Demidov pulled back, reaching for her knife, ready for a fight. Her backpedaling saved her. Just in front of her, Yelagin scrabbled her hands to get a grip to keep from falling into a hole in the tunnel floor, an opening that seemed to drop away into nothing. Air flowed steadily up from the hole.

"Kristina!" Demidov called, glancing around, trying to figure out how she could help.

Yelagin had already managed to drag one leg up, prop her knee on the edge of the abyss, and now she hauled herself to safety on the other side of the five-foot gap. She'd seen the glow, but had been moving too fast to stop, so instead she'd jumped. And almost not made it at all.

They stared at each other across the gap, neither of them wanting to be left alone. Yelagin used her torch to search the edges of the hole, and it looked to Demidov as if she would be able to get around it—if she was extremely careful—

without falling to her death. She lay flat on her belly and dragged herself to the edge to stare down into the depths, drawn by the soft glow that emanated from within. On the other side, Yelagin did the same.

Demidov went numb.

It was Yelagin who spoke first. "Is that...? Is it a kind of... *city*, do you think?"

Far below, perhaps hundreds of feet, were loops and whorls of stone, a kind of labyrinth of strange tracks and bowls and twisting towers. From those strange spires of rock hung innumerable tendriled things, either asleep or simply static, dreaming their subterranean dreams or contemplating the labyrinth of their underground world, and perhaps the new world they had discovered above them.

"Oh, my God," Demidov whispered.

"Captain," Yelagin said quietly.

Demidov looked up and saw that Private Yelagin had risen to her knees. Now the woman took to her feet, braced herself against the wall, and reached out across the gap. The message did not require words–*get up, don't look, don't think, and let's get the hell out of here.* Demidov ought to have been the one in command, but in that moment she was quite happy to let Yelagin guide her.

She glanced one more time at the sprawling, glowing city-nest below and then she stood, never wanting to see it again. Taking a deep breath, she put one foot on the bit of stone jutting out from one side of the hole, and then she shook her head.

"No," she told Yelagin. "Back up."

"Captain..."

"Back up, Private."

Yelagin withdrew her hand, hesitated a moment, and then backed away, giving her plenty of room to make the leap. Demidov got a running start and flung herself across the gap. She landed on the ball of her left foot, arms flailing, and then stumbled straight into Yelagin, who caught her with open arms.

For a moment they stood like that, then Demidov took a single breath and nodded. "Lead the way."

They followed the beam of Yelagin's light, passing several places where the tunnel branched off in various directions, until they found one that sloped up. Demidov paused to feel the flow of air and then gestured for Yelagin to continue upward. They'd been moving for only a minute or two, Demidov staring over Yelagin's shoulder, when she realized she could see more details of the tunnel ahead than ought to have been possible. Her breath caught in her throat and she reached out, grabbing a fistful of Yelagin's jacket.

"Stop," she hissed into the other woman's ear. "Quietly."

For long seconds they stood in the tunnel, just listening. Demidov felt her heart thumping hard in her chest as she stared ahead. Sensing the trouble, Yelagin clicked off her flashlight, confirming what Demidov had feared. Not only did the tunnel ahead gleam with the weird photoluminescence of the tumblers, but the glow was becoming steadily brighter. They could hear the slither of tendrils against rock.

Part of Demidov wanted to just forge ahead. But she remembered all too well the glimpse she'd had of the tumblers killing Zhukov, and she thought perhaps they ought to retreat, find a side tunnel, and wait for this wave of creatures to pass them by.

Demidov took Yelagin's arm and turned to retrace their steps.

The same glow lit the tunnel behind them.

"No," Yelagin said quietly.

Demidov slipped out her knife. They had no other weapons and nowhere to run. A numb resignation spread through her, but her fingers opened and closed on the hilt of the knife, ready to fight no matter the odds.

The tumblers sprawled and rolled and slunk along the tunnel, arriving first from one direction and then the other. Some slipped along the ceiling or walls, filling the tube of the tunnel with their undulating tendrils and their unearthly glow until it looked like some kind of undersea nightmare.

"Captain," Yelagin whispered. "Look at the little ones."

Demidov had seen them, miniature tumblers about the size of her thumb, maybe even smaller. They clung to the others and moved swiftly amongst them. The little ones seemed to cleave more to the ceiling, creating a kind of mossy mat of shifting, impossible life. The tumblers flowed in until the only bare rock was the small circle where Demidov and Yelagin stood.

And then the smothering carpet of creatures parted and a pair of dark silhouettes emerged, like ghosts against the creatures' strange light.

Demidov could not breathe. For a moment, she could not speak, and then she managed only to rasp out a single word.

"Vasily?"

As Yelagin swore, frozen in shock, Demidov lowered her knife. Vasily Glazkov–her lover and best friend–came to a halt just a few feet away, with Amanda Hart behind him. The small tumblers clung to their clothes and flesh. Hart's face seemed to bulge around her left eye, as if something shifted beneath the skin, near the orbit. Demidov wanted to look at Vasily, but that bulbous pulsing thing in Hart's face made her stare.

"Hello, Anna," Vasily said. His voice seemed different, somehow both muffled and echoing. The tunnel turned it into a dozen voices. He looked sad, and sounded sadder.

"Vasily, you're..." She didn't know *what* he was.

"It's such a shame," he said. "So many dead."

"We're all that's left," she said. But when he next spoke, she thought perhaps Vasily wasn't talking about the soldiers who had died.

"You must understand that they are no different from us."

"What?" Yelagin said, shaking her head in confusion. "They're nothing *but* different from us."

Vasily did not so much as glance at her. He focused on Demidov. "There's beauty here. A whole world of wonder. When the shaft opened above them, they went up to explore, just as we came down. They're studying us, beginning to learn about our world. Already they have touched us deeply. Amanda suffered a terrible injury and they have repaired her, strengthened her."

Things moved beneath the skin of Hart's neck, and something twitched under her scalp, her hair waving on its own. Demidov stared at Vasily, gorge rising in her throat, hoping she would not see the thing she feared more than anything. Was that his cheek bulging, just a bit? Where his temple pulsed, was that merely blood rushing through a vein or did something else curl and stretch his skin?

"Who's speaking now?" she asked.

Vasily frowned. "Anna, my love, you must listen. There's so much we can learn."

She could not find her voice, did not dare ask who Vasily meant by *we*.

"Dr Glazkov," Yelagin said, shifting nervously as the small tumblers skittered above her head. "Whatever there is to learn, we'll find time for that. But some of our team has died and I don't see Professor Brune with you. Captain Demidov and I have to report in. You know this. Can you get us to the surface? Whatever these things are, whatever you've discovered, our superiors will want to know. We need to—"

"Stop, Kristina," Demidov said.

Yelagin flinched, stared at her as if she'd lost her mind.

"This isn't Vasily talking," Demidov said. "Not anymore."

Vasily smiled. Tiny tendrils emerged from the corners of his mouth, like cracks across his lips. "The truth is the truth, regardless of who speaks it."

Demidov raised her knife.

They swept over her.

Yelagin screamed and they both fought, but there were simply too many of the creatures, binding them, twisting them like puppets.

Dragging them down, deeper than ever before.

***

It made her think of what drowning must be like. Tendrils gripped and caressed her, surging forward, one creature passing her to another like the ebb and flow of ocean currents. Sometimes, tendrils covered her eyes and other times she could see, but the eerie phosphorescence of their limbs–so bright and so near–cast the subterranean labyrinth into deeper shadow. It was difficult to make out anything but crenellations in the wall or the silhouettes of Vasily and Hart. The sea of tumblers brought her up on a wave and then dragged her under again, carrying her onward. Demidov caught a glimpse of Yelagin, and felt some measure of relief knowing that whatever might happen now, they were together.

She tried not to think about Vasily, tried to focus just on her own beating heart and the desperate gasping of her lungs. Had it been Vasily speaking, lit up with the epiphanies of discovery? Or had these things been masquerading as her man, recruiting for their cause, attempting to find the proper mouthpiece through which to communicate with the hostiles they'd encounter aboveground?

The image of the things twisting beneath the skin of Hart's face made her want to scream. Only her focus on surviving gave her the strength to remain silent. Every moment she still lived was another moment in which she might figure out how to *stay* alive.

The ocean of tumblers surged in one last wave, dumped her on an uneven stone floor, then withdrew. She blinked, trying to get her bearings. Glancing upward, she saw they had brought her to the bottom of the original vast sinkhole. Demidov stared up the shaft, the gray daylight a small circle far overhead, just as beautiful and unreachable as the full moon on a winter's night.

Not unreachable, she told herself. You could climb it if you had to.

But she'd never make it. For fifty feet in every direction, the glowing tumblers shifted and churned, rolling on top of one another, piled as high as her shoulders. Demidov didn't know what they wanted of her, but she had no doubt she was their prisoner. The tumblers parted to allow Vasily and Hart to approach her once more.

"Anna," Vasily began. "They need an emissary. There is so much—"

"Where's Kristina?" Demidov demanded. "Private Yelagin. Where is she?"

With a ripple, the ocean of tumblers disgorged Yelagin onto the ground beside Demidov, choking and spitting, tears staining her face. Demidov took her arm, helped her to stand. In the weird phosphorescence she looked like a ghost.

Yelagin whipped around to face her, madness in her eyes. "I saw Budanov! He's down here with us!"

"Budanov is dead."

"No!" Yelagin shook her head. "I swear to you, I saw him clearly, just a few feet away." She swept her arm toward the mass of writhing tumblers. "He's in there somewhere. They've got him!"

Demidov stared at Vasily, or whatever sentience spoke through him. "Give him to me."

Vasily and Hart exchanged a silent look. Things shifted beneath Hart's skin, bulging from her left cheek. A tiny bunch of tendrils sprouted from her ear for a moment, before drawing back in like the legs of a hermit crab.

"He is injured," Vasily said. "They can help him. Heal him."

Demidov heard the hesitation in his voice, the momentary lag between thought and speech, and she knew this wasn't Vasily speaking. Not really. Not by choice.

"Give him to me," she demanded, "and I'll carry your message to the surface."

The things pulling Hart's strings used her face to smile.

Vasily nodded once and the mass of tumblers churned. Like some hideous birth, Budanov spilled from their pulsing mass. One of his arms had been shattered and twisted behind him at an impossible angle. Broken bone jutted from his lower leg, torn right through the fabric of his uniform. His face had been bloodied and gashed, but it was his eyes that drew Demidov's focus. The fear in those eyes.

"Private—" she began.

"No, listen!" Budanov said, lying on the stone floor, full of madness and lunatic desperation as he glared up at Demidov and Yelagin. "There's an airstrike coming! Any minute now… Fuck, any *second* now! They're going to—"

Demidov stared up at that pale circle so high above.

She could hear them now–the MiGs arriving–the familiar moaning whistle of their approach. They had seconds. A terrible sadness gripped her, a sorrow she had never known. She looked at Vasily, feeling a hole opening up inside her where the rest of their lives ought to have been. He gazed back at her, mirroring her grief. Then she saw the twitch beneath his right eye.

"All the things we could have taught them," he said, and she wasn't sure whether it was her Vasily talking about them, or them talking about everyone else.

The scream of bombs falling. The roar of an explosion high above–a miss. A shower of rock cracking off the walls of the shaft.

The sea of tumblers closed around Demidov and she shouted, reaching for Yelagin. They covered her, lifted her, hurtled her along as the MiGs roared and she felt the first explosion, the impact, the flash of searing heat as the tumblers rocketed her into their tunnels. They burned, and her skin burned along with them, and then she felt nothing at all.

***

Just a pinch, at first. That's all it was.

Then a scrape.

Demidov flinched, surprised that she was still alive, but in pain. Searing pain, scraping pain that made her moan and wince and whisper to God, in whom she had never believed.

Her eyes fluttered open and for a moment all the pain faded, just a little. The city around her–city was the only word–could not have been real, and yet she was certain it was no dream. For a moment, she let her head loll from side to side, gazing at the beauty and wonder of its whorls and curves and waves, and the strange spires that looked more like trees, towering things whose trunks and branches were hung with thousands of tendriled creatures, all glowing with that pale, ghostly light. She and Yelagin had glimpsed it from far above, but now she was here in the midst of it. She was in their home.

Another scrape and the pain roared back in.

Groaning, Demidov looked down and saw them on her naked skin, a hundred of the tiny things, their tendrils caressing and scrubbing her raw, burned flesh.

"No!" she cried, trying to shake them off and then whimpering with the agony of movement, lying still as her thoughts caught fire with the horror of their touch.

She remembered the bombing, the blast that scoured the tunnel even as they rushed her away.

"They saved your life," a voice said.

Demidov recognized the voice without turning toward him. She steeled herself, because she knew that when she let herself see Vasily it would look like him, but it wouldn't be him. He surprised her by not speaking again.

Swallowing hard, feeling the gently painful ministrations of the tumblers, she looked to her right and saw him standing nearby, watching over her. They clung to his clothes and skin and hair. When he spoke again, she might have glimpsed one inside his mouth, but it might have been a trick of the light.

"Yelagin?" she asked. "Budanov?"

"I'm sorry."

Demidov sighed, squeezing her eyes shut. "Why save me?"

Vasily's reply came from just beside her. "I told you. They need an emissary."

She opened her eyes and he was right there, kneeling by her head, studying her with kindly, almost parental concern.

"There are other shafts. Other holes. They've been opening up all over this area. Some will be destroyed, as this one was. But not all."

Her burnt skin throbbed, but she could feel that the stroking of those tendrils had begun to soothe her. Slowly, she sat up.

Demidov exhaled. "Vasily…"

He ignored her, forging ahead. "They'll share some of their gifts with you," he said. "Teach you wonderful things, including how it is possible for them to heal the damage to your flesh—"

"Vasily?"

"—and then you will carry their message to the surface."

"Vasily!"

Blinking as if coming awake, he looked at her. Vasily had stubble on his face and his dark hair was an unruly mess, just as it always had been. For that moment, he looked so much like himself.

"What is it, Anna?" he asked, eyes narrowing, as if daring her to ask the question.

She almost didn't. Just getting the words out cost her everything.

"Who am I speaking to?" she said.

Vasily did not look away, but neither did he give her an answer. Several seconds passed before he continued to describe the mission the tumblers intended for her to undertake.

Demidov tasted the salt of her tears as they slid down her scorched cheeks and touched her lips. She hung her head, Vasily's words turning into nothing but a low drone.

Her right arm had not been burnt. That was something, at least. She stared at the smooth, unmarked flesh.

A shape moved beneath her skin.

The End

Biographies

Mort Castle has won three Bram Stoker Awards®, two Black Quill awards, the Golden Bot (Wired Magazine), and has been nominated for The Audie, The Shirley Jackson award, the International Horror Guild award and the Pushcart Prize. In 2000, the Chicago Sun-Times News Group cited him as one of Twenty-One "Leaders in the Arts for the 21st Century in Chicago's Southland." The author's most recent book is *Knowing When to Die* (Independent Legions Publishing). A film based on his classic, award-winning horror novel *The Strangers* is in development with New Zealand's Light at the End Productions. Castle and his wife, Jane, have been married forty-nine years and live in Crete, Illinois.

Greg Chapman is a two-time international Bram Stoker Award®-nominee, horror author and artist based in Queensland, Australia.

Greg is the author of several novels, novellas and short stories, including his award-nominated debut novel, *Hollow House* (Omnium Gatherum) and collections, *Vaudeville and Other Nightmares* (Specul8 Publishing) and *This Sublime Darkness and Other Dark Stories* (Things in the Well Publications).

He is also a horror artist and his first graphic novel *Witch Hunts: A Graphic History of the Burning Times*, (McFarland & Company) written by authors Rocky Wood and Lisa Morton, won the Superior Achievement in a Graphic Novel category at the Bram Stoker Awards® in 2013.

Visit www.darkscrybe.com

Tracy Cross was awarded the Boston Accent Literary Journal Prize in 2016. Her work has appeared in several anthologies and magazines, including *Big Book of Bootleg Horror, Things That Go Bump, Arc City Stories* and *D'Evolution Z Horror Magazine*. She has appeared on several websites, such as *Midnight and Indigo, New American Legends* and *Dark Fire Fiction*. She is an active member of the Horror Writers Association. Tracy hails from Cleveland, Ohio, and loves her current home, Washington, DC.

Matthew R. Davis is an author and musician based in Adelaide, South Australia. He recently won two Australian Shadows Awards in the same year–only the second author to do so–and has been repeatedly shortlisted for both the Shadows and the Aurealis Awards. His first collection of horror stories, *If Only Tonight We Could Sleep*, was released by Things in the Well in January 2020; his first novel, *Midnight in the Chapel of Love*, will be released by JournalStone Publishing in 2021. Find out more at matthewrdavisfiction.wordpress.com.

Steve Dillon was nominated for a Shirley Jackson Award in 2020 for best novelette. He also wears the face behind the mask at *Things in the Well* and is the executive editor and publisher of over 30 anthologies and single-author collections, he considers himself fortunate to have worked with some of the biggest names in horror including Ramsey Campbell, Clive Barker, Christopher Golden, and many more, as well as hundreds of emerging and award-winning writers. He has published two collections of his own short stories and poetry and his third is looking for a home. He's very active in too many Facebook communities and is a former president of the Australasian Horror Writers Association.
Facebook: SteveDillonWriter. Twitter: @ThingsInTheWell Website: www.ThingsInTheWell.com

Neil Gaiman is the *New York Times* bestselling author and creator of books, graphic novels, short stories, film and television for all ages, including *Norse Mythology, Neverwhere, Coraline, The Graveyard Book, The Ocean at the End of the Lane, The View from the Cheap Seats,* and the *Sandman* comic series. His fiction has received Newbery, Carnegie, Hugo, Nebula, World Fantasy, and Will Eisner Awards. *American Gods,* based on the 2001 novel, is now a critically acclaimed, Emmy-nominated TV series, and he was the writer and showrunner for the mini-series adaptation of *Good Omens,* based on the book he co-authored with Sir Terry Pratchett. In 2017, he became a Goodwill Ambassador for UNHCR, the UN Refugee Agency. Originally from England, he lives in the United States.

Christopher Golden is the New York Times bestselling author of *Ararat, Snowblind, Red Hands,* and many other novels. He is the co-creator, with Mike Mignola, of the *Outerverse* horror comics, including *Baltimore, Joe Golem: Occult Detective,* and *Lady Baltimore*. As editor, his anthologies include the Shirley Jackson Award winning *The Twisted Book of Shadows, The New Dead,* and many others. Golden is also a screenwriter, producer, video game writer, co-host of the podcast *Defenders Dialogue*, and founded the Merrimack Valley Halloween Book Festival. Nominated ten times in eight different categories for the Bram Stoker Award, he has won twice, and has also been nominated for the Eisner Award, the British Fantasy Award, and multiple times for the Shirley Jackson Award. Golden was born, raised, and still lives in Massachusetts.

Heather Graham is the NYT and USA Today bestselling author of over two hundred novels including suspense, paranormal, historical, mainstream, and Christmas stories. She lives in Miami, Florida, her home, and an easy shot down to the Keys where she can indulge in her passion for diving. Travel, research, and ballroom dancing also help keep her sane; she is the mother of five, and also resides with two dogs, and two cats and considers family and friends her greatest assets in life. She is CEO of Slush Pile Productions, a recording company and production house for various charity events. She has been honored with the Romance Writers of America Lifetime Achievement Award, a Thriller Writers Silver Bullet for charitable contributions, and in 2016, she will receive the Thriller Master Award. Look her up at theoriginalheathergraham.com.

Joe Hill is the #1 New York Times bestselling author of *The Fireman, Strange Weather,* and *Heart-Shaped Box*. His most recent book, *Full Throttle*, a short story collection, was released in 2019. Joe's third novel, *NOS4A2*, is now a TV series on AMC, and stars Zachary Quinto. Joe is also the Eisner Award winning writer of the six-volume *Locke & Key* comic books, which are now a TV series on Netflix. Most recently, Hill has returned to comics—his latest include *Basketful of Heads* and *Plunge* for D.C., and *Dying is Easy* for IDW. Hill lives in New England.

Eugene Johnson is a Bram Stoker Award®-winner, a bestselling editor, author and columnist. He has written as well as edited in various genres, and created anthologies such as the *Fantastic Tales Of Terror, Drive In Creature Feature* with Charles Day, the Bram Stoker Award®-nominated non-fiction anthology *Where Nightmares Come From: The Art Of Storytelling In The Horror Genre* and many more. He has had stories published by award winning publishers such as Apex Publishing, Crystal Lake Publishing and Things In The Well Press to name a few. He is currently an active member of the Horror Writers Association.

Alexis Kirkpatrick is a second-year writing student at Columbia College. Though originally a Massachusetts native, she had found a home in Chicago, where she works as a freelance writer and educator. She has true fascination with horror stories, and hopes to write fiction as engaging as the books she admires. During this difficult time, she has been occupying herself by consuming a concerning amount of tea, and writing stories of places and things far more exciting than her now-indoor life.

Tim Lebbon is a New York Times bestselling writer from South Wales. He's had over forty novels published to date, as well as hundreds of novellas and short stories. His latest novel is the eco-horror novel *Eden*. Other recent releases include *The Edge, The Silence, The Family Man, The Rage War* trilogy, and *Blood of the Four* with Christopher Golden. He has won four British Fantasy Awards, a Bram Stoker Award, and a Scribe Award, and has been a finalist for

World Fantasy, International Horror Guild and Shirley Jackson Awards. His work has appeared in many Year's Best anthologies, as well as Century's Best Horror.

The movie of *The Silence*, starring Stanley Tucci and Kiernan Shipka, debuted on Netflix April 2019, and *Pay the Ghost*, starring Nicolas Cage, was released Halloween 2015. Several other projects are in development for TV and the big screen, including original screenplays *Playtime* (with Stephen Volk) and *My Hunted House*.

Find out more about Tim at his website www.timlebbon.net

Vince A. Liaguno is the Bram Stoker Award-winning editor of *Unspeakable Horror: From the Shadows of the Closet* (Dark Scribe Press 2008), an anthology of queer horror fiction, which he co-edited with Chad Helder. His debut novel, 2006's *The Literary Six*, was a tribute to the slasher films of the 80's and won an Independent Publisher Award (IPPY) for Horror and was named a finalist in *ForeWord* Magazine's Book of the Year Awards in the Gay/Lesbian Fiction category.

More recently, he edited *Butcher Knives & Body Counts* (Dark Scribe Press, 2011)—a collection of essays on the formula, frights, and fun of the slasher film—as well as the second volume in the *Unspeakable Horror* series, subtitled *Abominations of Desire* (Evil Jester Press, 2017). He's currently at work on his second novel.

He currently resides on the eastern end of Long Island, New York, where he is a licensed nursing home administrator by day and a writer, anthologist, and pop culture enthusiast by night. He is a member (and former Secretary) of the Horror Writers Association (HWA) and a member of the National Book Critics Circle (NBCC).

Author Website: www.VinceLiaguno.com
Facebook: https://www.facebook.com/vince.liaguno
Twitter: https://twitter.com/VinceLiaguno
Goodreads: https://www.goodreads.com/VinceLiaguno

Chris Mason lives in the Adelaide Hills, South Australia, often dubbed "the murder capital of Australia," with her husband, a cat, and five goldfish. Her stories have appeared in numerous publications, including the *Things in the Well* series of anthologies, and the Australasian Horror Writers Association's magazine *Midnight Echo* issues #12 and #14.

Ben Monroe grew up in Northern California, and has spent most of his life there. He lives in the East Bay Area with his wife and two children. His most recently published works are *In the Belly of the Beast and Other Tales of Cthulhu Wars*, the graphic novel *Planet Apocalypse* and short stories in a number of anthologies. He can be reached via his website at www.benmonroe.com and on Twitter @_BenMonroe_.

Lisa Morton is a screenwriter, author of non-fiction books, and award-winning prose writer whose work was described by the American Library Association's *Readers' Advisory Guide to Horror* as "consistently dark, unsettling, and frightening". She is the author of four novels and 150 short stories, a six-time winner of the Bram Stoker Award®, and a world-class Halloween expert. Her most recent book, *Ghost Stories: Classic Tales of Horror and Suspense* (co-edited with Leslie Klinger) received a starred review in *Publishers Weekly*, who called it "a work of art"; forthcoming in 2020 is *Weird Women: Classic Supernatural Fiction by Groundbreaking Female Writers 1852-1923* and *Calling the Spirits: A History of Seances*. Lisa lives in the San Fernando Valley and online at www.lisamorton.com.

John Palisano has a pair of books with Samhain Publishing, *Dust of the Dead*, and *Ghost Heart*. *Nerves* is available through Bad Moon. *Starlight Drive: Four Halloween Tales* was released in time for Halloween, and his first short fiction collection *All That Withers* is available from Cycatrix press, celebrating over a decade of short story highlights. *Night of 1,000 Beasts* is coming soon. He won the Bram Stoker Award in short fiction in 2016 for *Happy Joe's Rest Stop*. More short stories have appeared in anthologies from Cemetery Dance, PS Publishing, Independent Legions, DarkFuse, Crystal Lake, Terror Tales, Lovecraft eZine, Horror Library, Bizarro Pulp, Written Backwards, Dark Continents, Big Time Books, McFarland Press, Darkscribe, Dark House, Omnium Gatherum, and more. His non-fiction pieces have appeared in Blumhouse, Fangoria and Dark Discoveries magazines.

He is currently serving as the Vice President of the Horror Writers Association. Say 'hi' to John at: www.johnpalisano.com and http://www.amazon.com/author/johnpalisano and www.facebook.com/johnpalisano and www.twitter.com/johnpalisano

Christina Sng is the Bram Stoker Award-winning author of *A Collection of Nightmares*, Elgin Award runner-up *Astropoetry*, and *A Collection of Dreamscapes*. Her poetry, fiction, and art have appeared in numerous venues worldwide, and her poems have garnered multiple nominations in the Rhysling Awards, the Dwarf Stars, the Elgin Awards, as well as honorable mentions in the Year's Best Fantasy and Horror, and the Best Horror of the Year. Christina lives in Singapore with her children and a menagerie of curious pets. Visit her at christinasng.com and connect on social media @christinasng.

Lucy A. Snyder is the Shirley Jackson Award-nominated and five-time Bram Stoker Award-winning author of over 100 published short stories. Her most recent books are the collection *Garden of Eldritch Delights* and the forthcoming novel *The Girl With the Star-Stained Soul*. She also wrote the novels *Spellbent*, *Shotgun Sorceress*, and *Switchblade Goddess*, the nonfiction book *Shooting Yourself in the Head for Fun and Profit: A Writer's Survival Guide*, and the collections *While the Black Stars Burn*, *Soft Apocalypses*, *Orchid Carousals*, *Sparks* and *Shadows*, *Chimeric Machines*, and *Installing Linux on a Dead Badger*. Her writing has appeared in publications such as *Asimov's Science Fiction*, *Apex Magazine*, *Nightmare Magazine*, *Pseudopod*, *Strange Horizons*, and *Best Horror of the Year*. She lives in Columbus, Ohio and is faculty in Seton Hill University's MFA program in Writing Popular Fiction. You can learn more about her at www.lucysnyder.com and you can follow her on Twitter at @LucyASnyder.

Luke Spooner is a freelance illustrator from the South of England. At 'Carrion House' he creates dark, melancholy and macabre illustrations and designs for a variety of projects and publishers, big and small, young and old.

Francois Vaillancourt is a Montreal artist who specializes in images illustrating dark worlds and stories where horror and macabre meet. His images are characterized by a highly textured, emotionally evocative and sensitive universe. Even through his darkest images, we can recognize a certain beauty and fragility.

Although Francois is trained as a classical artist, his work and creative methods have been transposed into the digital world, allowing him to rework his images in a more fluid way until the desired result is achieved.

Francois Vaillancourt: http://www.francois-art.com

Tim Waggoner is a bestselling author who has published close to fifty novels and seven collections of short stories. He writes dark fantasy and horror, as well as media tie-ins. He's won the Bram Stoker Award, the HWA's Mentor of the Year Award, and he's been a finalist for the Shirley Jackson Award, the Scribe Award, and the Splatterpunk Award. He's also a full-time tenured professor who teaches creative writing and composition at Sinclair College in Dayton, Ohio.

Bram Stoker Award-Winning Author
Website: www.timwaggoner.com
Blog: http://writinginthedarktw.blogspot.com/
Facebook: http://www.facebook.com/#!/tim.waggoner.9
Twitter: @timwaggoner

Kaaron Warren is an award winning author of horror, science fiction, and fantasy short stories and novels. She is the author of the short story collections *Through Splintered Walls*, *The Grinding House*, and *Dead Sea Fruit*. Her short stories have won Australian Shadows Awards, Ditmar Awards and Aurealis Awards

Stephanie M. Wytovich is an American poet, novelist, and essayist. Her work has been showcased in numerous anthologies such as *Gutted: Beautiful Horror Stories*, *Shadows Over Main Street: An Anthology of Small-Town Lovecraftian Terror*, *Year's Best Hardcore Horror: Volume 2*, *The Best Horror of the Year: Volume 8*, as well as many others.

Wytovich is the Poetry Editor for Raw Dog Screaming Press, an adjunct at Western Connecticut State University and Point Park University, and a mentor to authors with Crystal Lake Publishing. She is a member of the Science Fiction Poetry Association, an active member of the Horror Writers Association, and a graduate of Seton Hill University's MFA program for Writing Popular Fiction. Her Bram Stoker Award-winning poetry collection, Brothel, earned a home with Raw Dog Screaming Press alongside *Hysteria: A Collection of Madness, Mourning Jewelry,* and *An Exorcism of Angels.* Her debut novel, *The Eighth,* is published with Dark Regions Press.

Her next poetry collection, *Sheet Music to My Acoustic Nightmare,* is scheduled to be released late 2017 from Raw Dog Screaming Press.

Follow Wytovich at http://www.stephaniewytovich.com/ and on twitter @JustAfterSunset.

Acknowledgements

First we want to thank all the essential workers and everyone who has stepped up during the pandemic to help everyone in need!

I would like to thank the following people for their help and support making this amazing project become a reality. Steve Dillon, my co-editor.

All the amazing authors who jumped right in, helping out with a story or poem; Greg Chapman, Tracy Cross, Matthew R. Davis, Neil Gaiman, Heather Graham, Christopher Golden, Joe Hill, Alexis Kirkpatrick, Tim Lebbon, Vince A. Liaguno, Chris Mason, Ben Monroe, Lisa Morton, John Palisano, Christina Sng, Lucy A. Snyder, Tim Waggoner, Kaaron Warren, and Stephanie Wytovich.

To Mort Castle for the insightful introduction.

Francois Vaillancourt and Luke Spooner for providing the amazing artwork for the book. Lee Murray for taking the time to read the book and provide a fantastic blurb for the cover.

Jason, Anna Ray Stokes, and Alain Davis Of Gestalt Media for Jumping in to help with proofreading, formatting, and so much more.

Plaid Dragon Publishing support staff, Essel Pratt, S. Alan Berry, John Stroud, and Teddy Claypool.

My family Angela, Hannah, Bradley, Oliver and Ethan, Fred and Debbie, The Ricketts and Gibsons, my grandparents, Lois and Ben Muncy. My wonderful friends Luke Styer, John Stroud, Paul Moore, Scot Tanner, Lia Staley, Thom Erb, Chris Sartin, my agent Cherry, Ethan and Scott Berry, John Palisano, and Dave Simms.

I want to thank everyone who supported The Plaid Dragon Publishing campaign; May Budd, Alain Davis, Patricia Medeiros, Paul Moore
Dr. Ross Patton, Vasilia Staley, Luke Styer, Jason Stokes, James Ward and those supporters that chose not to be named. Thank you for helping make Plaid Dragon Publishing's first book a reality.

And last but not least, you the reader!

Tales of the Lost

Volume 2
Tales to Get Lost In

Coming Soon

TALES OF THE LOST

Volume 3

Watch out for more themed anthologies, collections,
and more from

Plaid Dragon Publishing

www.Plaiddragonpublishing.com